Rajani Chronicles III
War

Brian S. Converse

ISBN: 978-1-7339334-0-7

Cover Art by
Lawrence Mann
www.lawrencemann.co/uk

For LAZDE
Always

Thank you to all who contributed in some way to the
publication of this book, including
my excellent editor, Melissa.

I'm eternally grateful.

This one's for Lisa
You ugly head

Recap

James Dempsey was a Detroit Police Lieutenant until he inexplicably awoke aboard an alien spacecraft. He and four other Humans, Yvette, Gianni, David, and Kieren, learned they had been kidnapped by a group of Rajani who were fleeing their home planet. Rajan had been invaded by intergalactic pirates known as the Krahn Horde. The Rajani pleaded for assistance in ridding their world of the Krahn invaders, offering in return a gift beyond measure: objects that, when implanted into their hosts, gave them incredible powers.

With the Humans in dire need of training in the use of these powers, the Rajani ship, the *Tukuli,* stopped at a space station in search of someone who could build a training area aboard the ship. The station offered its own dangers, though, in the form of the Alliance Society for Peace, the police force of the Galactic Alliance. Led on the station by Ries an na Van, the ASPs would immediately jail the Rajani if they were discovered.

Amidst the new experiences and dangers, James and Yvette allowed their attraction for each other to become a fierce romance. Loners by both choice and chance, the two Humans were surprised and happy to find someone while so far from home.

With a daring escape from the station and the ASPs, the *Tukuli* made its way toward Rajan, only to be shot down over the planet's surface by the Krahn Horde's enormous mothership. The Humans abandoned ship, separated into escape pods, while the Rajani crew stayed aboard in hopes of steering the ship away from the capital city of Melaanse.

The Humans and Rajani crew of the *Tukuli* found themselves separated on the surface of Rajan, with no way of communicating with each other. They found their own way to Melaanse, though, each facing their own perils before reuniting.

James met up with the Jirina; Gianni and Kieren with the Sekani; and Yvette was reunited with Rauph and Bhakat, and later, David, who had been with Jonan, until they were captured by the Krahn. David managed to escape with the help of his comrades, but Jonan remained a prisoner.

The five Humans were able to help the scattered remnants of the Rajani society come together to form a Resistance movement, which began to make inroads in their fight to reclaim their planet from the Krahn Horde invaders.

Prologue

The Krahn home world was covered with lush, green vegetation, much of it poisonous. Most of the light gray stone of the immense Qadira stronghold was covered in moss and ivy that thrived in the boiling Krahn summers. It held a pattern of light and dark in the waning afternoon sun as the tall trees surrounding it swayed in the breeze.

The rocky stronghold rose above the forests and swamps, yet was still a part of the adjacent land. Large bat-like creatures flew en masse over the structure, their immense white wings shining in the sunlight as their strange calls filled the air. Krahn warriors stood guard throughout the palace and surrounding grounds. They were dressed in leather jerkins and vests bearing the Qadira Clan's sigil: two crossed spears that created a pyramid, and over and between the spearpoints was a red sun, symbolically rising over the Qadira Empire. It was an emblem of power known throughout the Krahn world.

On a flat stretch of rock near the palace rested the Qadira Clan's colossal warship and several smaller ships, most of them unused since the treaty was signed with the Galactic Alliance, making the Krahn an official member nearly twenty Standard years before. The Krahn had fought hard to stave off the Alliance's advances, but in the end, there was really no doubt as to the outcome.

The previous Vasin had united the various clans on Krahn into one force to battle the Alliance, becoming the High Vasin of Krahn in the process. When the treaty had been signed, he'd stayed in that position, and had ushered the Krahn into a larger universe, whether they were ready for it or not. They'd needed to adapt, or they would have been destroyed by the sheer power of the Alliance.

The Qadira Clan's throne room sat in the very middle of the stronghold. The throne was tall and created entirely from a single slab of stone. It was draped with a swath of royal black cloth with the Qadira Clan's sigil upon it. There were no cushions upon the throne; the Vasin sat without comfort as a symbol of his commitment to his clan. Sitting upon the throne was a large Krahn dressed in royal black but with no other sigil of rank. This was Maliq, Vasin of the Qadira Clan, and High Vasin of the entire planet of Krahn. He was currently gripping the arms of the throne in rage and disbelief. "Is he mad!"

Standing on the top step in front of the throne was his counselor, Xenic. This Krahn was much older, but his eyes were still very sharp—as was his tongue. "It would appear he is, Maliq," Xenic said. "Bating the beast in its own lair was once a sign of courage, but I'm afraid this strays beyond courage into folly."

Word had reached Kran of Ronak and his so-called 'horde' attacking the planet of Rajan. Though many light years away, Maliq did his best to keep track of his younger brother, and recent reports told him that just keeping track was no longer enough. Ronak was too unpredictable, and his leash was a bit too long.

Maliq scratched his throat as he thought about his

brother. "I believe it's long past time to collect my nest brother. Send word to Ronak that playtime is over. He's to return to Krahn under armed escort to await sentencing yet again."

Xenic bowed before asking, "And the Rajani?"

"Send a gift of medical aid and food, with the promise of more in the future. Send at least three full ships. And then pray that we're not too late."

Chapter 1

Galactic Intelligence Agent Level Two Ries an na Van sat on the bridge of his new starship, the *Digger*, and wondered what he was going to do. He'd been ordered by his new superior at GI to find his former superior's Sekani contact on the planet Rajan and either bring him in for debriefing or silence him for good. How he was going to do that in the middle of a war zone, he had no clue. He looked over at his pilot, a Sh'kallian, who was waiting for his orders, his tail twitching idly. The Sh'kallian was named Jerboxh and was not himself an agent of GI. GI employed a myriad number of support personnel, who knew enough not to ask questions if they wanted to stay employed and alive. He would be of no help in deciding what to do, and from the brief introductory conversation Ries had engaged in with him, he wasn't the sharpest claw in the nest, as his mother used to say. *At least he's not an Asnurian,* Ries thought gratefully, remembering the stench usually associated with those creatures.

To make matters worse, he didn't even know the contact's real name. He only knew that it was a male Sekani. That narrowed it down to thousands of individuals on Rajan. He took a sip of kolan using his upper right arm, while both his lower arms tapped incessantly on the armrests of his captain's chair. His two brains were able to think independently of each other, which helped to do more than one thing at once. This had benefited him on more than one occasion.

Ries looked over at his pilot to see that the Sh'kallian was looking at him, an annoyed expression on his face.

"Could you not do that?" Jerboxh asked with a growl. The pupils of his eyes had contracted into slits.

"It helps me think," Ries answered, not stopping his tapping. "I don't need commentary on my habits from a pilot. All I need is for you to do what I say, when I say it, understand?"

Jerboxh sat a moment, looking at Ries, before turning toward his control panel. "Yes, sir," he said quietly, though his tail was like some independent creature as it wagged behind him, and he pushed the buttons before him as if they were his mortal enemies.

Confident that he would get no more interruptions from the hired help, Ries sat and pondered a while longer, while he ate his second meal of the day. His high metabolism meant that he needed to eat frequently, so he usually ate anywhere from six to eight meals on a given day. He finally threw the container from the meal down on the floor in frustration. He had resigned himself to his task. He had to find T'van and get the name of the former agent's Sekani contact.

◊

Ronak, Vasin of the Krahn Horde, woke up feeling that something was wrong, but not knowing what it could be. He'd been plagued by nightmares recently, and had not slept well. His chief counselor, Kalik, had assured him that it was only stress, but he still felt like he was missing something. Something important, either about his present, or his past; or maybe it was just anxiety about the future.

That the feeling was now invading his dreams was both worrisome and distracting. He sat up, still close enough to his bloodmate, Mariqa, to feel her breathing softly next to him. He looked at her. So vigorously alive when she was awake, it was only when sleeping that her intensity was muted. He thought about waking her to mate, but decided that he wasn't really in the mood. She was as dangerous in the act of love as she was in battle.

He walked, naked, down the hall of the Rajani house that he'd made his temporary headquarters since arriving on the planet's surface. The entire building was most uncomfortable. It was nothing like his colony ship, where the temperature was regulated to the heat of a spring Krahn night, and everything was covered in soft furs or plump pillows, and the toilets were made for those who had tails, even if they were only vestigial. The Rajani weren't used to enjoying the good things in life, he decided. He walked to a room that had been set up with electronic equipment, including a communication system to contact his colony ship and a computer that was linked with the ship's central computer inside his private quarters. He sat down in front of the computer screen and spoke. "Computer." The screen instantly came to life. "Check messages. Personal account."

"Voice recognition confirmed, Mighty Qadira," the computer said. "One new message in your communication account."

"Proceed," he said, rubbing the sleep from his eyes with his left hand.

"Message is classified as 'Eyes Only' by Galactic Intelligence. Unfortunately, I am forbidden to read it out loud to you, Mighty Qadira. Please verify that you are the only one present in the room."

"Verified, on screen," he said. He was used to receiving

these messages, so he wasn't surprised every time the computer informed him of its inability to read them to him for security purposes. It was annoying, but it wasn't the computer's fault. A message appeared on the screen, written in Krahnish, instantaneously translated from the original Talondarian Standard. Ronak began to read, feeling his anger rise as he read the reply to the demand for support that he'd sent to his new Galactic Intelligence handler. For some reason, his original contact, T'van, was no longer assigned to him. They'd refused his demands for weapons and support troops, yet again. It was the second request he'd made since receiving the communiqué from GI stating that he would no longer have their support in his search for the Johar Stones on Rajan. He hadn't wanted to believe it at the time, but it seemed they were holding to their decision, and he was powerless to do anything about it.

Ronak stood and punched his hand into the screen. It shattered, its pieces flying everywhere in the small room. This wasn't the first screen he'd destroyed in his anger with GI, and probably wouldn't be the last. He pulled his hand back, blood running in thick trickles from the knuckles. How could they do this? he thought. They had promised him, and now they were reneging on that promise. It felt like the situation on Rajan was falling apart quickly. He would never be able to return to Krahn in a position of strength. Maliq would stay High Vasin. He sat back down in the chair, his aching hand now forgotten, and brooded. He thought about his brother, giving in to the hatred, remembering the past.

◊

The young Krahn male ran down the hallway of his father's stronghold, past the tapestries and weapons mounted on the walls. The pictures of former Vasins flew by him in a blur of colors. His bare feet felt the rough grain of the granite floor and the soft cushion of the black rug that ran interspersedly down the middle of the hall. The small toy ship clutched in his hand had been a gift from his mother, and he imagined as he ran that he was flying through space, on his way to some exotic Alliance destination, like Tritteran, or even Talondaria. Or perhaps, instead of one of the original Alliance worlds, he was headed to some uncharted planet on the outer rim of the galaxy, on a mission for the Alliance as it continually expanded its borders.

His steps slowed as he approached the throne room. His father would be angry if he was disturbed. The Krahn leader's temper was well known, and his children were not immune from his wrath. He slowed even more when he heard voices arguing loudly. They sounded angry.

"Be quiet," a voice whispered to his left. He looked over to see his older brother standing in a recessed doorway.

"Are you eavesdropping?" he asked his sibling.

"I said be quiet, Ronak," his brother said, pulling him into the doorway. His brother's plumage was up in a display of dominance. Ronak's brother was always so bossy. He'd been hatched a few minutes earlier, so he thought he was somehow superior. He certainly acted that way.

"I can talk if I want," Ronak said, a bit petulantly. His plumage stayed close to his head. "What are they fighting about?" he asked quietly. His brother didn't answer, just stared straight ahead as he concentrated on listening. They could hear their father and his chief counselor talking in the throne room now, their voices quieter.

"What would you have me do, Xenic, kill one of them?" his father asked, his voice rising again. "I'm sure their mother would be thrilled to hear your opinion."

"No, Mighty Qadira," Xenic answered. "I'm only saying that having both of your Seventh Sons reach maturity would cause . . . complications in the succession to the throne. With the Alliance treaty having just been signed, now is the right time to make it known who the next ruler of Krahn will be."

Ronak realized that his father and Xenic were talking about him and his brother. It was tradition that the seventh generation male would succeed to the throne of the Clan. Normally, only one male hatched from the seventh clutch of eggs. But in this case, two had hatched from the eggs produced by their mother, Vasina of the Qadira Clan and High Vasina on the planet of Krahn and all of its holdings. Usually when this happened, one of the offspring would be sickly, and not last more than a week, or was even killed outright, but whether it was a misplaced sense of pity or the fact that both males had been strong enough to withstand the culling time—that period just after hatching, where the hatchlings were left without food or water to test their will to live—both had survived.

"Careful what you say next, Xenic," his father said, softly. Ronak, though, could hear the steel in his voice. Even though it wasn't directed at him, he still felt a shiver of fear run through his body. His father yelled a lot, but it was when he used this tone of voice that he was at his most dangerous. His enemies never had time to know the difference; if they heard this tone, they usually didn't survive long enough to have a second chance.

"Mighty Vasin," Xenic said, "my only wish is to serve you, as my father did before me; you know this. What are your wishes in this matter?"

"Maliq was first born," his father said. "Maliq will sit on the throne when old enough. It's the law, and the law will be obeyed. Ronak will live, and he'll come to no harm. But he shall never be Vasin. Now get out of my sight."

"Run," Maliq whispered to him, and then quickly did just

that, running down the hallway and around the corner, out of sight.

Ronak was about to follow when he saw Xenic quickly walking down the hall toward him. He backed up, his back touching the door, hoping not to be noticed by his father's new chief counselor. The old chief counselor had just been killed in an honor duel, and so his oldest son had taken over the position. Ronak had no such luck.

"Ronak?" the counselor asked when he caught sight of the young Krahn. "Listening, were you?" He stopped to look at the young Krahn, who was clutching a toy to his chest. "Well, then I guess you heard your father's wishes. I'm sorry, child. I really am." He turned and walked away down the hallway.

Ronak stood there a moment longer, thinking about what he had just heard and trying to understand what it meant. Finally, he looked down at his toy spacecraft. After a moment, he let it fall and slowly walked away, leaving his childhood lying broken on the floor.

◊

Ries arrived at the Mandakan Space Port, hoping that his fake credentials would pass through port security without any problems. He let his pilot deal with the port authorities as the ship docked. He needed to keep a low profile, and having his former officers know that he had returned was not the way he was going to do it. As the former Commander of the Alliance Society for Peace unit that patrolled (and some say controlled) that sector of Alliance space, he had taken a few liberties with his position and power. Maybe more than a few, but that wasn't important at the moment. He'd lost enough because of those minor weaknesses in his character.

He'd been brought in to ASP headquarters on Asnuria for questioning concerning the events that had taken place with the Rajani starship that had disabled his own ship and another ASP ship. He'd subsequently been arrested for sticking his antennae where they didn't belong, losing everything he'd managed to gain while Commander on the Mandakan Space Port. He hadn't known at the time that researching the Rajani would lead to such problems. He'd been demoted within the ASPs, and then let his curiosity get the better of him once again. That had led him to the attention of Galactic Intelligence. He'd thought then that he was out of the mess he'd gotten himself into when he was recruited by an agent of GI who called himself Odorey T'van.

His first official mission had been to return to Asnuria and strong-arm the ASPs into dropping their investigation of the Rajani starship. Although he had relished the opportunity, the ASPs weren't likely to forget it. But the port was also where many of Ries's contacts were, and while a few of them were legitimate, many were less so. There was also a chance that T'van may have stopped there on his way to wherever it was he had gone to ground. It was a slim chance. Alliance space covered an immense area, and there were any number of hundreds of stations and planets where T'van could have gone to escape GI scrutiny. Yet word traveled quickly, even in the vast areas of space. He was betting that someone had heard of a rogue Sekani being spotted somewhere. It was the best he could hope for at the moment.

He'd learned while researching the species for his current mission that the Sekani of Rajan never left that planet unless piloting ships for their Rajani masters, so they were rarely seen in public. And most of the other Sekani stayed on their home world, Sekan, secluded from the Alliance.

◊

Ronak had just finished his final molting, his childhood down falling out, never to return, when his father fell ill. The average Krahn lifespan was sixty years, and his father was pushing seventy at the time. His seventh sons had come later in his life than was usual. Fighting the Alliance had taken its toll on him in more ways than one, it seemed.

Ronak's mother had died some years earlier, and since that time, he and his brother Maliq had been raised by various nursemaids, counselors, and tutors. But only Maliq had been permitted to spend time with his father and the chief counselor, Xenic, while they attended to the affairs of state. It was his right as heir to the throne.

Ronak, on the other hand, was shuttled off to military school as soon as he was old enough. He'd gone to the classes, but found it wasn't very interesting, and he also wasn't good at military strategy. He didn't have the mind for it, nor the inclination to learn. He wanted to be a starship pilot, someone who explored the known and the unknown. The other students at the school either hated him for who his father was, or looked up to him in a kind of awe, but none of them wanted to be his friend, not even several of his cousins who attended, sent there by his father's younger brothers.

He'd felt lost and alone ever since his mother had died, and now his father was sick as well. When his father had collapsed suddenly while holding court, both of his sons had been informed at once. Ronak hadn't talked to his brother for several years at that point. Their lives had caused them to grow apart. Now, as he walked down the hallway toward his father's sickroom, he hoped that his brother wouldn't be there. He had nothing to say to Maliq. He was relieved to see that his father was alone when he reached the door to the room, which was open. The two guards who stood on either side of the door lowered their weapons in deference to the High Vasin's son, but neither of them spoke a word to him, or looked him directly in the eye. He was accorded deference due to his station, but not respect.

Ronak didn't pass through the doorway at first. He stood and looked at the old Krahn who was lying on the bed within the room. His father seemed to have changed into an elderly Krahn in only a few months. When Ronak had last seen him, he'd been vibrant and full of fire. Now that fire had almost been extinguished. He could smell the sickness emanating from the room. His father was thin and haggard as he lay on his sick bed, his sallow chest hardly moving at all when he breathed.

Ronak slowly walked through the doorway and approached the bed, not knowing exactly what to say. The truth was, he had too many things to say, too many questions to ask his father, and had no idea how to begin. His father saved him the trouble of choosing. As Ronak opened his mouth to speak, alarms began to sound from the various medical machines in the room. Krahn medical staff in dark green smocks flooded into the room, pushing him out of the way as they attempted to bring his father back to life. Ronak watched the proceedings from the corner of the room until the frantic attempts at resuscitation had ceased. He then slipped from the room unnoticed and walked slowly down the hallway, his mind full of half-formed thoughts and bitter disappointment. He didn't need to be told that his father was gone.

He'd hoped to be able to talk to his father; find out why things had to be this way. He was tired of always being on the outside. He didn't want to be in the military any more than he wanted to become High Vasin of the Qadira Clan. He only wanted to know why his family had pushed him so far away.

◊

Ries's ship was directed to a birthing port, and his pilot successfully docked. He knew there wouldn't be a problem with the ship docking at Mandaka. Port security was not as concerned with a ship that was docking as they were with who the crew of the ship were and why they had come to Mandaka. Getting himself through the security checkpoint and then back afterward would be trickier to pull off.

He ordered Jerboxh to stay with the ship and make sure it was restocked with food and provisions. He made a point of telling the Sh'kallian to make sure the store of kolan was full. He didn't know how long it was going to take to find T'van, and there was no reason to run out of the drink, especially when it was much easier to procure it from Mandaka, where it originated. Jerboxh just nodded without looking at him. Great, he thought. *Of all the pilots they could have assigned to me, I get a sullen Sh'kallian.* He'd have to deal with Jerboxh's attitude problem later. He needed to talk to his contacts first, and before that, needed to get through security.

Ries left the ship and walked toward the security checkpoint, hoping that Loese wasn't working. The blind security guard relied on a sort of sonar to 'see' who was coming through his checkpoint, and he was both too smart and too principled to allow someone through with a false identification, even one set up by Galactic Intelligence. He knew Ries too well to not know it was him. Ries walked up to the end of the line, waiting to pass through the checkpoint. He was unable to see who was working. After a few moments, as the line slowly moved forward, he finally caught a glimpse of who was performing the inspections. He was relieved to see that it was Dzan. The multi-eyed Zord would be much easier to deal with than Loese. Plus, the blind security guard sort of gave Ries an uneasy feeling every time he spoke to him. The fact that he didn't have any eyes was disconcerting.

What most visitors to the Mandakan Space Port didn't realize was that although the port was patrolled by the

Alliance Society for Peace Officers, the port was owned by the King of Mandaka, and it was his security force that controlled the dock and security checkpoints that led to the interior of the port. The ASPs were a courtesy offered to the king by the Alliance, but they were not the ultimate power on the port. The port security guards reported directly to the king's Security General, though a copy of their daily logs were given over to the ASPs as a courtesy. The Security General was also the Commander of the Mandakan Imperial warship that patrolled around the planet. Luckily, Ries hadn't run into that ship as he approached the port. He and the Security General had experienced their share of differences, but had gotten along well enough professionally. Their history together wouldn't mean much now, though, Ries knew. The SG was smart enough to allow some of the black market trade that benefited his planet's coffers, but also ruthless enough to take care of any problems quickly and efficiently.

Ries slowly approached the security checkpoint. One thing to his advantage was the fact that his species all looked alike to most others. While it was true that members of his species looked very similar, there were certain characteristics that differed among individuals. Antennae length, abdominal plate shape and size, and eye color pattern all could be used as a differentiator, but the differences were difficult to detect, even by a trained security guard. Ries pulled out his fake identification card provided by GI. As he came to the checkpoint, he handed it to Dzan.

"Reason for coming to the Mandakan Space Port today?" the guard buzzed, his words translated into Talondarian Standard by the translating device.

"Supplies, and maybe a little gambling," Ries replied, doing his best to change the quality of his voice, as he had been taught during his agent training. He also slumped a little at the shoulders to disguise his true height.

The Zord paused a moment. Ries imagined that many of the Zord's optical parts were looking at Ries as he studied Ries's features. Finally, the guard passed the ID card over the scanner next to him. "Ship name *Digger* verified," the computer said. Ries inwardly cringed at the name of the ship, but it fit in with his cover of being a freelance ore miner.

Dzan handed the card back to Ries. "Welcome to Mandaka," he said in his buzzing, though not unpleasant voice. "Next, please."

"Thank you," Ries replied gruffly, taking the card and walking onto the port.

◊

Ronak was confused, torn by his feelings about his father's death. The High Vasin had been a relatively old Krahn, but his sons were still young, though they had passed their Ascendancy Day. Most male Krahn were raised to be warriors, and on their Ascendancy Day, (which was informally referred to as Clipping Day by most), were turned from males to genderless warriors. Only the royal male blood lines were allowed to breed on Krahn, and only a portion of those offspring lived their entire lives intact. Those who remained intact due to political wrangling or sheer luck were allowed to breed with any female, whether royal or not, which ensured that there was a large enough gene pool for the species to survive.

Now the entire Qadira Clan was present for the royal funeral and the crowning of his brother, Maliq, as the new High Vasin. It had been decided long before that Maliq would be the royal heir who would follow his father as Vasin, and not Ronak. He felt his resentment for his brother growing as he watched him strut before the assembled clan leaders of Krahn. He turned to look away from the ceremony, not wanting to display the anger that threatened to overwhelm him. His attention was caught by his father's royal black burial case. It was elaborately adorned with jewels and silver, as befitted his station. He looked at his father's face, visible through the clear top of the case. He looked like he could just open his eyes at any time and stand up, ending the pain in Ronak's heart.

His relationship with his father had been complex, and he hadn't spoken to him for months before his death. He was surprised by the raw sense of grief he now felt looking at his father's body. He watched as a stream of commoners walked past the burial case, saying their farewells to their ruler. It was a custom to allow all the members of the clan to do so.

Just then a tall female who was approaching the case caused him to suddenly lose focus on his hatred for his brother. She wasn't looking at the case, though her shoulders were set low in respect for the dead. Instead, she was looking directly at Ronak. Her eyes seemed to blaze with some emotion Ronak could only guess at. He returned her stare. She saw that she had his full attention and finally dropped her eyes in a show of deference, but it was not directed toward his father or his brother, it was to him. She passed by his father's body, forgotten now as he watched her. She gave him one last glance before turning and walking away, not paying any attention to the crowning ceremony.

He had to follow her. Find out who she was. He no longer cared about the ceremony, or about the lifeless flesh in the burial case, all that was left of his father.

He began to walk toward her retreating figure. He knew he was breaking protocol, and that it would be frowned upon, but he didn't care. He couldn't let her just walk away without knowing who she was. He finally caught up to her as she turned the corner of a building, now out of sight of the ceremony. She had stopped just a few Standard feet past the corner, as if she knew she was being followed. When she saw him approaching, she dropped her eyes again, as well as her shoulders, but he saw that she was also smiling.

"What is your name?" he almost blurted out as he came nearer to her position. He composed himself a moment before actually asking the question, though his tongue still felt like someone had drugged him, and his words sounded clunky in his ears.

"Mariqa," she answered, looking up at him and still smiling broadly, her sharp beak flashing in the sunlight.

◊

Ries made his way through the port's central concourse with his head held high. The quickest way to get caught was to act suspicious, as if he didn't belong. He knew that he was on surveillance cameras, but he didn't see any ASPs as he headed directly for the hydrolifts, so he knew that his cover identity was still working for the moment. As he entered one of the lifts, surreptitiously looking around to make sure he wasn't being followed, he pushed a button and waited for the car to move. As the door closed, his lower set of arms straightened out his clothing, while he thought about what he planned to do once the lift stopped.

He was heading toward the main casino level, where one of his better informants, Keiss, owned a small casino called The Invader. Although it wasn't one of the large three-story gambling establishments that dominated the port's interior, it was a successful business, as it catered to a select set of clientele. The rich and powerful of Mandaka, as well as special off-world dignitaries and business representatives, were given preferential treatment at the casino. These high rollers were usually guests of the King of Mandaka, or his son, the crown prince. As Commander of the ASP unit stationed at Mandaka, Ries had needed to keep tabs on all of them. That's where Keiss had played a part. The casino owner kept his aural buds open, and Ries had kept his paw lubricated, as the saying went.

The hydrolift car stopped a floor below Ries's destination, and he was disappointed to see a Makerfy waiting to board. Ries knew who he was, and was sure it wasn't just a chance meeting. As the stout, hairy Makerfy came aboard the car, Ries did his best to ignore the large, toothy smile he bore. Punjor worked for Zazzil, a Carterfan gangster who lived aboard the space port, and the last time he'd talked to the Carterfan, it hadn't ended well.

"Officer Van," Punjor said. "So good to see you again. Happy to see you are well."

"I'm sure you are," Ries replied as the door shut. He ever so slightly moved away from the Makerfy, while also keeping an eye on him, just in case he attacked in the close confines of the hydrolift.

"My employer would like nothing better than to have you come for a visit," Punjor said. "If you have time in your busy schedule, that is." His smile was really beginning to annoy Ries, but he showed no outward sign of it.

"Send him my sincerest apology," Ries said. "I have others I must talk to before I leave." The truth was, he didn't trust that he'd ever leave Zazzil's room if he entered it. They were not on friendly terms.

"That is disappointing," Punjor said. "Almost as disappointing as it would be to have to inform the Security General of your presence on his space port. But I am sure he would understand that you are here under a false identification for a very good reason."

Just then the hydrolift car came to a stop and the doors opened. Ries walked a few paces ahead before turning back toward the Makerfy. "I have an appointment to keep at the moment, but tell Zazzil that I might just have time to speak with him later." He turned away from Punjor before he would have to see those large teeth smiling at him once again.

◊

Ronak struggled to free himself from the chains that wrapped around his ankles, wrists, and neck. His rebellion had finally failed, after years of fighting. His followers, most of them fellow military school students and a few high-placed warriors who were disillusioned by the new High Vasin's peaceful ways, were either dead or imprisoned like himself. He only hoped that his bloodmate, Mariqa, was still alive somewhere. She carried his first clutch of descendants in her abdomen and would be Vasina when he finally won this war.

The final battle had been decisive, and he'd been separated from her when he'd been captured by Maliq's forces. All would be lost without her. She was the reason he'd begun the rebellion in the first place. He stopped his struggles when his brother entered the jail cell room. He wouldn't give Maliq the satisfaction of knowing he was uncomfortable, even though his injured shoulder was screaming at him with pain every time he moved it. A bullet was still lodged within it from his capture. He kept his eyes on the floor, not willing to look at his brother's face and see the smugness in his eyes.

"I've been advised that the easiest way to quell your little rebellion is to just kill you," Maliq said, walking up to the cell bars. "A private trial followed by a public execution, for you and your followers, including Mariqa."

Ronak's head snapped up at his brother's words. Mariqa was still alive, for now at least. He looked back at the ground quickly, not wanting his brother to see the relief in his own eyes.

"But I've talked to Xenic," his brother continued. "There's been enough bloodshed already." Maliq sighed, rubbing his throat in exhaustion. "I never wanted this, Ronak. I wish things were . . . different between you and me."

"Then step down," Ronak said. "Give up your false claim to the throne and free me."

"You know I can't do that," Maliq said, quietly.

"You mean you won't," Ronak said. His shoulder throbbed with every word he spoke.

"Either way," Maliq said. "It won't happen. The clan needs a strong leader. They wouldn't follow you, even if I were to do all that you ask. You've already been defeated. You cannot lead the Qadira Clan."

Ronak knew he was right, and it made the flame of hatred burn even brighter inside him. He was in no position to lead the clan. His dominance would be challenged at every turn. Then he thought of his only alternative. "Release me," he said, raising his eyes to finally look his brother in the face, "and I will take my followers elsewhere. We will not return." *Not until I'm strong enough to conquer you all,* he thought. It was the only way to regain his stature among the clan. His brother stood and stared at him, and Ronak recognized the expression on Maliq's face. It was a cold, calculating look that he'd come to know well when dealing with his older sibling. Finally, he turned away, and Ronak smiled, knowing that he'd won this battle, at least.

"You will be banished forever," Maliq said, standing up straight as he proclaimed his decision. He turned back to look at Ronak. "You'll receive no assistance from any clan on Krahn other than a ship and whatever supplies and followers you can take on it." He stepped closer to the cell and looked at his younger sibling. "Listen to me well, brother. If you ever return to Krahn, your life, as well as any others on your ship, will be forfeit. I will kill you myself." He turned before hesitating again. "Don't make me regret my decision," he said softly. He left without another backward glance.

"Don't worry, brother," Ronak said, spitting out the word as if it pained him to even say it. "You won't live long enough to feel regret. I swear it by the blood of my unborn children."

Chapter 2

Kedar tuc Tinaane looked around at the collection of Rajani, Sekani, and Jirina fighters assembled before him, his lone eye appraising each of them individually. There were twenty in all. Not a large force, but one that should prove to be enough for the mission he had planned. The Rajani he knew and trusted from previous battles; a few of them he'd even known before the Krahn invaded. The Jirina were total unknowns, but he had faith that they would do well, as they always did when called upon. The Sekani were on loan from Zanth, the leader of their species. Kedar was told that these Sekani were more than capable, but he knew that part of the reason they were sent was so that the objective of their mission would be shared equally among the three species. Although that had always been his intention, he didn't mind Zanth's forcefulness if it meant he had more troops to use on the raid.

"Thank you all for coming," he began. "If you don't already know, the structure we'll be assaulting contains the city's central computer. This means we have to be careful not to destroy it while in the process of liberating it from the Krahn." He smiled, before adding, "I don't think Tumaani would be very happy if we erased thousands of years of

Rajani history with a few stray weapon shots."

The other Rajani at least smiled, thinking about the Keeper of the Past's reaction to that kind of news. The Jirina and Sekani only stood waiting for their orders. It was understandable. They didn't know him very well, didn't know if he could be trusted to lead this mission. The only one they all would trust was James the Human, and unfortunately, he wasn't available to come give a pep talk, though Kedar had asked. It was a strange feeling, knowing that the only being they all felt that way about wasn't even an inhabitant of Rajan.

The Human was an outsider, but he was special. James was more than just some alien who had come to help them in their darkest hour of need. He was a symbol of hope, an inspiration for all of them to fight for their own future.

While growing up and eventually becoming a Priest of the Kaa, Kedar had always been the optimistic type. That was until his future had been taken away by the Krahn. His mate was gone, and his youngling as well—a female, but still, she'd been his only child. Both had been killed in the initial attack, when Krahn ships had come screaming from the skies in a wave of destruction. He'd also lost his left eye as his house came crashing in around him. Afterward, he'd been so full of rage that he'd fought the Krahn out of a pure sense of hatred, not caring if he lived or died, as long as they died as well.

He still felt no mercy for the Krahn and would kill them whenever he was given the chance, but now he knew it served a greater purpose. His species—no, not just his, every species on Rajan—was on the brink of extinction because of the Krahn invasion. He must have survived for a purpose. There was a reason why he had lived and everyone he loved was killed, and this was it. It was all he had left to fight for anymore.

◊

Ries finally arrived at the casino and casually walked through the open front door. There was no need to ask to speak to the owner; he knew that he would be on the casino's private surveillance system as soon as he crossed the threshold of the doorway. He walked to a nearby bar and ordered himself a glass of kolan. He'd almost finished it when the casino's private security guard approached where he sat.

"Please follow me, sir," the guard said quietly.

Ries nodded to the guard and stood, noticing the tell-tale bulge of a weapon within easy reach of the guard's tentacled appendage. He drank the last of the kolan in a gulp, and wordlessly followed the guard to a private hydrolift. When the doors to the lift opened, he was met by two more security guards, who asked politely to search him. He had to act like he had nothing to hide, so he let them. He wasn't there to kill anyone unless it became necessary, and they wouldn't find the weapons he had hidden on his body anyways.

The hydrolift began to move soon after he was cleared by the guards, and in a short amount of time he arrived at the top floor. He walked down the small corridor to Keiss's private office, followed by one of the security guards from the hydrolift, a Mantak who looked like he could carry a small starship on his broad shoulders. Ries knew the way; he'd been there many times before. He was surprised, though, when he was met with the barrel of a large energy weapon as he opened the door.

"You checked him for weapons?" a voice he recognized as Keiss's asked. The casino owner sounded tense.

"Of course, sir," the guard answered, frowning, his four eyes closing to slits as he did so.

The door opened wider, and Ries could see that Keiss himself was holding the weapon. "Check him again," Keiss said, his eyes wide as he looked at Ries.

Ries was beginning to grow impatient. "I see your hospitality hasn't improved since I was last here, Keiss," he said as the security guard rubbed and prodded him in various areas of his body, yet still didn't find his weapons.

"I'd have felt better if you had made an appointment," Keiss said. "Or better yet, never came back here at all. Word is the ASPs are hot for you. Not to mention you were just chatting with Zazzil's pet, Makerfy."

"Him?" Ries said, trying to sound casual. "He's nothing. Zazzil was just sending his regards. At least someone missed me since I've been gone."

"I'm sure that was it," Keiss said sarcastically, as he finally lowered the weapon away from Ries. He nodded to the guard and turned away from where Ries stood. Ries followed him into the small room. The office was relatively sparse of decor, with only a desk, computer, and two chairs occupying the cramped space. This was where Keiss did business, not where he lived.

Ries sat down in the chair in front of the desk before Keiss could proffer it. He wasn't there to be courteous. He stretched out his antennae, feeling the tension in them lessen after his walk through the port. "So what's new?" he asked, smiling.

Keiss sat his large frame down in his chair and frowned across the desk at Ries. "What do you want? I got enough trouble coming down from this new ASP commander, I don't need any from the old one."

"You're mistaken," Ries said. "What you don't need is Galactic Intelligence taking an interest in your activities on this space port. It could prove to be most inconvenient."

"Oh no, don't tell me you're one of them now, Ries," Keiss said, holding his head in his hands.

"That's Agent Ries to you," Ries replied. He was enjoying himself. His antennae were picking up waves of discomfort from the casino owner.

"Well, I'm sure Commander Complin would be interested to know that a GI agent was aboard the station illegally," Keiss said, looking up at him.

Ries's smile disappeared. "Commander Complin?"

"Yeah, like I said, the new ASP Commander assigned to the port," Keiss answered. "I take it you know him?"

"Yes," Ries said. He was sure that Complin had been stationed at Mandaka just to piss him off. It had worked. And Complin was probably still angry about his damaged starship. Ries would have to hope he didn't get picked up by the ASPs. It could turn ugly. "Enough small talk, Keiss," he said, trying to change the subject. "I'm here on official business, not to trade threats with you. I need some information."

"What can I do for GI today?" Keiss asked, still frowning.

"I'm looking for a former agent," Ries said. "A Sekani named Odorey T'van. Ever heard of him?"

"Can't say that I have," Keiss said, looking down at his desk and half-heartedly moving around some data disks that were piled there.

"You're lying to me," Ries said, leaning forward in his chair. "Why?"

"Oh, c'mon, Ries," Keiss said, looking up at him with real fear on his face. "I have a business to run here. I can't compromise my clients, or else they'll either go somewhere else, or they'll come after me."

"What client?" Ries asked. He was close, he knew. His antennae were almost humming.

Keiss sighed and rubbed his snout in defeat. "The Sekani has protection from the Talondarians."

This brought Ries's antennae straight up in surprise.

"What?"

"The Talondarian royals," Keiss said. "They're the ones who've been supporting him for years. At least since the king came into power, if not before the Tragedy."

The Tragedy. It was an event that everyone knew about, so much so that two words would evoke memories of where you were when the King and Queen of Talondaria had been overthrown. "Then they're the ones behind all of this?" Ries asked, absentmindedly, trying to take this new information in.

"Behind all of what?" Keiss asked.

Ries looked across the desk at his former contact. Did he really not know what was going on between the Rajani and Krahn Horde? "Is T'van on Talondaria?" he asked, changing the subject.

"I don't know," Keiss said. "The Talondarians have grievances that go back generations, and the current ruler has his share of personal enemies, as well. But the Talondarians are still powerful, Ries. They're more powerful than many realize. Powerful enough to have a number of GI agents in their employ, as well as some high-level ASPs, from what I've heard. That's all I know, I swear."

"Who do the Talondarians have on Mandaka?" Ries asked, standing up.

"He's not on Mandaka," Keiss said, sighing. "He's on the port."

"He's staying at your casino, isn't he?" Ries asked, leaning all four arms on the desk.

Keiss just hung his head in his hands, his snout now almost touching the top of his desk.

◊

Kedar briefed his team on the building's logistics in exact detail. He'd had Tumaani attempt to draw a layout of the rooms surrounding the computer room. Even as an Elder, Kedar had never stepped foot in the central computer room. It had been restricted to the three Keepers alone. The team would have to strike quickly to keep the element of surprise, and also to prevent the Krahn from destroying the computer, if they hadn't already. But they had to go in thinking that the computer was still operable. In a way, this was a rescue mission. Besides holding the history of the Rajani in its extensive memory, the computer also had the ability to send and receive messages across vast distances of space. If they could get a hold of the computer, they could call for help. While they hadn't been able to restore regular electrical power to the section of Melaanse they had so far liberated from the Krahn, they had recovered several working generators. They would have more than enough power to run the computer adequately.

Firearms weren't as scarce as they once were, so all of the members of the team were given one, whether trained with them or not. After they'd defeated the Krahn at their northern base, the Resistance was able to confiscate a large number of weapons stored there. After issuing weapons, they headed toward their destination in downtown Melaange.

The team fanned out just as James had taught them and made their way down the narrow street. James the Human was the only one who had ever been a professional soldier. He'd done his best to teach them all what he knew about military tactics. In theory, it should have been enough to outwit the undisciplined Krahn warriors. The horde relied on their strength of arms and ferocity in close quarter fighting, not on superior strategy.

According to the scouts' reports, the building housing the central computer was lightly guarded. But it was located in an area that was still occupied by the Krahn, so Kedar knew that things could get out of control quickly if they were discovered. The Krahn could call in reinforcements, even a few ships, and their mission would be a failure.

They didn't see their first Krahn until they were only a few hundred Standard feet from the building. The Krahn was dispatched quickly and quietly with a knife through its ribs from behind. They met two more before they reached the building. One of the Krahn they killed outright, with a knife through the ear canal. The other surprised one of the Sekani and ripped out his throat before others from the team smashed in its skull with the butts of their weapons.

Finally, they reached a building that stood across from their target. Kedar could see that it was surrounded by only six Krahn guards. There was no telling how many were still inside. He motioned for his team to fan out around the building's perimeter, as they had planned. When the signal came back that all were in position, he carefully took aim at one of the guards and fired. At the sound of his shot, the rest of his team opened fire as well. The Krahn all fell where they stood. Kedar quickly stood and rushed toward the building, his weapon up and ready. He scanned the windows on the second floor to make sure there were no snipers. He reached the door and waited a beat for his team to catch up. Then he crashed through the door, his team pointing weapons in all directions as James had taught them. There were no Krahn in sight.

The team split up, half going to check out the main and second floors, and half down to the basement, where the computer was located. According to the map that Tumaani had drawn, the computer was located in a reinforced bunker. Kedar led the smaller team to the door that led to the stairs going down to the basement. Suddenly, a Krahn warrior jumped from behind the door where it was hiding and pointed its weapon at Kedar. It fired. Then something strange happened. The projectile never reached where Kedar was standing, as if it hit something in between that could not be seen. Kedar had been caught by surprise, but then he pointed his own weapon at the Krahn and fired, spraying its brain all over the wall behind it.

Kedar looked at the dead Krahn a moment, unsure at what had just happened, but happy that he wasn't the one lying on the floor in a pool of his own blood. Just then, he heard gunfire erupt above them. The other half of his team was under attack. He had a choice to make, either go help his team or make sure the computer was safe. He looked at the open stairwell door a moment before turning to his team. "We go up," he said.

◊

Ries left his meeting with Keiss knowing the name of the Talondarian dignitary who was staying at The Invader. He had no idea how he was going to talk to him. He couldn't just stroll up to the room and introduce himself. There would surely be guards posted, both those provided by the casino and by the Talondarian government. He made his way back down through the casino and out the front door and walked toward the hydrolift. As he was pondering his next plan of attack at the door to the hydrolift, the door opened, revealing Punjor standing inside. Ries frowned, but entered the car. "Do you just ride the hydrolift all day? Doesn't seem like much of a job."

Punjor smiled as the door closed. "My boss pays me very well to do what he asks. If it means riding the hydrolift, then that is what I do. I do not question him." The Makerfy pushed a button, and the car began to move. "He is anxious to speak with you, Agent Van."

Ries noted the change in his title from his earlier

encounter with the Makerfy. Zazzil must have had Keiss under surveillance somehow. He knew the Carterfan was good, but he was impressed by his reach. "If it's about our last conversation, I'm sure Zazzil can appreciate someone who's just performing his job."

"It is not my job to know what Zazzil thinks," Punjor said, still smiling. "If it is any reassurance, if he truly took offense to your last meeting, you would not still be alive to have this one."

"Oh, yes," Ries said, "I feel much better."

The hydrolift car came to a stop and Punjor stepped off, motioning for Ries to follow him. They walked through a maze of corridors until Punjor finally stopped in front of a doorway. Ries knew it well. He'd visited Zazzil on many occasions, but he was still a bit awestruck every time he saw the Carterfan's home away from home. The chill air hit him like a wall as he walked through the doorway. He followed the Makerfy toward the Meeting Room, and noticed that someone else was just leaving. She was a young Talondarian, one he'd never seen aboard the port. *Curious,* he thought, wondering if there was a connection somewhere. He slowed as he passed her by and looked into her eyes, seeing the disappointment on her face. Her meeting with the Carterfan must not have gone well. As he reached the Meeting Room, he overheard Zazzil speaking to Punjor through the translator on the wall. As usual, Zazzil couldn't be seen in the cloudy miasma inside his tank.

"Make sure she returns to her room safely," the Carterfan was saying. "If you must, keep her locked in. Her welfare is my only concern. She's becoming much too headstrong for her own good."

Punjor bowed to his employer before flashing his smile once again at Ries. It was an annoying habit, Ries decided.

Especially because of how long and sharp the Makerfy's teeth appeared. Punjor more than likely knew this and used it at every opportunity he could to intimidate others.

Ries walked into the bubble in the side of the Carterfan's enormous tank and sat in the chair there. "Domestic problems, Zazzil?" he asked casually, watching Punjor escort the young Talondarian female from the room. "She doesn't seem like your type."

"She's none of your concern, Agent Van," came Zazzil's voice from the speaker near the chair.

Ries looked into the cloudy mixture of gases within the tank but couldn't see the Carterfan anywhere. Another habit that annoyed him to no end. "Why am I here?" he asked. "I'm sure this isn't a social visit."

"You're correct, for once," Zazzil said. "As much as it pains me to say it, in this instance, our goals seemed to have aligned."

"You want to find a rogue Sekani GI agent too?" Ries said, smiling.

"Not exactly, but it amounts to the same thing," Zazzil answered. "I will get you access to the Talondarian dignitary. In return, you will make sure that he leaves this space port. The sooner, the better."

"And it's just a coincidence that the female who just left is a Talondarian as well?" Ries said. *Yes,* he thought, *very curious.*

"As I said," Zazzil responded, "she's none of your concern. You are not to approach her or try to contact her in any way. The repercussions of this action would result in severe consequences. Severe."

"Are you threatening a Galactic Intelligence Agent, Zazzil?" Ries said.

"Of course not," Zazzil responded. "Do you want access

to the Talondarian representative or not?"

"Yes," Ries said after a moment. "Who is he, by the way?"

"His name is Creon," Zazzil answered. "He's the youngest son of King Tordor of Talondaria."

This got Ries's attention; Keiss hadn't told him that Creon was the king's son. He sat up quickly. "And you can get me access to him? Today?"

"There are certain elements within the Talondarian society that are still loyal to the former king and queen," Zazzil answered. "Some of them happen to be within the current security command structure. They are closer to the king than he realizes."

Ries was speechless as he thought of the implications of what Zazzil was telling him. He'd stumbled once again into something for which he was altogether unprepared. All he'd wanted was to find T'van, and now he was caught up in a possible coup. He also had no doubt that if he didn't agree to go through with Zazzil's plan, he would find himself in a dangerous predicament. He'd been told too much for Zazzil to just let him walk away. He really had no choice in the matter that he could see. "Okay, then let's get it done quickly," he said. "I need to be alone with the princeling, and I need time to question him adequately."

"That can be arranged," Zazzil said. "Do you guarantee that the delegate will leave the port afterward?"

"Of course," Ries answered, knowing that if everything played out right, he'd be off the port and on his way to find T'van as well.

◊

Kedar cautiously moved along the corridor leading to the stairwell that accessed the second floor. His half of the team had checked out the main floor and found no one. The gunfire had lessened, but an occasional shot still rang out, which meant that at least one member of the team was still alive. He found a dead Jirina lying at the bottom of the stairwell, a wounded Sekani sitting next to him, holding a bloody hand over his side.

"We were ambushed," the Sekani said, painfully gasping as Elenden, one of Kedar's Rajani, attended to the wound in his side.

"How many are there?" Kedar asked the Sekani, whose name he couldn't remember.

"Only five or so," the Sekani said, grimacing as the Rajani probed his wound. "I don't know for sure. I was hit, and Doren carried me downstairs." He looked over at the Jirina. "I . . . I didn't know he got hit too."

"He'll be fine if we can get him out of here," Elenden said. "The wound goes all the way through."

"Then take him back to the compound once you have him ready to go," Kedar said. "Take two or three others to help carry him and provide security."

Kedar continued slowly up the stairwell, along with three Jirina and a Sekani. At the top, they found two more dead Jirina and a dead Rajani. He saw that there were two Rajani crouched down next to the corner of the corridor. One of them, Menttel, saw him coming and motioned for him to get down. Kedar crouched low and walked over to wall. "Where's everyone else?" he asked.

"Pinned down just on the other side of the corner," Menttel answered. "We killed two of them, but there are at least three others holed up in a room down the corridor. We didn't know if we had approval to take them out."

"Where are the explosives?" Kedar asked.

"Around the corner," Menttel answered.

"Stay here," Kedar said. He slowly looked around the corner to see members of his team crouched down in various doorways along the corridor. He looked farther down to see a bullet-riddled door at the end of the corridor, which was about a hundred Standard feet away. It was a dilemma. If they used explosives, they would alert other Krahn in the area to their activity. If they tried to rush the room, other members of his team could be wounded or killed. He turned back away from the corridor to think. Finally, he decided that they should use a small amount of the construction explosives they had brought as a diversion and send his team in with orders to shoot anything in the room. If it alerted a Krahn patrol in the vicinity, then they'd deal with it later.

Suddenly, a flurry of shots rang out in the corridor. He turned the corner to see two Krahn warriors in the doorway, shooting toward his team. A Jirina was hit in the arm as he leaned out to return fire. Kedar wasn't the best shot with a weapon, but he was skilled enough for the moment. He pointed his weapon around the corner and aimed at the first Krahn he saw, who hadn't yet seen him. He pulled the trigger, feeling the jolt of the butt against his shoulder. He kept his eyes on the Krahn long enough to see it drop, a hole appearing in its chest, before turning back. The firing stopped, and Kedar turned to look once again. The Krahn was lying where it fell. The other was nowhere to be seen.

Kedar used a loud whisper to convey his orders to the team. They were to throw two explosives down the corridor, followed by a rush from every member of the team. When all of them had nodded their acknowledgment, he held out his hand, counting down on his fingers. After he'd curled his last digit, two explosives were flung down the corridor as everyone covered their heads. The twin explosions seemed excessively loud in the close confines. Almost instantly, Kedar stood and motioned for everyone to move. He saw that the doorway was a ruin, the door blown in half and lying in the room. He ran down the corridor, confident his team would follow. When he got to the room, he saw that there were four Krahn, and they were holding their heads, stunned by the concussive blasts. He began to shoot any Krahn he saw, regardless if they were armed or not. Other shots rang out as his team caught up to him, and all of the Krahn were quickly killed.

The smoke-filled room had become an abattoir, with Krahn blood spattered on the walls and floor. He turned to see the members of his team looking at him, many of them with the same shocked looks on their faces as the Krahn had right before they were killed. He nodded to his team, trying to work up enough moisture in his mouth to speak. "Good job, everyone," he said, his voice sounding foreign in ears that still rang from the explosion and weapons fire. "Be on your guard, but I think that's all of them." He prayed that it was.

◊

Ries waited for word that everything was ready for him to talk to the Talondarian dignitary. Zazzil had set him up in an empty room on the space port; a room that was comfortable, surprisingly. As much trouble as Ries had caused him over the years, he wouldn't have been surprised if Zazzil had provided a maintenance closet. He sat and sipped from a glass of kolan and wondered how he became entangled in such intriguing but dangerous situations. What was more surprising to him was how he felt. He had to admit, he was having fun. He did regret the loss of his houses on Mandaka and his small fortune, but in his short time in GI, he'd learned to live on his wits and not much else.

He'd only just received a ship for the first time since joining GI. Before that he'd been forced to find lodging space on whatever ship he could to get to a desired destination.

Thinking about the ship, he wondered if Jerboxh had even begun to resupply it as he'd ordered. The Sh'kallian was an able enough pilot, he supposed, but his attitude was atrocious. As he was musing about possibly making Jerboxh disappear, there was a chime from the door, and he stood to open it. He saw on the monitor next to the door that it was his favorite Makerfy, Punjor. Ries pushed the button that opened the door and frowned at the grinning face that appeared.

"Zazzil wants me to inform you that the package is ready for your inspection," Punjor said. "If you will follow me?"

"Lead the way," Ries said, standing up.

He stayed behind the Makerfy the entire way, so he wouldn't have to talk to him. After a maze of twists and turns that not even Ries could follow, they came to a door that Ries assumed was somewhere close to the outer hull of the space port. He waited a moment while Punjor tapped in a security code, and then the door opened. Punjor stood to the side and motioned for Ries to walk in. Ries tentatively looked into the room and saw a surprisingly young Talondarian male sitting in a chair. The room was basically adorned, so he assumed it was some type of storage room, or possibly even a meeting room for port staff.

"My father will hear of this," the Talondarian said, angrily.

"Hear of what?" Ries asked, innocently.

"Of how I was kidnapped from my own room in the middle of the night and brought to this place against my will," the prince said. Ries noticed that he was not just sitting in the chair, he was attached to it. There were small, clear bands of some type of material around his wrists, ankles, and waist.

"I apologize if you've been treated poorly," Ries said. "I assure you, it wasn't my doing. When I heard what had happened to you, I came straightaway to make sure you weren't being treated harshly by your captors."

The Talondarian looked at him suspiciously. "Who are you?"

Ries walked closer to him, and noticed for the first time how scared the Talondarian appeared. *He really is young,* Ries thought. *Pity.* "I'm an agent of Galactic Intelligence."

"If that's true, then you should be able to get me out of here, correct?" Creon asked, eagerly sitting forward in his chair and stretching the clear bands to their limits. "I don't understand why I'm here, and my hands and legs are starting to go numb."

Ries patted the prince on his shoulder with one of his lower hands. "I'm sure I can work it out with your captors, don't worry." A palpable look of relief came over the prince's face. *So young,* Ries thought. "By the way, while I'm here, I was wondering if you could help me with a little matter, just as a professional courtesy."

"What?" the prince asked, now looking skeptical again.

"Just a small matter," Ries said. "I'm searching for a rogue agent. I was hoping that you may have some idea of where I can find him. His name is Odorey T'van."

Ries watched as Creon's expression changed yet again. Ries couldn't tell whether it was fear or dread he saw on the prince's face, but either way, it was a look of quiet guilt. He knew where the Sekani was, and he probably wouldn't just tell. It was time to move from friendly banter to interrogation. He pulled the small pain inducer from where he'd hidden it in a hollow section on his thorax. He turned it to a medium setting and pressed it against the prince's neck. He pushed the button. The prince screamed at the unexpected and excruciating pain.

"I know, I know," Ries said. "That was just to let you feel

what would happen if you lie to me." The prince struggled against his bonds, but Zazzil's employees had been thorough. The bonds didn't budge.

"Now, will you tell me where I can find T'van?" Ries asked.

"I . . . don't know anything," the prince responded, thrusting his chin out in defiance. He was young—he would learn. Ries touched the inducer to the prince's chest and hit the button, and then hit it again. Once again the prince screamed as the pain radiated throughout his body.

"Tell me what I want to know and the pain will stop," Ries said. "I need to know the location of T'van. Is he here? Is he nearby? Is he on Talondaria?"

The prince just sat, panting in the chair, tears streaming from his eyes. Ries thought of turning the pain inducer up to its highest level, but knew it would kill the prince quickly, especially if he had any heart problems. *No, I have time,* he thought. Better to make sure he had all the information he could get from the Talondarian dignitary.

"I don't enjoy this," Ries said. "I don't like to see you in pain, but it's critical that I find T'van. He's the only one who knows the name of his Sekani contact on Rajan."

At this statement, the prince looked up at him sharply. Ries stopped where he was, surprised at the reaction. "Do you know the name of the Sekani?" he asked, bringing his face near to the prince's. Could it be that he wouldn't have to find T'van at all?

The prince lowered his head swiftly, closing his eyes. Ries turned the pain inducer up a notch and stuck it in the prince's ribs. The prince screamed again, this time doubling over as the pain coursed through his body. Ries pulled back the inducer as the prince vomited on his own legs.

Ries paced around the chair, becoming truly irritated.

He was so close. He could practically feel the answer within reach. "Where is T'van? What is the name of his contact? Tell me what I want to know."

"T'van . . . is out of your reach," the prince said. Ries hit him again with the inducer. This time the prince lost consciousness.

"Blast it!" Ries said, looking at the still form of the Talondarian, knowing that if he kept this up, he was going to kill the prince without learning what he knew. The Talondarian was stronger than he thought he would be when he first saw him, and this was going to take longer than he would have hoped. He was going to have to take the prince back to his ship and interrogate him properly. But that meant getting him there.

◊

Kedar walked down the stairs in the computer building. At least his ears were ringing less from all the recent explosions and weapons fire. His team had searched the entire structure and hadn't found any more Krahn warriors within it. He walked to the door that Tumaani had pointed out on his improvised map and tried to open it. It was locked. He'd sent half of the remaining members of his team to guard the doors of the building in case the earlier explosions had alerted any more Krahn to their presence, and brought the other half down to the basement with him. Now he motioned for them to take position around the door in case there was a Krahn warrior within the computer room. Fortunately, Tumaani had left the key to the room at his estate when he was captured by the Krahn. The Keeper had gone back to retrieve it and had given it to Kedar before the mission. Kedar pulled the key from his pocket and inserted it into the lock. He looked at his team before quickly turning the key, and then the handle, pushing the door open in one quick motion.

His team piled into the room, guns pointing in all directions.

The room was empty. *Could it be that the Krahn had been unaware of what was in the basement of the building?* Kedar thought. It seemed unlikely, but it didn't appear as if any of them had entered the room. The computer was undamaged. It would just need to be powered up and turned on. The computer interface terminal was a simple seat with a monitor and keyboard. The computer itself was made up of a large network of memory modules that lined the walls and a central control box that sat under the monitor. The Rajani were conservative in their use of technology, so they were still using a manual interface and years-old computer model, but it would do for now.

Kedar motioned for Mentell to bring him a large backpack that they had brought with them. He opened the bag, revealing the small power generator. It was one of the few the Resistance had, but he knew that it should be powerful enough to at least boot up the computer and send a message for help. He plugged the generator into one of the computer's power jacks and turned it on. The generator hummed softly. Kedar reached over and turned on the computer. There was a moment when he thought it wasn't going to work, but then the screen came to life. He waited for it to run through its startup protocol before opening up the communication system application.

He typed in a simple message telling of the situation on Rajan and imploring help from the Galactic Alliance. Then he pushed the 'send' button on the screen. The screen showed the word 'Sending' for a moment before a message came up. "Unable to send message. Interference from extra planetary source. Please check all connections and try again."

"No!" Kedar said. He'd been afraid of that. The Krahn were jamming communications from orbit. He tried sending the message again, just to make sure, and soon received the same alert. He hung his head down a moment in frustration before standing up. At least it wasn't a total loss. They had the computer, and would set up guards around the room and the building until they were sure the area was secure. He looked around at the assembled team and smiled, hiding his disappointment. "I need volunteers to stay here and guard the computer until reinforcements arrive. You all did an exceptional job today. I commend you for your dedication. I have to go talk to the Elders, as well as the leaders of the Sekani, Jirina, and James the Human." He was not surprised when all of them volunteered to stay.

◊

Ries was at a loss as to how he was going to move the Talondarian prince to his ship. Finally, he knew he was going to have to ask Punjor for help. As much as he would have liked to hit the Makerfy with his pain inducer until his insufferable smile was purged from his lips forever, he knew that only Zazzil and his employees had the resources to pull this sort of thing off successfully. But would they consent to his plan? That was the question. He had a feeling that keeping the prince in that room and doing what he wanted with him was fine, but Zazzil might object to a kidnapping. A disappearing prince would cause a lot of trouble on the port for anyone who wasn't pure as the egg, as his mother used to say. He also knew that he was probably under Zazzil's watch at that very moment.

"I need to move the prince to my ship for further questioning," he said in a conversational tone. It was only a few Standard minutes before there was a chime at the door.

He pushed the button that opened the door, to see Punjor waiting for him, smiling widely. "My employer wishes me to tell you that if we agree to this course of action, the prince must never be found again. Ever."

"Agreed," Ries replied. He'd never intended for the prince to live past his questioning. It would be too dangerous to allow him to survive. The Makerfy nodded, stepping aside to make room for a cart that was being pushed by a large, ugly creature. It was a Xerbian. Suddenly, pieces began to fall into place about the riot that had occurred on the port right before his demotion. But why? Why risk a fight with the ASPs? Ries was sure that Zazzil had a reason, but it wasn't worth speculating about at the moment. They needed to move the prince. Yet Zazzil and Punjor had to know that Ries was smart enough to link the Xerbian to the riot. Perhaps they no longer cared if he knew, which meant he had to be extra careful, in case they were planning on making him disappear, along with the prince.

"Zazzil's transporter can offer the cover you seek," Punjor said. "It is a common sight to see it moving from place to place at night." The Xerbian easily picked up the unconscious prince and placed him in the cart. It was a quick, if nerve-racking walk to the hydrolift and then through security to the docking area. Loese, the blind security guard, only nodded to him as he passed through, and he wondered if Zazzil was in control of port security as well. They finally arrived at Ries's ship.

"Remember," Punjor said. "The prince must never be found again, dead or alive. It is imperative that he disappears."

"I understand," Ries said as he punched in the security code for his ship's outer hatch. He was met at the inner door of the airlock by Jerboxh.

"What's going on?" the pilot asked, his eyes wide as he watched the Xerbian push the cart past. "What exactly is that?"

"None of your concern," Ries said. "Prep the ship for

departure immediately and get clearance. We're leaving."

"But—" Jerboxh began.

"I said, we're leaving," Ries repeated. "No more questions."

"Fine," Jerboxh said, turning and heading for the bridge, his tail twitching with displeasure. Soon the Xerbian returned and left the ship, pushing the transporter before him, and not even glancing in Ries's direction.

"There's something I don't understand," Ries said to Punjor as he was about to leave as well.

"What is that?" Punjor asked, turning back toward him.

"Why start a riot on the port?" Ries asked.

"Why not?" Punjor responded, smiling. He bowed slightly to Ries and walked off the ship.

Chapter 3

James Dempsey, leader of a team of Human Beings brought to Rajan and de facto leader of the Rajani resistance forces, waited until he'd left the computer building to disengage his invisibility mode. Kedar could handle things from there, he was sure. He had come along strictly as an observer, and an indiscernible one at that. He wanted the three species of Rajan to be able to fight and win on their own, not rely on the Humans or their powers. It was the reason why he rarely went out to fight and hardly ever used his great strength. He wanted the combined species of Rajan to have pride in themselves as they won the war against the Krahn. He'd intervened just once inside the computer building, when he had saved Kedar's life, and that had been a lucky case of being at the right place at the right time.

He remained powered up until he reached a section of the city that he knew was controlled by the Resistance. He felt the familiar pangs of hunger from using his powers for so long. He mentally kicked himself for not bringing along something he could eat afterward, even if only a protein bar. He shrugged and waved to a passing group of Sekani males, who looked like they were going out on patrol from their nearby compound. He thought of stopping to say hello to

Kieren, but then his attention was caught by a figure sprawled out next to a building within the compound.

As he came nearer, he could see that it was Gianni. He walked through the gate, nodding silently to the two Sekani guards posted there. They knew who he was and didn't say a word, though they both smiled widely at him. As he approached the Sekani building, he saw that the other man was sleeping, an empty bottle that had once contained fernta lying next to him.

James had heard about the fight between Gianni and David and the resulting argument between Gianni and Kieren. He'd been so busy with the Resistance that he hadn't had a chance to talk to them, though Yvette had filled him in on the particulars of the situation. He bent down next to Gianni's head as the other man started to snore softly. He decided he couldn't just leave him there, as much as he wanted to. The Humans had a reputation to uphold, such as it was. If anything, he was surprised it was Gianni lying there drunk and not David. He'd noticed on the *Tukuli* how much and how frequently David partook of the alcoholic beverage known as fernta, many of the times with Janan'kela, the Sekani pilot. Yet he seemed to have straightened himself out once they had all crashed on Rajan. Yvette had mentioned, though, how the man had become more and more distant after Janan had been taken by the Krahn. Just then, Gianni snorted loudly and opened his eyes. His gaze finally focused on James's face.

"Still not in heaven," James said, smiling.

"Very funny," Gianni said, wincing. "Ah, my head."

"Tell me you haven't been lying here for long," James said.

"That depends," Gianni said, sitting up slowly. "Is it morning?"

"Long past," James answered, standing up and extending his hand down to the other man.

"Then I'd be lying," Gianni said, grabbing onto James's hand and pulling himself to his feet. He just as quickly bent over, and James took two steps back, just in case Gianni got sick. He'd just received new shoes that actually fit him from the Rajani, and he didn't want to ruin them.

Gianni stood back up slowly. "Sorry," he said. "Stood up too fast."

"We need to talk," James said. "But first you need to get cleaned up. You smell like a distillery."

"They don't have enough clean water to drink, let alone take a bath," Gianni said.

"Then go take a dip in the ocean or something," James said. "At least go brush your teeth, man."

"Okay, okay," Gianni said. "I know, I'm pathetic. Kieren and David already told me."

"Yeah, I heard about that from Yvette," James said. "You know, I'm not one to give advice about women. Before Yvette, it had been a long time since I was in any type of relationship."

"I'm certainly not doing well in the romance department," Gianni said. "I could use all the advice I can get."

James chuckled before turning serious again. "Well, I guess my point is, when an opportunity presents itself, you need to do all that you can to not blow it."

"Funny you should say that," Gianni said.

"And even when it seems like you've done everything right," James continued, "you can still lose it all. Believe me, I know."

"But I haven't done anything right, that's the problem," Gianni said. "Kieren's right, I did blow it. I don't think I could fix things with her if I tried."

"You'd be surprised," James said. "Women can forgive a lot of things. Look, I know now that the tough-guy smartass routine was mostly an act. I've heard how helpful you've been to the Sekani since you've arrived. I think it's time to be honest with yourself and with Kieren."

Gianni gave him a wary look.

"I don't care about your past, if that's what you're thinking," James said. "Hell, I don't even consider myself a cop anymore. As far as I'm concerned, the slate was wiped clean the moment we woke up on that ship. I'm sure she feels the same way. She wants to know the man you are now, not the man you were. It's as simple as that."

"It's not that simple," Gianni said, quietly.

"I won't say any more," James said. "Just think about it. And take a bath before you talk to her again. You really do stink."

◊

Yvette had fallen into a comfortable routine since reuniting with James and the others. She spent her days either helping on patrols with the Vaderren, the Rajani troops, or with Bhakat, who was doing what he could to set up medical facilities for all three species on Rajan. At night, James would return from a busy day of strategy sessions with the three species or diplomatic meetings between them. She didn't mind so much not seeing him during the day—they were both busy—as long as he came home to her at night. Neither of them had said the 'L' word to the other as of yet; she knew about his first and only marriage, but she sometimes resented having to compete with the memory of a dead woman. But she was also afraid of saying "I love you" and not receiving the same response from James.

She was a strong woman, but this one thing made her feel like a helpless schoolgirl. It was aggravating and discouraging at times. She had woken up that morning determined to talk to James about their relationship before it drove her mad with anxiety, but he'd already left, presumably to attend another meeting, and she'd felt a little lightheaded and nauseated when she'd first attempted to get out of bed.

It was puzzling, because none of them had been sick since they'd arrived on Rajan, as far as she knew. This was strange in itself, when she thought about it. They were exposed to countless new viruses and germs, both on Rajan and on the space port they'd visited before arriving there, and yet none of the new bugs had any ill effects on any of the Humans. It was a riddle for which she had no answer. It seemed that she had finally succumbed and caught something. She just hoped it wasn't anything serious. She'd have to ask Bhakat when she saw him next. For now, she decided, she just needed to rest.

◊

Gianni hadn't meant to drink the entire bottle of fernta the night before. He'd sat and thought about Kieren and about all of things he wished he could change, not only his relationship with her, but his entire life. Yet something that James had said earlier had struck a chord with him. James had said that he didn't consider himself a cop anymore. He hadn't known James at all before the abduction, and not very well aboard the ship, but he could tell that the man had changed even from the person he was when they all first woke up aboard the *Tukuli*. Most cops he'd met were lifers, so he assumed that James was the same—dedicated more to his work than to anything else in his life. It must have been difficult for him to change the way he thought of himself.

Gianni had been thinking about Kieren quite a lot, even before his run-in with James that morning, and it both scared him and thrilled him at the same time. He'd never really been much of a ladies' man, so he didn't have a lot of experience wooing a woman properly. Most of the time it was some lady he met at a club and his work was halfway finished for him, depending on how much she had been drinking, and how many inhibitions she had to begin with. He wasn't always proud of his sexual conquests, but those weren't the type of girls you brought home to Mama anyway. He almost never called them again, which didn't exactly earn him a glowing reputation in the New York club scene.

He'd been somewhat relieved to be sent to Detroit and let the New York situation die down for a while. He hadn't gone out much in Detroit. There were too many country bars and strip clubs. Not that he didn't like seeing a naked woman as much as the next guy, but a strip club wasn't the best place to pick up women. Usually it was his cousin Tomas who dragged him along to play wingman, but that meant Gianni was stuck with the cute girl's friend, running interference so Tomas could get in good with the looker without having to worry about her bulldog roommate getting in the way.

Of course, he and Tomas had not been in Detroit for pleasure. Tomas's father had sent them to scout out new territory. They were thinking of making a move to seat Tomas in Detroit to better cover the drug routes through the Erie Canal. Cocaine and marijuana would come in and was then sent through Windsor and Detroit to supply their businesses in those regions. The Feds didn't even know yet that the entire system had been set up and was overseen by the New York family. They also had a finger in most of the casinos in the region, whether tribal casinos in Michigan or the Canadian ones across the border, and they owned hotels in both places as well. The real money in that region of the country was in the gambling.

He'd wondered at times while on the *Tukuli*, and then on Rajan, what might be going on back on Earth. His family had probably given him up for dead, figuring he'd ended up with cement shoes at the bottom of the Detroit River or some similar fate. Maybe they retaliated by killing a rival's man, but they would have moved on by now.

The fact was, he and the other four Humans had all been given a second chance. Whatever had happened before was in the past. He had to let it go if he was to become the person he wanted to be. It was all about choice. Kieren had said she had chosen him. He hoped he hadn't truly blown it. There was only one way to find out. He'd agreed to go out on patrol with the Sekani that afternoon for a short time, but after that, it was time to change for good.

◊

Kieren had been living with the Sekani for a few months before she realized that she enjoyed their culture immensely. She still wasn't sure how much it had changed from the time before the Krahn had attacked, but she suspected that now they were much freer to practice their own customs, since escaping from under the thumb of the Rajani. When the Krahn had first attacked, they had rounded up all of the Rajani, regardless of gender or age. They had not considered the other races of Rajan a threat, and so had only rounded up Jirina males of a certain age, and any Sekani they caught were immediately sent to the main Krahn base in the south of Rajan as food stocks, and then on to the colony ship as well. It was no wonder that the Sekani had been the ones to go farthest underground.

She'd learned, from Zanth mostly, the Rajani had outlawed some Sekani traditions when they had conquered them. In their effort to integrate the Sekani into their own culture, the Rajani had ruthlessly crushed any sense of independence the Sekani felt. Even the Sekani language had been officially banned from use, though, as she had discovered upon first being found after her escape pod crashed to the surface of Rajan, the Sekani still spoke the language when they gathered together. She had also been fascinated to learn about the Sekani religion, which had also been banned by the Rajani. Because the Sekani had evolved as nocturnal hunters, their goddess was known as the Blue Moon Goddess. She was also known as the Huntress. She was depicted as a large Sekani female with a spear strapped to her back, riding on the back of a Slan, a monstrous beast that looked like a cross between a bear and some type of big cat.

She'd learned that the male Sekani were the primary workers, although some females were used as servants in the Elders' houses. Mainly, though, the females stayed at home with the younglings, who were brought up and taught in a communal setting until they reached the age of twenty-three seasons. At that time, they would start an apprenticeship to work for the Rajan.

Kieren had to do something to pass the time each day. The conditions had improved a great deal since they had first been captured by the Sekani and brought to Zanth, but there was still a lot of work to be done. The scouts had just found a number of wells, which provided fresh water for all of the Resistance. Since they had begun attacking Krahn outposts and troop caravans, their security had improved to the point where they were not in constant fear of being captured. Because of this, the Sekani had been able to begin rebuilding their society, at least on a limited basis.

Their time amongst the Sekani had also begun to bring her and Gianni closer together, or at least that was what she had thought until David had appeared and everything had gone wrong. She was frustrated with herself, because she realized that despite what she'd told Gianni, she knew she still had strong feelings for him. He refused to make any effort to learn the languages, whether Sekani, Rajani, or Talondarian Standard, so most of the time they could be found holding hands so he could understand everything being said. It was going to be an awkward situation now, whenever they needed to hold hands. Many times he would go out on patrol with the Sekani, where he only needed to know when to shoot or raise a force shield to protect his companions. He'd gained notoriety amongst the Sekani for his fearlessness and ferocity in battle.

Of course, Kieren knew that when powered up, they were almost invulnerable. The only weakness she knew of at least, was they must stay conscious or else the energy field surrounding them would drop. Also, to her eternal consternation, if they lost concentration. It had happened to her only a few times, but enough so that she and Gianni had gotten into a number of arguments over her involvement in any fighting whatsoever. She had relented, only because she was secretly happy not to have to fight. She was just not a warrior. She would much rather help the Sekani in their struggle to become a free society once again. Her greatest joy came in working with the Sekani younglings. They were all inquisitive and able pupils. They wanted to know all about her and the others, especially their hero, James the Human.

She was returning from a visit with the younglings, and was headed to the room she had been given at the Sekani compound, when she ran into Gianni. It looked to her as though he had just come back from a patrol. His four Sekani companions were bidding him goodbye, using the Sekani nickname that they had given to him. They called him *Sedan'ka*. The closest translation she had for it was 'Bright Finger' or 'Fire Finger.' She was a little disappointed she hadn't been given a Sekani nickname, but she supposed it must have been a guy thing, even way out here on another planet.

"I'm starving," Gianni said when he saw her.

"Well, I'm not your cook," Kieren answered.

"No," he said, wincing. "That's not what I meant. I just, I mean, I was just going to ask you if you'd like to, you know, have dinner with me. Tonight."

"Oh, I—" she started to say before he interrupted.

"Never mind," he said. "I'm sure you've been invited by Zanth or someone important to dinner. It's okay."

"No. I mean, yes, I'll have dinner," she said. "With you. Right now?"

"How about half an hour?" he asked. "I should get cleaned up first. We ran into a small Krahn scout party, and I chased them for at least a mile. Worked up a pretty good sweat."

"Okay," she said. "Half an hour."

"At my place?" he asked.

"Okay," she said.

Gianni turned and quickly headed for his own room, which was on the other side of the compound from hers. He turned back once to look at her, and gave her a little wave that she found endearing. She returned the wave and watched him until he was out of sight in the maze of buildings.

"Shit," she said, and ran for her own place. It was the strongest swear word she ever used. She was thinking about everything she could do to get ready in the time she had left. Her hair was a mess, and she didn't have any makeup or nail polish or anything—the Sekani didn't use it. Her hair had been about to her neckline when she'd first been brought aboard the *Tukuli*, and now it was to her shoulders—not a great length to work with for any type of styling. Most of the time she kept it tied with a piece of string in a ponytail to keep it out of her face. At least she'd been able to find a hairbrush that seemed to work for her hair. It had probably belonged to an Elder at some point.

She went back to her room and washed up with some of the water ration she'd been given for the week—they still didn't have running water. She brushed her hair and cleaned her teeth as best she could. The Sekani did have perfume, but to her it smelled like wet cat, and she was afraid of what it might be made of, so she refused to use it. She took a good look at herself in her mirror, something she hadn't done since first arriving in the Sekani compound.

She had lost weight since coming to Rajan. Her cheekbones were more prominent, but surprisingly, she didn't look gaunt or unhealthy. Her face looked plain without makeup, but she'd always had a good complexion, so at least there were no embarrassing pimples. She'd never been a heavy makeup user back on Earth, but she wished she at least could have found some lipstick. She sighed and resigned herself to the fact that she looked how she looked, and that was just the way it was. She had shaved that morning, so her legs and armpits were still smooth. She knew that Yvette had chosen not to shave, letting nature take its course, but Kieren felt creeped out by even a little hair on her legs.

Why didn't I say an hour? she thought, hurrying to change her clothes. They'd been able to find some Rajani clothing that fit her and Gianni well enough. The clothes must have been made for adolescents, but at least it was something better than a black robe. Finally, she felt ready and took one last look in the mirror. She had to admit, she looked pretty good, when it came down to it. She stuck her tongue out at herself and turned to go, rolling her eyes at her own lack of modesty.

◊

Yvette hadn't had any plans for the day, so she spent most of it lying down. She felt better as the day went on, and by the quality of the light outside the room, could tell that it was now late afternoon. James was somewhere else, presumably preparing for the meeting between the three species, so she knew he'd be gone most of the day and probably not come back until later that night. She thought of going out on her own to find a little action with the Krahn, but it didn't really interest her at the moment. She was tired of killing. Frankly, it had begun to bore her—at this point, it was just too easy.

Kieren was busy with the Sekani, and Gianni was best left alone until he could deal with his problems. David was becoming a real cold fish. He hardly talked to anyone anymore. It wasn't that she felt unwanted, but she was practical enough to know she was unneeded at the moment. On top of all that, she was fighting off some bug that didn't seem real serious, but could become so for all she knew. She had no idea what types of illnesses the Rajani had on their planet. Did they catch colds? The flu? Pneumonia? She decided it was time to talk to Bhakat about it, if only for her own peace of mind.

She found him outside the medical clinic he was setting up for the Jirina, getting ready to pick up a stack of tables to carry inside. There didn't seem to be anyone else around. The Jirina had no one educated in medicine in their community, so they were in dire need of medical care, if only for the types of injuries, sicknesses, and preventative care that came up on a typical day.

Bhakat had been searching for any Rajani he could find who were medically trained. Most of the doctors were also Elders, and many had been killed in the first attacks by the Krahn, but Bhakat had been able to find a handful and had put them to work at the various clinics he had helped set up. They in turn were training their Sekani and Jirina assistants in basic first aid and emergency response. They were also training some of the Rajani, Sekani, and Jirina to treat the types of wounds encountered on the battlefield. There had been a high attrition rate among the troops who were injured while fighting the Krahn, but it was beginning to lower significantly as they trained more and more troops to keep the injured alive long enough to receive proper medical care. It was a slow process, but Bhakat had made a great deal of progress already.

He smiled when he saw her coming down the street toward him, and she smiled in response, if only because he still looked like he was ready to bite someone whenever he attempted to smile. "I'm happy to see you," Bhakat said once she was within talking distance.

"Why, do you have something that needs a hole poked in it?" she asked. It was an old joke between them, about her skill at poking holes and his at patching them up.

"No," he replied. "I just enjoy your company."

She was still surprised at times at how different he was from her first impression of him when she had woken up aboard the *Tukuli*. "I'm afraid this isn't a social call," she said. "I think I'm coming down with something."

"Coming down . . . ?" he asked, a puzzled expression on his face.

"I think I'm getting sick," she said. She was taken aback as his expression quickly changed to concern.

"That shouldn't be possible," he said.

"Why?" she asked, beginning to grow concerned as well by the sudden change.

"You've been implanted with a Johar Stone," he responded simply, as if that explained everything.

"Yes, but what does that have to do with anything?" she asked.

"Rauphangelaa asked me not to tell you all too much

about the Stones when we brought you aboard the ship," Bhakat said. "For that, I am sorry. You should have been told everything, but he was afraid you would not agree to be implanted, and if you weren't, that you wouldn't agree to help us."

"So what are you saying?" she asked. "Are they somehow dangerous?" *Is this why I'm getting dizzy spells?* she thought. *Is it doing something to my brain?* "Tell me the truth, Bhakat."

He looked around a moment, as if making sure they couldn't be overheard. "You must not share this information with anyone, do you understand?"

She reluctantly nodded, though she knew she would tell James later, no matter the seriousness of what Bhakat was about to divulge.

"The truth is," he began, "the Johar Stones are not truly . . . stones. Implanting a mineral substance in the brain, no matter what properties it exhibited, would only cause the body to treat it as a foreign object or as a tumorous growth."

"So you gave us all brain tumors?" she asked, shocked.

"No," he said. "Quite the opposite. Please just let me explain. The Stones are not truly stones. They're what are known as symbiotic organisms."

"You put some type of creature in my brain?" she asked. "Are you crazy?"

"Yes," he replied. Then after a moment he smiled. "And no."

"Oh my God," she said, feeling like she was going to faint. She walked unsteadily and sat in the closest chair.

"It's safe, I assure you," he said, seeing the look on her face. "I didn't lie on the *Tukuli* when I told you all that. I would not have performed the operation if it was unsafe. In fact, you and the rest of the Humans are very close to your peak physical conditions, if not there already. The Stone restores any physical impurities within its host organism. According to what we know, it keeps you at the height of physical perfection."

"You're saying we can't die?" she asked, looking up at him.

"No, you can die," he replied. "Lose enough blood, get stabbed in the heart or shot in the head while your power fields are down—whatever doesn't allow your body to heal itself fast enough, can kill you. Barring that, no, you won't die."

◊

'Shit happens' used to be one of his father's favorite sayings. *Yes, it certainly does,* Gianni thought as he cleaned himself with his meager water ration. He took bites of a protein bar as he got ready. He couldn't wait any longer. He'd used his powers quite a bit that day, and it always left him starving. He'd still be hungry when Kieren arrived, but he needed to get something in his system or he'd be grouchy, and he didn't want that with her coming over. He felt like this might be his only chance to put things right with her, and being a slave to his metabolism would only hinder that goal.

He noticed how long his hair was getting as he washed it. Then he shaved the rough stubble on his cheeks and neck. It was easier to leave the goatee and mustache than try to shave around his mouth and nose with the crude razor he'd fashioned. He'd lost the original one he'd come up with aboard the *Tukuli* when it crashed. The razor wasn't the only thing he'd seemed to lose when the *Tukuli* crashed.

He'd been born into a world where his aggressiveness and confidence could be the difference between life and death. When he'd woken up on the *Tukuli*, naked except for a robe, with no weapon and no clue where he was or who he was with, his only defense had been his attitude and guarded nature.

It was also spooky as hell to find out he'd been kidnapped by aliens. And having to live side by side with a cop wasn't great, either. But things had changed over the course of the journey. They had all stopped identifying themselves by their past lives, and starting identifying themselves as simply Human Beings. By the time they crashed on Rajan, he didn't think of himself as a made man, or even as an Italian American so much as just a member of the team. It felt liberating for him that he could just be Gianni, instead of trying every day to live up to being the nephew of a New York City crime boss.

Now, he just wanted to start over with the others. He'd been a jerk aboard the ship, and even after the *Tukuli* crashed, he hadn't been on his best diplomatic behavior with the Sekani. He needed to make it up to Kieren. He couldn't just come right out and tell her that he loved her, even though he was pretty sure he did. In their present situation, his feelings would cause more problems than it was worth if she didn't feel the same way about him.

There were times when he thought she might, and times, usually when they were arguing about something trivial, when he was sure she loathed him. He had no frame of reference in his life. His parents certainly didn't love one another. He couldn't tell her if he wasn't sure, so his time with Kieren was spent secretly burning inside at the feel of her hand in his. He thought he should tell her eventually that his Talondarian Standard and his Sekani were coming along well enough for him to understand most conversations with the Sekani he went out on missions with, but he hadn't felt like losing that contact with her.

After his talk with James that morning and thinking about

it while on patrol with the Sekani later in the afternoon, he'd made up his mind that he needed to tell her the truth. About everything. He sat and fidgeted nervously as he waited for her to arrive, going back and forth in his mind about how he should approach the evening. If he did this wrong, she might hate him forever. He didn't think he could bear that.

There was a knock on his door just as he was beginning to change his mind about the entire thing. What had he been thinking? *Why didn't he say an hour?* He opened the door and was instantly struck again by Kieren's natural beauty. Everything, from her hair, which was now free and flowing, to her eyes, to her smile, was radiant. She was quite possibly the most beautiful woman he'd ever met.

"Hi," she said.

"Hey," he replied. "Oh, um, come in." He moved out of the way. "Sorry. Can I get you anything to drink?" he asked her as she sat down on the small couch-like piece of furniture that was all he had besides a small cot where he slept. "Fernta? Water?"

"Water would be great," she said.

He had never invited her to this room. For one thing, there wasn't much to it, and for another, the opportunity had never materialized. He poured them both a glass of tepid water and handed one to her. They still hadn't been able to turn on the power in the Rajani-controlled part of Melaanse, so refrigeration was out of the question.

"Thanks," she said, taking a small sip. "They didn't give you a very big room," she said, looking around.

"I don't need much," he said, sitting down next to her. "As long as I have a place to sleep, I'm good. Although I do miss TV sometimes."

"Me too," she said. "There are some nights where I'm just bored out of my mind."

"There aren't any alien books or magazines to read?" he asked jokingly.

"My power seems to only be auditory in nature, not visual. I can't read anything but English, I'm afraid," she answered wistfully.

"Damn," he said. "That sucks."

"Yeah," she said.

The silence stretched on for an awkward moment as the conversation stopped. Finally, he took a deep breath and began to speak.

"Look, I . . ." he said.

"Gianni . . ." she said at the same time.

They looked at each other a moment, and then both started laughing at the absurdity of the situation.

"Why is it," he said, "that we can never get out of our own way with each other?"

"I don't know," she said. "Maybe we're just . . . trying too hard."

"Look, just hear what I have to say, and then you can think of me what you will," he said.

She leaned forward, her face only inches from his. He could smell her fresh, clean scent. "How about we just shut up for once?" She kissed him lightly on the lips and pulled back a little, looking into his eyes. She seemed a little uncertain.

He leaned forward for another kiss, one hand finding the small of her back and the other going to the back of her head as he pulled her near. He could feel her breathing rate increase to match his own. After that, there were no more words for a while.

◊

Bhakat waited patiently while the Human female processed the information he had just given her. He was surprised when she smiled up at him from her chair.

"Immortality? Really? We'll never grow old or sick? You know, Bhakat, I always thought you were the serious type, but you really had me going there for a minute."

He only looked at her a moment, wondering if he should tell her that he was being serious, but then thought better of it. If she needed to think it was a joke to help deal with it better, then so be it. He just shrugged, instead. "You can believe what you would like. What symptoms are you experiencing?"

"What?" she asked, seemingly confused by the change of subject.

"You said that you were becoming ill," he said. "What are your symptoms?"

"Dizziness, mostly," she replied. "Although I felt sick to my stomach this morning, and rundown, like I didn't sleep very well last night."

"May I?" he asked, motioning toward her with his hands. She nodded, and he felt her neck just below her jaw, checking for swollen glands. He'd found aboard the *Tukuli* that there were several similarities between Rajani and Human physiology, but it was also strange examining so small a patient. He looked into her eyes, comparing pupil sizes and looking for jaundice. "Have you been drinking your full ration of water?"

"Yes," she said.

"Drinking a lot of fernta?" he asked, though he knew she wasn't much of a drinker.

"That stuff is disgusting," she said, wrinkling her nose.

"Any rashes, dry mouth, dry skin . . ." he trailed off as he tried to think of anything else.

"Not that I know of," she said.

"I don't see anything wrong, but then, I don't have a medibot here, either. If you want to come with me, I can give you a thorough examination."

"No," she said. "I don't want to take you away from your work here."

"I'm done here, for tonight, at least," he said. "And you have me curious." He also had a suspicion growing in the back of his mind that he chose to keep to himself, for the moment.

"Well, okay," she said. "As long as it doesn't take too long. James will be worried if I'm not home for dinner." She smiled at her own joke. There was no such thing as simple domestic routine on Rajan. And it wasn't like she and James were married. But she knew he would be worried if he came home and didn't find her there, without any explanation as to where she'd gone. Life in a war zone wasn't a good place for assumptions.

Bhakat knew that 'okay' was the same as 'yes,' though there was no equivalent word in the Rajani language. "Good," he said. They began to walk together in companionable silence.

They made their way north toward the main medical clinic, where they'd found the Human named David a prisoner of the Krahn months before. It seemed like so much had happened since then, but the clinic also brought back good memories for Bhakat, of learning the Human language, English, from Yvette and spending his days tending to Rauphangelaa's injuries; just happy to have returned to Rajan after being away for so long. As they walked they talked in low, familiar tones about the war and the other Humans and the medical centers that he was trying to build before they finally arrived at the clinic. The sky was growing dark, and Bhakat guessed that there was only an hour or so of light left. The days were growing shorter, and the rainy season would start in earnest soon, he knew. They were met in the clinic's waiting room by a Rajani doctor named Andraal and two Sekani assistants, a male and a female whom Bhakat had never met.

"Hello, Andraal," Bhakat said. "May I use the medical robot to examine the Human female? I shouldn't be long."

"Of course, Bhakat," Andraal responded, looking at Yvette curiously. Everyone was curious about the Humans, it seemed.

"Yvette, if you could lie down," Bhakat said as they walked into the examination room. He turned to look at her, noticing how tired she appeared. She complied, and he began inputting information into the medibot. Soon the machine's arms were moving over her, taking vital statistics such as blood pressure, pulse, and breathing rate. The bed measured her weight and height.

"I need to take a blood sample," he told her.

"Why?" she asked, turning her head to look at him.

"I . . . need to check your blood oxygen level, and for any pathogens that might be present," he replied.

"All right," she said. One of the machine's arms pricked her earlobe lightly, then used a small straw-like appendage to suck out a quantity of blood. Bhakat kept his eyes on the machine's monitor as he read her vitals. The blood test results were quickly displayed, and his suspicions were confirmed. There was nothing wrong with her. He couldn't help but smile as he looked down at her.

"What? What is it?" she asked, seeing his expression.

Chapter 4

David Morris had fallen into a deep depression since his friend Janan'kela was captured by the Krahn upon their arrival on Rajan. It wasn't the first time he'd battled depression, but he'd never done it while fighting a war on an alien planet before. *Of course, I'm just crazy enough to think I was abducted by aliens,* he thought. *I could be in a loony bin in Detroit for all I know.*

He also didn't have his usual medications with him, since the Rajani had not known about them when first bringing him aboard the *Tukuli*. Being kidnapped by aliens had provided him with enough motivation to rise above his various psychological problems for a little while, at least, but losing his friend and being rejected in his romantic advances by Kieren had taken any form of hope out of his life. He found himself closing off from the others, just as he had done back on Earth. At least his father wasn't around to bully and abuse him.

His father. David hated and feared the man in equal shares. His mother had left them when David was four years old. David had no illusions as to why she would leave the man and his only spawn, considering all he'd been through with the man. His father, though, had missed few opportunities to share his views about her and women in general as disloyal, money-hungry temptresses who only pretended to love you to get what they wanted. Sometimes his views came as part of a beating, sometimes not. But there were few days when David didn't have a bruise somewhere on his body while growing up.

David had thought the man was wrong, until his girlfriend, Lisa, said no to his proposal, leaving him feeling both embarrassed and furious in turns. After that, he knew his father had spoken the truth all along. It had been the last time he'd had a conversation with anyone on Earth, and his feelings of rejection had lasted until he woke up aboard the *Tukuli*. None of that mattered, until his first real friend in years was taken from him. Then it seemed like all hope that he'd be able to start over and begin a new life, and forget what had happened to him and the things he'd done back on Earth, were dashed. He found it hard at times to even get out of bed, and he did the absolute minimum expected from him by the Resistance.

So far he was able to resist the urges that had plagued him back on Earth when he felt this way, but he didn't know how long he would be able to in the future. Killing the Krahn he'd encountered or sought out had provided a brief respite, but he knew it wasn't the same as back on Earth. It no longer excited him to kill the vile, reptilian aliens. Some hero I turned out to be, he thought, lying in his cot and feeling tears of rage and frustration stream down his face. He'd thought that he could come to Rajan and forget his past—begin a new life without all of the worries of the old one dragging him down—but he had been wrong.

◊

Janan'kela wasn't sure how long he'd been locked in his prison cell, but after a while he'd started to think that maybe he was already dead. The Rajani didn't believe in any type of afterlife, but the old Sekani who worshiped the Goddess held that after a Sekani died, their spirit would either go to the Eternal Hunt in which he would serve the Goddess, or to the Forever Darkness. He sure wasn't hunting, so the alternative seemed real.

The only way he knew that he wasn't dead was the daily torment he received from the Krahn guards and the masagas, which had learned to keep their distance after he'd killed a few of them, but the small creatures were still an ever-present and unwanted presence. His abdomen still bothered him, where the Krahn guard had raked its claws across it in his escape attempt, but it had finally started to heal.

His jailer, Toruq, had come down once to ask him questions but had not returned since then. Janan hoped that meant the war was going badly for the Krahn, but he had no way of knowing for sure. If the rebellion by the Rajani failed, he would spend the rest of his life in the same jail cell until he died. Or he would be eaten by the Krahn as the main course of a victory feast. His captors never let a chance pass where they could torment him about how good his kind tasted to them.

Suddenly, there was a shaft of light as a door was opened somewhere close to his cell. Janan could hear the sound of footsteps coming down the hallway toward his location. It was Toruq, but he wasn't alone. He had a Sekani with him. The Sekani was beat-up and bandaged, with a swollen eye and a bloody cloth covering his entire left shoulder.

"I've brought you a friend," Toruq said in guttural Krahnnish. "Perhaps you'll both be the main course of the banquet celebrating Ronak's arrival." He laughed as he shoved the prisoner into the cell. The Sekani fell to the ground with a gasp of pain and curled up into a protective ball, breathing raggedly.

Janan waited until Toruq was gone, leaving the cell once more in darkness, before he spoke. "Who are you?" he whispered.

There was a moment of silence, and he wondered if he had only imagined the prior events and was sitting alone in the darkness talking to himself, his seclusion finally pushing him over the edge into madness. Then a hoarse voice sounded from the darkness, and he almost cried out in surprise, having halfway convinced himself that he was crazy. Maybe he still was, but at least he didn't feel so alone. "I'm Golena," the voice said. "Who are you?"

"Janan'kela," he replied, almost crying at the pain from his sore throat. It had never healed correctly from the kleng beast attack in the Desert of Ambraa, and grew painful when he hadn't had anything to drink for a while. His small ration of water had come the day before.

"How long have you been here?" Golena asked.

"I don't know," Janan answered. "I've been here long enough to wonder if you're even real or if I'm just talking to myself."

Golena chuckled weakly. "So, a long time, then."

"I was pilot for Rauphangelaa, the Elder," Janan said. "We crashed upon our return to Rajan. We were carrying—"

"Quiet!" Golena hissed, interrupting him. "They are listening to us," he said so quietly that Janan could barely hear him.

Of course they are, Janan thought, mentally kicking himself. He was so out of the reality of the situation that he was happy to talk to someone, and had almost said exactly what he'd been stonewalling the Krahn about for who knew how long. "We were carrying supplies for the Elders in hiding," he said weakly. "As far as I know, everyone on the ship died except for me."

"Good," Golena's voice said softly in his ear. The other Sekani had moved up closer to Janan's position. "I know who you are. All I can say is that you have not been forgotten." Janan could feel tears begin to creep down his face as he heard Golena's words. All of a sudden, the shaft of light returned as footsteps hurried down the hallway toward the cell. "Please," Golena continued in an urgent voice. "Let them know what happened to me. The Krahn said they'd kill me if I didn't get you to talk, but I just couldn't do it. Remember me."

"That will be enough out of you," Toruq's voice came from the hallway. Janan could see now that the Krahn had returned with two guards in tow. They stopped at the door to his cell and Janan watched as they dragged Golena away. Janan never saw him again.

◊

David woke up, unaware of what time it was, and not really caring. He still hadn't become used to the Talondarian Standard time that the Rajani used. He walked to the door and opened it, seeing that it was light outside, but not all that warm, which meant it was either early morning or late afternoon. Either way, he made up his mind, he was leaving. He had to find Janan. If his friend was alive, then he needed to be rescued. David had been so busy fighting the Krahn in the north of the city that he hadn't had time to really think about his friend much, and the last few days he hadn't wanted to do anything at all.

David had also spent too much time trying to be normal. His failures with Kieren and Gianni showed him it just wasn't possible. He was different from the others, which was obvious. Janan was the one being he'd met who had been willing to be his friend, warts and all. They'd become close on the ship after David had been taken by the Rajani, and even closer in their short time on Rajan after the ship had crashed and they'd found themselves marooned in the Desert of Ambraa.

David rubbed a hand over his face, feeling the rough sandpaper-like stubble. He hadn't shaved in a few days. He also hadn't bathed, which was something he would have to take care of before he left. He'd spent enough time locked away in his room. It was time to leave his self-imposed prison. He washed and shaved using his allotted water ration. He felt much better afterward, as he always did when recovering from a serious bout of depression. Life always seemed to look better after spending time wondering if it was worth living, for some reason. He dried off and got dressed in clean clothes, taking his time, as if dressing in ceremonial robes.

As he was leaving his room, he saw Bhakat walking toward him. "Good morning, David," the Rajani said. "I pray your rest was peaceful. Are you going out on patrol?"

"Yeah," David replied. "I should be back soon." It was a small lie, inconsequential in the grand scheme of things.

"Then I wish you luck," Bhakat said, bowing slightly to him and beginning to walk away.

"Bhakat?" David asked before the big Rajani had gone very far. Bhakat turned back to look at him. "Nothing," he said. "Never mind." He found that he was unwilling to tell Bhakat what he was going to do. If he failed, then Bhakat would just be disappointed in him, and he couldn't take disappointing anyone else at the moment. He powered up quickly and sped off, wanting to be alone again.

◊

Sendok had passed his Clipping Day still intact, for which he was eternally grateful. No genderless Krahn warrior could climb the ranks to gain real power in his cousin Ronak's army. Ronak had given him command of a company of warriors, and he'd been the one to capture one of the off-world creatures who had crashed on Rajan. Although the creature had somehow later escaped, Sendok had been promoted, an honor few received from Ronak.

He now commanded most of the warriors still left on the ground in Melaanse. The pilots and their support staff were commanded by Mariqa from the colony ship, which was still in orbit around the planet. He reported directly to Kalik, Ronak's chief counselor. Yet he was hesitant to report the true state of affairs, lest he end up clipped or working in the dungeon like his cousin Toruq. But there was no doubt, they were losing the war against the Rajani. They had won a victory against them in the south with the help of the Sekani traitor, but it was only one victory. The borderline between Rajani and Krahn-occupied space in the city moved southward on an almost daily basis. It was almost imperceptible. The city of Melaanse covered a vast area, but he knew that if affairs continued in their present course, it was only a matter of time before they would be defeated. Unless they somehow were able to obtain more weapons and ammunition, they would fail. In the initial attack on Rajan, they had used too much of their stores of each, and now they were beginning to run low. They had miscalculated the resiliency of the Rajani. Ronak and his counselors had counted on the initial shock and devastation to keep the population subdued, and they'd been mistaken.

He knew Ronak well enough to know it wouldn't be too much longer before he gave up and left Rajan, and Sendok meant to be with him when he did. There was nothing on Rajan for him. The weather was too cold, even on the warmest days, and it was much too dry. His skin felt like it would split wide open if he didn't keep applying moisturizer on a daily basis. He also bled from his beak-like snout every now and then for no reason except that his nostrils were too dry. It was safe to say he hated everything about the planet.

Until it was time to leave, he had to do what he could to stay in his cousin's favor. He didn't want to be left behind on such an uninhabitable rock like Rajan. That meant days spent like the one he faced that day, sitting, bored to death, at a road checkpoint, as if he had nothing better to do. He'd swallowed his pride and lowered his plumage in respect, and set out with his guards to sit at his checkpoint like a loyal warrior should, though he dreaded what was turning out to be another tedious day.

◊

David made his way south through the city. He hadn't gone far to the south since arriving on Rajan. The devastated city's broken buildings sat like a landscape model made of Legos that a child had discarded in a fit of frustration. David was amazed that anyone had survived the Krahn attack. The center of the city was a wasteland. He was still powered up but moving slowly now, not familiar with his surroundings. He was surprised that he hadn't seen a Krahn since starting his search. They must have pulled back farther south than anyone thought. He'd have to tell James when he returned. If he returned.

He finally grew tired of stepping around rubble and slowly making progress through the city. He ran east, and made it to the outskirts of the city within a few minutes before turning south. He saw that the southern part of the city was bordered by mostly grassland to the east. He turned back to a westerly course as he came to the southernmost section of Melaanse. He saw a checkpoint of Krahn warriors ahead, and increased his speed as he approached. As fast as he was going, he was almost invisible, he knew. As he got closer, he could see that the five warriors were equipped much better than the normal Krahn that he usually fought.

Perhaps they could tell him what he wanted so desperately to know.

He slowed down enough for them to see him. He had to find out which one was in charge. It didn't take long to see one of the Krahn yelling orders at the others. David made quick work of the four others, picking them up and smashing their heads against buildings at a high rate of speed, and then stopped in front of the leader. It looked at him with wide-eyed fear. Now the problem was two-fold. First was getting the Krahn to tell him what it knew. Second was being able to understand what it said. He hadn't thought of bringing one of the translating devices with him. He'd have to bring the Krahn to the translating device. He quickly ran around to the back of the Krahn and picked it up. The enhanced strength the Johar Stone gave him was more than enough to carry the struggling and hissing Krahn warrior. It wasn't close to what James could do, but it was enough.

He began to run back east to clear the edges of the city once again. He then turned north and ran along the border of Melaanse until he came to a place that he recognized as the road he and Janan had taken into the city when they had first arrived. *How fitting,* he thought. He slowed down and made his way toward the Rajani compound.

◊

Janan realized something as he thought about the ploy that the Krahn had used to get him to talk. The Krahn were still fighting the Rajani, otherwise, they wouldn't need to know anything from him. If they had already won, he would be dead. While it was a comforting thought, it didn't really help him in his present situation. He'd been wrong. His wounds from the Krahn he'd fought were not getting better. They weren't hurting much anymore, but he'd woken up feeling muzzy-headed and feverish. He'd touched his wounds in the darkness, and they felt hot under his hands. A warm, thick liquid had oozed onto his fingertips. *Infected,* he thought. He wasn't surprised. He wasn't exactly living in sanitary conditions.

He didn't have a choice; he would have to ask Toruq for help. He waited until the Krahn came to give him his daily ration of water. When the light broke into the inky blackness of his cell from the open doorway, he quickly looked at the large scratches on his stomach and saw the redness surrounding them and extending out in lines in all directions. He stood up feebly and stood next to the bars of his cell. "I'm sick," he said when Toruq approached the cell. "I need medical attention."

"Oh, really?" Toruq replied, holding a cup of water out to him. "And why should I save you? You've been nothing but trouble for me since I brought you here. You're uncooperative and refuse to answer even the simplest questions."

Janan drank the proffered cup of water, making sure he got every drop into his mouth. He handed the cup back to the Krahn.

"Now, if you were to answer a few questions," Toruq said, "I might be able to help you."

Janan had expected that response. He wouldn't do it, even if it meant dying a slow, horrible death from infection. He walked away and sat in the muck on the floor of his cell.

"No?" Toruq asked. "Then you can rot, as far as I'm concerned." He walked away, and Janan heard the door slam as the light disappeared once again.

◊

David took his Krahn prisoner east across Melaanse. There were a limited number of translating devices in the city, but he remembered hearing that the Valderren had one. He didn't know Kedar or Welemaan very well, but he did know they would be more willing to let him borrow the device than the Elders, considering how he intended to ask his questions. The Elders were clinging to an antiquated view of non-violence, even after everything that had happened to them and their city. He hadn't even talked to Rauph since reuniting with the other Humans during the battle at the Krahn's northern base. Of course, it seemed he'd been slowly pulling away from everyone he knew.

As he came nearer to the Valderren's building, he realized he should have at least made sure his Krahn captive was unarmed. It posed a problem, seeing as he couldn't just stop and try to pat the creature down now. He was in the heart of Rajani territory. They were likely to kill any live Krahn they saw, and David would be forced to go back and find another one. Finally, he decided to just run the Krahn into a building, though not hard enough to kill it. He turned and did so, knocking the still-struggling Krahn unconscious. He stopped and checked to make sure it was still alive, and seeing that it was, hoisted it over his shoulder and made his way to his destination.

The Velderren building was a hive of bustling activity. There were Rajani coming and going through the doors as David came to a stop there. Many of the Rajani looked at him in surprise. Clearly, they were astonished to see the Human carrying a Krahn warrior over his shoulder like a sack of potatoes.

"I need to speak to Kedar," David said to a shorter Rajani, who was walking by and looked like he was heading into the building. "Can you tell him to come out to talk to me?" The Rajani listened to David's stuttering Talondarion request and then put his hand out to David, as if telling him to wait there. David did, and after a few moments, the large Rajani named Kedar came out of the front doors.

"Um, hi," David said. "I was wondering if you could lend me the use of a translating device so that I could ask this Krahn some questions."

Kedar looked at him quizzically for a moment, and David thought at first that he had said something wrong. His Talondarian Standard wasn't great. But then Kedar smiled at him. "I assume that James told you about his last time here?"

"No," David said, confused. "He didn't."

"Oh, well, yes, we have a translating device you can use," Kedar said. "You can take the Krahn down into the basement of this building, if you need privacy."

David was confused even further. James hadn't told him he had also brought a Krahn there for questioning. But he also didn't want to bring his prisoner down there. It didn't feel right. He wanted more privacy than he was likely to get in the Valderren building. "No, thank you. I'll bring the device back, I promise."

"Of course," Kedar said. "I'll be right back." He smiled again, then turned to go back into the building.

David waited a few minutes, still powered up, outside the building. He was growing tired of the curious and sometimes suspicious looks he was getting from the Rajani who passed by. Finally, Kedar reappeared with one of the bulky translating devices and handed it to David.

"Whatever information you seek, I hope he tells you," Kedar said, bowing slightly.

"Thank you," David said. He thought he should say something else, but couldn't think of anything, so he just repeated his thanks and then quickly took off, heading for the coast. When he came close enough to see the waves of the ocean crashing on the sandy shore, he headed north to his familiar dumping ground, a cliff that was at least a hundred feet above the jagged rocks that created a landing below. He let the Krahn unceremoniously fall to the ground from his shoulder, and then set down the translating device. He dropped his power field and sat under a large plant that looked like a tree but had spikes instead of leaves, more like a cactus. It provided little shade, but it was better than nothing. David made sure not to let any of the spikes touch him. He'd experienced enough of Rajan's wildlife after he had first arrived. He was wary of everything now. The plant could be poisonous for all he knew.

It was ten minutes later that he saw Kieren fly over his position, though she was high enough not to notice him under the tree. She was heading north along the coast. He wondered where she was going. As far as he knew, there wasn't anything up that way except more coast. Nothing worth flying to, at least. His musing was interrupted by the Krahn, who began to move. It was waking up. David reached over and turned on the translating device and waited a few minutes more for the Krahn to fully wake up. The Krahn slowly rolled over and looked at him. David watched as its eyes grew wide when it saw him.

He knew, from his experience with the alien named Punjor on the Mandakan Space Port, that the translating device would need the Krahn to speak before it would be able to work properly. He was surprised when the Krahn began to speak and the device worked right away. That meant it had been used to translate the Krahn language before, presumably when James had interrogated his Krahn prisoner.

"Why have you brought me to this place?" the Krahn asked, sitting up. It rubbed its head where David had rammed it into a building. It winced and then hissed as its hand came away bloody. There were a few scrapes still bleeding slowly, but nothing that wouldn't stop in a few more minutes, David saw.

"I need answers," David said.

"I do not answer to the Rajanis' puppets," the Krahn said, the feathers on top of its head rising up. At least they looked like feathers to David. "Whether you kill me or not doesn't matter. Eventually, you will lose this war."

"I don't care about the Rajani or if they win or lose," David said. As he said it, he knew it was true. He'd tried to be the team player, the hero helping the Rajani to win their war against the Krahn and let them live happily ever after. But he found he just didn't care enough about any of them to do any more for their cause. He only wanted to rescue his friend.

The Krahn looked at him, its eyes narrowed suspiciously. "What do you want to know?" it asked.

"There's someone I'm looking for," David replied. "A Sekani. We were captured by the Krahn; I escaped and he didn't."

The Krahn's eyes widened once more at David's words before quickly narrowing again. "If I tell you what I know, will you let me go?"

"If you tell me what I want to know," David said, "I'll just walk away from this place. But if you lie to me . . ." As he trailed off, he pointed toward the cliff.

The Krahn followed where he pointed, turning toward the nearby drop-off. It turned back toward him, looking at him another moment before smiling. "I understand your meaning. I must say, you're not what I expected."

"Good," David said. "Is the Sekani still alive?"

"Yes," the Krahn said. "He's being kept prisoner at Nestbase One."

David leaned forward. He could feel his heart beating quickly at the news. "How do you know for sure?" he asked.

"My cousin Toruq is the jailer there," the Krahn replied. "And besides that, I'm the one who captured him. Captured you both, actually. The Sekani is named Janan'kela, true?"

"Yes," David said, feeling like he was going to cry, but not wanting to in front of the Krahn. He stood up. He was surprised to find that he didn't feel like killing the Krahn, even though he had every intention of doing so when he first began talking to it. Even after learning that it was the same Krahn who had first captured him and Janan, he felt no urge to end its life. "I would suggest you go out to the outskirts of the city before moving south. If you try to go straight from here, you're bound to get caught or killed. But you'd better hurry; they'll be coming soon."

The Krahn stood up. "I'm free to go?" it asked warily.

"That's what I said," David told it, preparing to power up.

"Tell me one thing," the Krahn said. "What are you?"

"I'm known as a Human Being," David said. "My planet is called Earth. My name is David." He had no idea why he told it his name; it was an impulsive act, he knew.

"Hu-man. I . . . my name is Sendok," the Krahn said.

"Goodbye, Sendok," David said, looking at the Krahn one last time. "Hopefully we'll never meet again. For the sake of both of us." He powered up and began to run southwest toward the city again, leaving the Krahn standing on the cliff.

Chapter 5

It had been a long day of preparation for James, and he'd had little to eat. He was starting to feel the effects of the fernta that Zanth had brought to their meeting, even though he had drunk only one glass of the powerful beverage. He pushed his cup away and adjusted the volume on the translating device he kept with him at these types of meetings. It was a crutch, he knew, but he didn't want anything important to be lost in translation, though he felt like his Talondarian Standard was probably good enough without it. Besides James, Zanth, Mazal, and Kedar were present for the meeting. Yvette, Kieren, and Gianni were also meeting with lower-ranking members of the various factions of Rajani, Sekani, and Jirina at a different location.

The Rajani Elders had refused to attend any war councils, so those Rajani who were willing to fight had chosen Kedar to represent them. The group had even taken on the name Vaderren, which, as far as James could tell, was translated to, 'those who will fight.' *Not very original,* he thought, but it was to the point.

He hadn't been able to find David when he'd looked, but Kedar had told him he'd spoken with him earlier, and had given him a translating device to use to interrogate a Krahn prisoner. He was probably locked away somewhere asking it questions. James hoped he'd be careful around the creature, but there was nothing he could do about it at the moment. He felt like he should talk to David, like he needed to try to find out what was happening with him, but he'd just been too busy with everything else. He had the feeling there was something important about David he was missing.

His mind wandered again as he studied the Rajani as they went through the pleasantries at the start of the meeting. He'd learned something of the Rajani culture since coming to their planet, so he knew Kedar was the Rajani's birth name, and not his second name; the name he was given after becoming an Elder, which was characterized by the double a's called Kaa'va and included as a sign of their status. The double a's essentially meant 'of the Kaa,' and were only used by the Rajani Elders. He also knew that Kedar must have been an Elder before the Krahn came because he had a mate and child, both of whom had been killed in the initial Krahn attack. Kedar had lost an eye, and apparently, his belief in the Kaa along with it. He had renounced his second name and gone back to his birth name. It was difficult to tell how old the Rajani was, but James guessed that he couldn't be much older than Bhakat, who was the equivalent of someone in their early to mid-thirties back on Earth.

James was about to call the meeting to order when there was a knock on the door. All conversation stopped, while everyone looked expectantly at the door, wondering who it could be. *Maybe it's David,* he thought.

"Enter," Zanth said. The door opened, and a Sekani entered and spoke in hurried whispers with Zanth for a moment. "What!" he asked after he had listened to his assistant. Zanth stood up and motioned for the Sekani to leave. "I apologize for the interruption, but word has come of our strike teams in the south." He sat down heavily. "I'm afraid that it's not good news."

"Tell us," Kedar said, leaning forward.

"No," Zanth answered quietly, looking down at the table. "Someone is coming who will." There was silence for a moment, and then another knock on the door brought Zanth out of his stunned reverie. Unbidden, the door opened and a bedraggled-looking Rajani entered.

"Welemaan?" Kedar asked, a stunned look on his face.

Welemaan sat down at the table and poured himself a small glass of fernta and drained it in one mouthful before speaking. "I only just arrived now," he began. "As far as I know, my strike team was the only one that survived, let alone was successful in stealing a Krahn ship."

"No!" Mazal said, a look of horror on his face. "But how?"

"They knew we were coming," Welemaan said, pouring himself another glass of fernta. "They were waiting for us. When the strike teams arrived from the north, they were ambushed."

"How is it that you made it through unscathed?" Zanth asked.

"Simple. I didn't arrive from the north," Welemaan replied. "I found a boat, and my strike team sailed down the coastline as I advised you we should do. We came through the inlet unseen, at night, as I thought we would. By daybreak we had set up an observation point just to the west of the airfield in a small grove of trees. We saw one of the strike teams get ambushed by a group of Krahn." He took another drink of fernta and then continued. "We were too late to save the team, unfortunately, but we were able to overcome the Krahn and take two prisoners. We pieced together what had happened to the other strike teams from what they told us." He took another long draft of fernta after his explanation, and then banged the glass down on the table.

"Bring the Krahn here so they can tell us themselves," Zanth said, still visibly upset.

"Wait, there's more to my story," Welemaan said. "One of the prisoners was a Krahn, yes. But the other is Belani'tola." He turned to Mazal. "I'm sorry, Mazal. The strike team we saw ambushed was Fajel's. He and Rachal are dead."

Mazal sat stricken for a moment before his eyes welled up with tears. "No," he whispered.

The room was silent for a moment before it erupted in shouted questions and accusations, with everyone speaking at once.

Finally, James stood up. "Please, be quiet. Wait until we've heard what happened."

The room slowly grew quieter as the occupants calmed down. James could see, though, that the situation could erupt again if he allowed it. He sighed, wondering if he could just place them all in timeouts, like his partner, Steve, used to do with his kids back on Earth.

Kieren and Gianni had told James about their experience on first arriving in the Sekani camp, so he knew there was a mole among them. It was still a shock when he and the others were presented with the spy in person. He'd known it would be a possibility during his planning with Zanth and Kedar, but he'd hoped it wouldn't make that much of a difference. He'd been wrong.

Two Rajani guards brought in the Sekani prisoner, shackled at the hands and feet with a crude rope. He was a pitiful-looking specimen. It seemed like his captors had been a little rough with him on the trip. One of his eyes was swollen shut, and he had blood still oozing slowly from a cut on his lower lip. He looked utterly defeated, like he had given up any hope of living. For a moment, James pitied him, but then remembered this Sekani was responsible for the death of many good troops, troops James had personally sent into battle. The Rajani sat him down and then turned and walked out of the room, closing the doors behind them. There was silence, but James could feel the tension sitting like a layer of fog, permeating the air of the room.

Finally, Zanth spoke, breaking the silence with an icy tone that James had never heard from him before. "Belani, you have been accused of treason. We are giving you a chance to speak, only because I want an explanation from your own mouth. Tell us what happened."

Belani sat still and silent for a moment, and James began to think he wouldn't speak. The Sekani finally spoke in a low tone that caused everyone present to lean in to hear him clearly. "It doesn't matter. They're dead. They're all dead."

"Of course they're all dead," Welemaan said angrily, standing up. "You've betrayed us all, you piece of filth!"

"Quiet, please, my friend, let him talk," Kedar said.

Welemaan nodded and sat back down, a look of disgust on his face.

"I'm not talking about the strike teams, you ignorant fool," Belani said. "My family, my two sisters and younger brother are dead." He looked down at the table. "They must be, for the Krahn to have tried to kill me like that."

James thought it sounded like the Sekani was talking to himself now, even though the crude translating device on the table made it difficult to tell.

"Where's the Krahn prisoner?" Kedar asked. "Can he verify what happened, at least?"

Welemaan looked sheepishly around the room before speaking. "Uh, the prisoner . . . had a little accident on the way here. He, uh, fell out of the ship at five thousand feet."

"Don't tell me you dropped him out of the cargo bay,"

Kedar said, holding his head, but smiling. Welemaan smiled as well and shrugged.

"I am so happy that you find this amusing," Zanth said. "But we now have no way to verify any of Belani's story. I, for one, would like to know how long he's been working for the Krahn." He turned to the prisoner. "Was it you that called them here to Rajan?"

Belani seemed to wake from a dream state at this question. "What? No! Of course not, Zanth." He looked around the room at the faces. He seemed to see something in James's, because he stayed focused on him as he spoke. "You must understand, I had no choice. When the Krahn attacked, they took my siblings captive. They . . . killed my mother in the process. I had to find out if they were all right. So, I-I made contact with the Krahn and pleaded for their safe return." He sat up a little straighter before continuing. "They told me they would release my siblings, if I would spy for them. That's all it was supposed to be. But then, they kept asking for more and more, finally wanting all the details about the strike team mission. They told me if I turned in my team, they would let my family go. They never said they would kill them. You have to believe me, I never wanted anyone to get hurt."

"You expect us to believe that?" Welemaan asked, snorting in derision.

James sighed before speaking. "There's nothing we can do about this now. We still have a war we must fight. Our strike team mission has failed; we'll have to deal with the consequences of that going forward."

"I agree," Zanth said. "The prisoner shall be dealt with at a later time. We need to get back to the real reason we've met here this night. For now, I suggest incarceration for Belani. He may still be able to provide information. Someone please remove him from my sight."

Welemaan stood up. "Gladly."

"No," James said, standing as well. "I would hate for him to have a similar accident as the Krahn before reaching the jail. Mazal, do you have anyone in the building who could perform this task? Mazal?"

The Jirina had been deep in thought. He jerked to attention. "Um, yes, James. I'll make sure he gets there safely." He stood up slowly.

"Are you sure you're okay?" James asked him. He knew how much his nephew had meant to him.

"I don't know," Mazal answered, truthfully. He turned and walked the Sekani out of the room.

"I know we may not feel like it, but we must continue our meeting as planned," Zanth said wearily, looking at the others. "Before we do, however, Welemaan must leave."

"What?" Welemaan asked angrily.

"I'm sorry, but the agreement was that we would all send one emissary from our species for this meeting," Zanth said. "And as you can see, Kedar is already here."

"But—" Welemaan began, looking at his fellow Rajani.

"He's right," Kedar said. "If not a little tactless in his assessment. It is what was agreed upon. I'm sorry, my friend. I will speak to you after the meeting concludes. I promise."

Welemaan stood a moment, and then walked quickly from the room, pausing long enough to give a dangerous look toward Zanth's back.

"I appreciate your support," Zanth said, nodding toward Kedar. "I didn't look for it from the Rajani."

"The Rajani cannot win this war alone," Kedar said. "Welemaan is proud, but it was that same sort of pride that has brought about this tragedy in the first place. The Elders claimed all of the inhabitants of Rajan were equals, but we all know this was a lie. The Rajani pride, as well as our prejudice toward the Sekani"—as he was speaking Mazal returned to the room, and Kedar continued, nodding toward him—"and the Jirina, have led to this disaster. If we are to defeat the Krahn, we must truly be equal. All of us."

James was impressed by the maturity of the Rajani. He could tell that the other two were, as well.

"Thank you, Kedar. With that," Zanth said, pausing to make sure that he had everyone's full attention, "we have received information that Ronak himself is on Rajan."

"What? When did he arrive?" Kedar asked, suddenly very serious.

"Two, maybe three days ago," Zanth replied. "He and his mate were brought down in secrecy to the main Krahn base in the south of Melaanse."

"If Ronak is really here," James said, "are we prepared for an all-out assault on the Krahn headquarters? We may not get a better opportunity."

"A bid to end this war once and for all," Zanth said.

"I say we do it," Mazal said quietly. "Before this war turns us all into monsters."

"Then I suggest we meet first thing in the morning," James said. "With our top staff, of course." He looked at Kedar. "We need to begin planning the assault. For now, I think it's been an emotional night. We should all get some rest."

"Agreed," Kedar said.

As they made their goodbyes, James stopped to talk to Mazal. "I'm truly sorry about your loss."

"I've been sitting here trying to come up with the words I need to use to inform my kin of his death," Mazal said, his eyes beginning to well up again. "I don't know how I shall do it."

"Do you want me to come along?" James asked. He'd had to inform families on too many occasions that a loved one would not be coming home again while back in Detroit. It was never a message he wanted to bear, but he would do what he could to help minimize Mazal's pain.

"No, thank you," Mazal replied. "This must be amongst family. It's our custom."

"I understand," James said. "Please extend my condolences to them as well."

They shook hands briefly, and then James was left alone in the room. He slowly walked over and turned off the translating device with a soft click, remembering the young Jirina he had met only once at the final briefing meeting before the strike teams had left for their mission. He hoped Yvette was still awake when he got home. He needed to talk.

◊

The Rajani had not set up a prison since the Krahn attacked. They never took Krahn prisoners—at least, not any who survived long enough to be sent to live in a prison. Their one prison had been commandeered by the Krahn and used to keep the Rajani and Jirina males prisoner until they were freed by James the Human. That prison was now used for the storage of supplies essential to the Resistance: explosives, ammunition, weapons, and food stores. This was why Belani found himself imprisoned in the cellar of a small Jirina dwelling that had been half destroyed. He was left in darkness; there were no windows. All he knew was the cold stone floor and the uncomfortable edges of the rock that had been used to build the walls. Food and water were brought to him once a day.

His Jirina captors didn't speak to him, and he didn't try to speak to them. He was alone and friendless. His family was dead; he knew it in his heart. He had nothing left to live for, which was lucky for him, seeing as he expected that he would probably be put to death for treason after the fighting had finally ended. Or else he'd be kept in prison for the rest of his life, years staring at the same walls until he died. He knew he would go mad if that was the case. He'd thought about killing himself, but couldn't think of a way to do it. There was nothing to hang from, and the rocky walls were uncomfortable, but not sharp enough to cut as deep as was needed. Besides, if he was going to kill himself, it would not be quietly in the dark. He had too much hatred built up inside toward the Krahn.

After a few days he could stand it no longer. The next time one of his Jirina captors came with food, he decided to ask to speak to James the Human himself. The Jirina just laughed at him. The next day he asked again, with the same results, but he was determined to talk to the Human. And then he waited.

◊

Mazal was dressed in his ceremonial robes. Each Jirina was given a set when they reached five Standard years old, and traded them amongst themselves as they outgrew them. It was a custom without a known past. Perhaps it was something leftover from their early history, before the Rajani had conquered their species. No one knew. But the robes were only worn on the most special of occasions. Unfortunately, this occasion was one of sadness as he walked to the burning grounds, along with many other Jirina. The area had been used for funerals among the Jirina for hundreds of years. He was just relieved that the Rajani named Welemaan had been able to bring back Fajel's body. To have a funeral without a body would have left them all feeling emptier inside than they already were.

Mazal walked a few steps behind Fajel's parents as they

said their greetings to various family members. It was custom that only family attended the funeral ceremony itself. Mazal had a sense of déjà vu, having attended the funeral of Fajel's brother only a few months before. It was heartbreaking for his sister and her husband. They had lost both of their offspring, and were of an age where it would be difficult, and possibly unsafe, for her to become pregnant again. As he walked along, he remembered when his nephews were born, when they'd first walked, and when they'd come into their horns. Mazal remembered when he would come over for dinner and be pestered by both younglings for stories or songs. He smiled sadly, feeling the moisture of tears run down his cheeks while thinking about all of the good memories he would have when he thought about them. He only wished he would have had more.

◊

Pregnant. The word both thrilled and scared her to death. Yvette could hardly believe her ears when Bhakat had told her. ◊ At first she'd thought he was kidding, just like when he'd been joking about the Johar Stones, but he'd shown her the readings from her blood test and explained the heightened hormone levels that could mean only one thing. And then it had really hit home. Bhakat had not been joking about the Johar Stones. He'd been telling her the truth, and somehow the Stones had healed her, allowing her to become pregnant. James had been the only one she'd told that she was incapable of conceiving, and now he was going to be a father. He'd trusted her when she'd said it was okay to not take precautions, and now she was pregnant.

Is this what it feels like to be a pregnant teenager? she thought. She was excited about the possibility of having a child, but she and James had not talked about it at all. It hadn't been an issue they needed to worry about. She had no idea what his reaction would be, and now was not the time to broach the subject. The species summit was later that day. He had a lot on his mind, and she didn't need to distract him with this now. She took her time cleaning herself, using part of her daily water ration. James had come in late, after she had already fallen asleep, and had already left for the summit. She wasn't expected to attend until later. She would stop by and walk there with Bhakat and David, if he was around. She never knew if he would be off on his own, and never knew what mood he would be in if he was present.

Besides the pregnancy, there was the fact that if Bhakat really was telling the truth, then she had to somehow think of a way to break the news to the others. It would have to come about on some future date, though. If she let her mind concentrate on it right then, she felt like it would overwhelm everything else in her life. She was preoccupied with one thing and one thing only at the moment. As she dressed, she made a decision. No matter James's reaction to her news when she eventually told him, she was keeping this baby. She smiled as she rubbed her abdomen softly. She wasn't certain what the future would bring, but she was ready to find out. She'd been given a second chance, and she wouldn't take it for granted this time.

◊

James wasn't sure what to expect from the day's meeting. He and the other Humans had done their best to keep the relationships between the three races amiable, at least. He had assigned them to stay with the different factions of Rajani and Sekani, while he'd stayed closer to the Jirina, and especially Mazal, when they'd first arrived on Rajan. Their roles had eventually evolved as the war went on and the situation had changed for each of the species.

Things were much different now than they were when

the *Tukuli* had first crashed on the planet's surface.

Kieren and Gianni stayed with the Sekani. She had cultivated her relationship with Zanth, and he trusted her more than any of the other Humans, including James. She seemed to love living with them, and was a favorite with the Sekani females and their younglings. Gianni had become a favorite of the young male Sekani troops, even garnering the honor of having a Sekani nickname. David and Yvette stayed with the two factions of Rajani, the Elders and the Valderren, but mostly they could be found with Bhakat. Bhakat had become a sort of liaison between the Elders and the Valderren. He and Yvette traveled together, and David would tag along, if he was in the mood, but most of the time it was just the two of them as Bhakat attempted to set up his medical clinics and keep the lines of communication open between the two Rajani factions.

The Rajani Elders were used to being in charge and not having to do the kinds of things necessary to win the war. James suspected that part of it was their belief in the Kaa, but some of it was the same obstinate arrogance that had gotten them into the situation they now found themselves in. The Sekani were trying to press their bid at freedom from the Rajani, and so were also unwilling to perform the menial tasks that they had performed previously for the other species. They no longer wanted to be viewed as servants, and James didn't blame them.

Kieren was doing her best to keep the Sekani focused on the Krahn and not on their rebellion against the Rajani. Their resentment had been building for years, and it was difficult at best to get them to cooperate in battle plans that had them fighting in an integrated unit with the Rajani.

The Jirina didn't seem to care one way or another. They just wanted to survive, and so were easier to deal with on a day-to-day basis. That, and they basically worshiped James as their savior. He had done his best to curb their tendency to place him on a pedestal, but there was only so much he could do. The Jirina were always willing to do whatever was needed, whether it was loading bullets into the weapons they had confiscated from the Krahn in the fighting, or assisting in the harvesting food from the large farms outside Melaanse—a job that was especially dangerous because they were so exposed—and yet, they never complained. They didn't seem to have the same egos as the Rajani or Sekani, for which James was grateful.

They were meeting that day in what had become the central headquarters for the entire resistance. What used to be a large Jirina dining hall was now filled with various stacks of papers and other supplies. It had a long wooden table with wooden benches on both sides that were large enough to accommodate everyone. Mazal had shown up early with his four lieutenants, and they had helped set up the room with glasses of water and some of the local fruits and vegetables that had been harvested from Rauph's farm. They were vegetarians, so they left the meat for the others to bring if they wanted it.

James had thought about becoming vegetarian as well, after seeing a pulko, the creature that was most commonly raised for its meat by the Rajani. It was about the size of a large pig, but had long hair covering its body, and its face had a wide mouth for chewing grasses and large nostrils set under small, almost useless eyes. But its appearance wasn't what turned James's stomach, it was the smell. It was enough to put him off meat for a long time. He'd just sat down to eat a quick breakfast when Yvette, David, and Bhakat arrived. James had been surprised when he'd discovered how close Yvette and Bhakat had grown in their time fighting the

Krahn. Bhakat always seemed so prickly in nature aboard the *Tukuli*, but he treated Yvette with the same respect as he did Rauph. David, on the other hand, had grown sullen and distant ever since Janan had been captured. Without Yvette there to drag him along, James believed that the young man may have just stayed in his room all day. He still hadn't found the time, but he knew he needed to talk to the younger man.

James stood up and greeted Bhakat, and then gave Yvette a hug and quick kiss. David slunk off to the table and sat without saying anything. James raised his eyebrows in question to Yvette, but she just smirked and shrugged. David sat with an obvious air of uncaring, but at least he was there. James sat and was able to take two bites of the local equivalent of an apple before Kedar and his lieutenants, including Welemaan, arrived. Shortly after that, Kieren, Gianni, Zanth, and his party arrived. The Sekani sat on the opposite side of the table from the Rajani, with noticeable glares shared between the two sides.

"Thank you all for coming," James began, the translation device stationed in the middle of the table translating his words into Talondarian Standard. Although he felt proficient in speaking the alien language, he knew the other Humans were at various levels in their own ability to speak and understand it; not counting Kieren, of course. "We are here today to plan an attack on the main Krahn headquarters, located in the south of Melaanse," he continued, looking at the faces around the table. "I would appreciate it if that is all we focus on today. We cannot afford to go off on any tangents, or this will take too long." He paused a moment to let the gravity of the situation sink in. "We are under a tight deadline, as we don't know how long Ronak will remain on the surface of Rajan. We must strike now, while we can still ensure a final end to this war."

After his opening remarks, the day seemed to drag on as they discussed logistics, expected casualty rates, medical treatment sites, and other pressing matters. The meeting stayed civil in tone, and James was satisfied with the way that all of the species had come prepared for the planning of the assault on the Krahn stronghold, even the Jirina. Sooner than he'd expected, they had agreed upon a plan and were breaking for a light dinner. James thought breaking bread together would go a long way toward forming a genial relationship between the factions, so he had arranged for food to be brought in, as well as plenty of fernta. There was still a lot of planning left to do, but for now, the most important thing he could think of was to build a more cohesive team. Up until that point, the three races had not worked much together in fighting the Krahn, liberating the Melaanse central computer being an exception that had proved successful. That needed to change if they were going to prevail in their fight against the invaders.

James mingled as the dinner went on, sharing a drink with the various members at the meeting and making sure the large number of guards outside the building received some food as well. Finally, he settled down between Mazal and Welemaan at the long wooden table.

"And I still say that one ship can make a difference," Welemaan said. James could tell that the Rajani had drunk a good portion of fernta. His words were a little slurred.

"One ship wouldn't stand a chance," another Rajani said. James thought that his name was Menttel.

"I'm not saying one ship could defeat that blasted colony ship of theirs," Welemaan continued, ignoring his peer. "But it could keep them occupied and away from our ground forces."

"And I'm saying it would be suicide," Menttel said. "So

who exactly are you going to get to fly it?"

"I . . . I don't know," Welemaan answered, taking another drink from his cup. "I hadn't gotten that far yet."

"That's what I thought," the other Rajani said, laughing and shaking his head.

"If it is a suicide mission," Mazal said, "then why don't you send that traitor Belani out there to get killed?"

"Yes, James," another Jirina said. "He's been asking about you, so why don't you go tell him?" All of the Jirina laughed at this, except for Mazal.

"What?" James asked, turning to look at the one who had just spoken. He caught the end of a dirty look that Mazal was giving his companion. "Why wasn't I told about this?" he asked.

"I'm not letting that piece of offal near my ship," Welemaan said.

"Your vehicle, is it?" Zanth said from the other end of the table.

James looked up and noticed that conversation had stopped throughout the room. He knew if he didn't intercede, there was a good chance that things would get ugly fast. So much for his idea of cooperation through food and drink. He'd have to try another tactic. "The ship belongs to the Resistance," James said, looking around the room. He had their full attention now. "Which means that it belongs to all of you, equally, of course. But I think that Welemaan and Mazal have worked together to come up with a wonderful idea on how best to use it in our fight against the Krahn."

"You're not actually serious, James," Kedar said.

"Of course I am," James said. "And since Belani has been asking for me," he said, looking at Mazal, "I will personally go and offer him this chance to serve the Resistance in this matter."

"But, James," Mazal said, "we were only talking—"

"Mazal is right," Welemaan said.

"We're not ready," Zanth said.

Everyone began talking at once. James noticed their use of we when they had spoken. *That's more like it,* he thought. Of course, now he would have to actually follow through on his words and go talk to the traitor named Belani, but at least it had given them all a mutual focus of disdain. The meeting once again broke into the distinct groups that had arrived earlier that day, but they seemed much more comfortable in each other's presence.

James was glad to see the other Humans take part in the strategy sessions and offer their input, without it seeming like their way was the only way. He wanted the inhabitants of Rajan to be at the forefront of any resolutions that came from their time together. The meeting wrapped up with promises to work together on the finer logistics of the upcoming battle from all of them. As they were all leaving, James felt optimistic they all could work without any petty differences getting in the way. He was surprised, though, that Yvette had left with Bhakat instead of waiting for him. He'd have to ask her if there was anything wrong when he had the chance.

◊

David waited for his chance to speak to James after the meeting. It was difficult, considering the new information he'd learned, but he waited patiently while James talked to first the Rajani, then Sekani leaders, then give the Jirina leader a quick squeeze on his shoulder as Mazal spoke to Menttel.

James looked surpised to see David standing before him, then he smiled. "David, good to see you made it today."

David decided it was best to get right to the point. "Janan is still alive."

"What? You know this for sure?" James asked. "C'mon, let's talk outside.

David waited until they were outside the building before speaking again. "A Krahn I interrogated told me that Janan is being held at their last base to the south," David replied.

"You believe him?"

"I was persuasive," David said.

James stood and thought about this for a moment. "I don't know if this changes any plans we may have, but it's good to know that we might be able to save him when we attack."

"But..."

"No," James said, putting his hand on David's shoulder to look him in the eye. "We can't change what we're doing. Not even for Janan. This attack is going to take time to plan and I can't risk any distractions. He's been kept alive this long, if your informant is telling the truth. There's no reason to believe that he won't still be alive when we attack."

David's emotions were crashing together inside his skull. He'd hoped that James would give him permission to try to rescue the Sekani before the battle. Now it looked like he'd have to wait, or he'd have to go without the blessing of the Resistance.

"And I don't want you trying anything stupid on your own," James said, as if reading his mind. "Do you understand, David? I can't let you endanger others. If you were to go in, they would be ready and waiting for us when we arrive later. At least right now there's a chance that we can have a small advantage. They know we're coming, they just don't know when."

David thought about this for a moment, and finally had to agree with James' assessment. He would just have to wait. For now. "Fine. But if I see a window during the battle..."

"Then you take it," James said, smiling.

◊

Yvette walked along with Bhakat for a while before she could work up the nerve to speak. She hadn't been able to think of a way to bring up the subject, so she went with the direct approach. "Bhakat," she began, "what you told me about the Johar Stones is true, isn't it?" The way she spoke could have been taken as a question or a statement, but Bhakat chose to treat it like a question. He must have known that she wanted to talk.

"Yes," he said, turning to look at her. "You've finally accepted it?"

"I guess I have," she answered. "How am I supposed to tell the others? Should I tell the others?"

"That's up to you," he said. "I don't know how they'll react any more than you do."

True, she thought. *But is that a reason they shouldn't know the truth?* She wasn't sure. She figured she'd have to think about it a while longer, which meant staying away from James as much as possible so she didn't slip up and tell him. It would be a difficult task.

"I meant to ask you," Bhakat said, breaking her concentration. "What is the normal gestation period for a Human female?"

"What?" she asked. "Oh, forty weeks. About nine months or so. What is it for Rajani?"

Bhakat thought for a moment. "I believe it calculates to a year in Earth time. We have big babies." He smiled, sadly.

◊

James found Yvette wasn't home yet when he arrived, which was strange, but certainly not that unusual. She could take care of herself, he knew. Perhaps Bhakat had something for which he needed her help. He decided to sit outside the building and watch the sun set. It was a pleasant night, with a light breeze that carried the scent of the Rajani ocean. James hadn't had a chance to just sit and think since he'd arrived on Rajan. Now that the Resistance was planning on attacking the Krahn's southern base, or Nestbase One as they referred to it, he didn't know when he'd have another chance. He sat with his back against the wall of the building, the stone still warm from the Rajani sun. With the beginning of the rainy season set to start any day, he knew he might not get another opportunity to enjoy the warmth for a while.

He used to love to sit on the fire escape back in Detroit at night and listen to the sounds of the city around him. It helped to settle his nerves if he'd had a tough day at work, which was often, toward the end of his police career. On especially rough nights, he'd sit and read poetry, the pages illuminated by the cheap lamp next to the window. Then he'd suddenly found himself aboard an alien spacecraft, caught in a situation he'd never even dreamed of being in while growing up. He'd made a quick decision to travel millions of miles away from Earth, and he'd never regretted leaving, except at night. Then he'd miss the city sounds and the poetry, at least on those nights when he wasn't exhausted from training with the others who'd come along on the trip.

After Rauphangelaa's ship, the *Tukuli*, was shot down and his escape pod had crashed on Rajan, it had taken him a long time to get used to the sounds of a Rajani night. Or lack of sounds, as it turned out. The city had been struck a near-fatal blow by the invading Krahn, and at night, the only sounds that could be heard were the rare call of strange nocturnal creatures, or more common, weapons fire between the Rajani resistance and roving bands of Krahn warriors.

Lately they'd managed to push the line between the Resistance and the Krahn farther and farther to the south of the city. The nights had become almost peaceful, though he'd barely had time to notice due to his various responsibilities to the Rajani. He was constantly in meetings of one kind or another with all three species on Rajan. When Rauph had asked him to help free Rajan, he'd had no idea he'd become the leader of the entire Rajani resistance movement. And now all the long, hard months of fighting were coming to an end, one way or another. So James sat, watching the clouds, red from the Rajani sun, pass by overhead. They were identical to the clouds at home, which shouldn't have been a surprise, but it somehow was. It would be dark soon, darker than any night back on Earth. There was still no electricity on Rajan, so no light reflected off the night sky as it did back in Detroit.

There were more stars shining down than he'd ever seen, and none of them he recognized. The constellations he knew were far away, and he wondered if he'd ever see them again.

Chapter 6

Belani had given up any hope of ever getting out of his stone prison. His only sense of time was the once-a-day feeding, and even that seemed like a dream some days. The Jirina never seemed to bring him food at the same time of day. He'd lost track of everything else. They kept him without light, and even with his keen nocturnal eyesight, it was still too dark for him to do anything but sit and think. His thoughts inevitably drifted to his family, no matter what the time of day or night. His father had died a few years before the Krahn invasion. His sister Beren, who was a year younger than him, had helped his mother raise his youngest sister, Kalani, while he did his best to provide for all of them. He would work any job he could find, while also training to fly starships for the Rajani Elders.

He'd finally graduated from flight training school and became a pilot and had thought all of his family's problems were solved, and they had been for a time. But then the Krahn had appeared, their ships screaming from the sky and destroying everything in their path. Ships had landed near their housing area, and Krahn ground troops had swarmed through their building, shooting indiscriminately and collecting prisoners. He'd been returning home from work and couldn't get to his house through all of the chaos of the attack. His mother had died trying to protect his sisters. He had found her inside their home, a look of terror frozen on her face, even in death. He'd sat next to her body and cried for a few minutes before coming to the realization that his sisters must have been captured. After burying his mother, he'd wandered aimlessly before being found by a small group of Sekani, which had been led by Zanth.

Belani was falling asleep as he remembered the events that had led him to a basement cell, when a light suddenly spilled into his room. His eyes filled with tears of pain at the blinding brilliance. He moaned unintentionally, covering his eyes with his arm and turning away from the light source.

"Why do I always get that reaction whenever I wake someone up?" he heard asked through a voice translator, its mechanical sound echoing off the stone walls of his prison.

◊

Ronak was thinking about the events that had led him to being stuck on the Rajani mud ball, light years from his home, with no end to the insurgency and no progress yet in finding what he had come there for in the first place. It was no wonder he lashed out at times in an impotent rage at his incompetent followers. Most of his warriors had been born and bred aboard his colony ship. He had taken a number of Krahn females, many unwilling, aboard his ship when he'd fled the Krahn home world, and these, as well as the females from future generations, were used to breed the largest number of males possible. These males had been raised for the single purpose of fighting and scavenging, whether in space or on a planet's surface.

Very few of the inhabitants of his ship had been with him before his banishment. None of the initial breeding females taken from Krahn had survived long; forced breeding had taken its toll. Many of his original warriors had been captured or killed in his rebellion against his brother, and the ones who still lived were languishing in Maliq's prisons on Krahn. He'd been allowed to take his counselor, Kalik, as well as some cousins who had sided with him in the rebellion. He'd also been reunited with his bloodmate, Mariqa, when Maliq had sent him into banishment. It had taken him years to build up his troops to the necessary numbers again, while he also pirated ships, finally making enough money to have his colony ship built.

After that, he'd almost felt ready once more to return to Krahn and finally overthrow his hated sibling. But his counselors had told him that they didn't think he could beat his brother's forces with the number of warriors he had. He needed an edge. It was Mariqa who had suggested the attack on Rajan, reasoning that it should be easy enough to defeat the now-peaceful Rajani and their servant races and recover the Johar Stones in their possession. And now it was Mariqa's suggestion, in private, of course, that they should abandon the planet and retreat to their colony ship, to start over once more. His stable of breeding females was still aboard the ship. It wouldn't take more than three or four years—five at the most—to build warrior numbers back up to levels sufficient enough to be able to attack his homeworld of Krahn.

His plan, then, was to abandon whatever warriors were still on the planet. It was not a difficult decision to make, but he still needed to get his bloodmate, his counselor Kalik, and himself on a ship without arousing the suspicions of any others, or there could be a full-scale mutiny among his warriors. And he'd have to do it quickly, because the rebellion on Rajan would probably attack Nestbase One soon, and he didn't want to be there when they did.

◊

James wasn't apprehensive as much as he was curious about Belani. It was true that the Sekani was responsible for the deaths of eleven resistance troops; four strike teams had been killed in the failed attack on the airfield. But James wanted to know more of the alien's story before he passed a final judgment of his own. He set the translating device down by the door and waited for Belani to become used to the light. James had been hit by a wave of odor that was part body odor and part excrement, so he decided to let the room air out a bit before entering. He'd gone to his share of crime scenes where a body had been found after decaying for a few days or even weeks, but that smell he could tolerate. The smell emanating from Belani's cell reminded him more of a visit to the zoo.

He remembered visiting the monkey house at the Toledo Zoo when he was a kid. He'd had to ask his mother to take him outside for some fresh air, and he hadn't been to a zoo since. His brother had teased him unmercifully about it, but James had been all right with that, as long as he didn't have to go back. He'd even gotten into a big fight with Jenny before they were married because she had wanted to go to the San Diego Zoo, and he had refused. It was one of the rare times he'd stood his ground with her; he'd rarely denied her anything. When she died, it was one of the things he regretted. There were so many things he regretted; so many experiences they would never share. It had taken him years to not wake up or go to bed thinking about her.

And now here he was in a relationship with a woman in the middle of a war zone, where she could die at any moment. Yvette was much different than Jenny had been, though. She was tough, and cynical at times, yes, yet she hadn't let herself become emotionally distant from the world around her, either. Jenny had maintained a sweet disposition most of the time. She actually was more like Kieren in that respect than Yvette. Yvette had a temper, and her tongue was sharp sometimes when dealing with people, but James liked her fire and appreciated her truthfulness. There was another side to her as well, once she let him into her confidence. It was a gentleness that was only on display in their most intimate moments together. James found that he was able to talk to her about anything when they were together, and she would always listen to him, even if it was only to vent his frustrations.

His thoughts were interrupted by the voice of Belani. "James?" the Sekani prisoner whispered. "James the Human?"

"I was told you were asking for me," James said. "Why don't you come out of there and we'll find a better place to have a conversation. Looks to me like you could use some fresh air."

Belani walked slowly from the cell, wincing and stretching his legs and arms. "How long have I been in there?"

"Nine days," James answered.

"Where are the guards?" Belani asked, still squinting as he looked around.

"I sent them away, for now," James said. "Am I going to have any trouble with you? Do I need to call them back?"

"No," Belani said, smiling. "Besides, you could break me in half with one arm."

"There is that, yes," James said, knowing that Belani could easily outrun him if he chose to escape. He led the Sekani up a flight of stairs and into a large furnished room that had one wall turned to rubble from the demolished upper level of the house. "Sit down. Maybe I can rustle up something to eat and drink."

James knew that whatever food had been in the dwelling had either been eaten or had gone bad. With no electricity, it hadn't lasted long. He knew Kieren and Gianni had overseen a task force of Sekani that had gone from house to house to collect whatever food could be found after they'd first arrived. He hoped that the Jirina guards had some provisions set aside, though, while they stayed in the house. His search was rewarded when he found bottles of water and two pieces of fruit. One, a guardo, was about the size of a grapefruit and had purple skin. James had eaten them before. He knew that the fruit had pink flesh and tasted something like an apple. The other piece of fruit he'd never seen before. It was the size of a cantaloupe and was dark green with small, spiky protrusions.

He left the mystery fruit and took a bottle of water and the guardo back to where he'd left Belani. "Here, eat," he told the Sekani, handing him the fruit.

Belani greedily bit into the fruit, barely taking the time to chew before taking another bite, the juice dripping down his chin. He wiped his arm across his mouth, looking like a cat that had just finished devouring a mouse. "My thanks," he said. He opened the bottle of water that James had set down on the table next to him and took a long gulp before sitting back, contentedly, in his seat, now eating at a more leisurely pace.

James waited until the urgency of the Sekani's eating seemed to lessen before speaking. "Now, everyone told me I should just leave you to rot down there." Belani looked up at him as he said this. James could see the fear in the Sekani's eyes at the mention of his cell. "But I'm willing to at least listen to what you have to say to me."

Belani swallowed a mouthful of fruit and took another drink of water. "Again, my thanks. I knew you would be reasonable the first time I saw you at your meeting with the other leaders. That's why I asked for you."

"Doesn't mean I can do anything," James said.

"No," Belani said, sitting forward again. "But I had to try, at least." He took one last bite and swallowed it. "You know, I don't even like guardo, but I think I would have eaten a masaga if you had given it to me," he said, referring to the rodent-like creatures found on Rajan. Their numbers had seemed to multiply after the Krahn attack, as they fed on the bodies of the dead.

James could see that the light, food, and water had gone a long way in improving the Sekani's demeanor. He seemed much different from the broken creature who had sat before them all after the failed attack on the airfield. "Okay, so talk."

"I'm aware that your time is important," Belani began. "So I'll be brief. I don't want to die here. Not in that cell, anyway. Put me at the front of the line with a club in my hand if you want, I don't care. If I'm going to die, let it be by fighting the Krahn, not by the so-called authority of the Rajani."

"You think they would put you to death for your crimes?" James asked. "After this war is over?"

"They've done it before," Belani replied. "They try to act pious and civilized, but below the surface they're what you've seen since you've arrived: a society of beings that can be ruthless, especially when it comes to members of another species."

James thought about the two bodies that they had discovered aboard the *Tukuli*. He knew the disregard that Belani was talking about, even if it was unintentional, as it had probably been for Rauph. He kept his thoughts to himself, however, and let the Sekani talk. There was no use muddying the situation with his own memories.

"Before the Krahn attacked us," Belani continued, "there was a court system. Or I should say two court systems—

one for the Rajani, and a separate one for the Sekani and Jirina. In both, it was a panel of Rajani judges that meted out punishments to those who broke the Rajani's laws. There was no death sentence for Rajani, except for one crime, but a Sekani or Jirina could be put to death for a variety of crimes."

"Such as?" James asked.

"Murder, of course," Belani answered. "But also stealing from an Elder, having an inappropriate inter-species relationship, mutiny aboard a Rajani ship . . ."

"When they first brought us aboard their ship, Rauph and Bhakat said that implanting oneself with a Johar Stone was punishable by death," James said.

"Yes, that is the one crime that I mentioned," Belani said. "It's the one crime that brings death to anyone. But no one has done it for so long now that it's almost not worth mentioning. Until now, of course. I don't know what the laws state about implanting a species other than those found on Rajan. Up until now it was thought to be outside the realm of possibility that the Johar Stones would wind up outside of Rajani control."

James thought about Bhakat, who had been forced to implant himself with a Stone to escape the *Tukuli* and rescue Rauph. He wondered what the Rajani's fate would be after the fighting was over. He knew that Yvette had grown quite fond of the big Rajani in her time there.

"All right," James said. "We're running out of time, and even though this talk about Rajani society and the legal system has been both interesting and informative, we should actually talk about why I'm here."

"I thought I made myself clear," Belani said. "I would rather die fighting the Krahn—"

"No," James said, interrupting him. "That's not what I meant. I meant the reason I actually came here."

Belani sat there a moment, a quizzical look on his face.

"As you know," James began, "the Resistance is planning on attacking the main Krahn base within the next couple of days."

"I've been locked up," Belani said. "The war could have ended and I wouldn't have known it."

"Oh, yes, sorry," James said sheepishly. "Anyway, we need someone to provide air cover, and to also draw away the attention of Krahn ships that might possibly attack our ground troops. Since we only have one ship at the moment, the individual who pilots it would be on their own up there. So I volunteered you."

"Because I'm expendable," Belani said.

"Yes, to tell the truth," James answered. "In war everyone is. Let's face it, we could all die before this thing is over." He sighed and rubbed his face, a habit he'd picked up since growing a beard—a beard that if he had looked in a mirror he'd notice was entirely black now. But mirrors were few and far between on Rajan.

"I'm going to be straight and truthful with you," James continued. "My volunteering you really had nothing to do with you. It was a means to an end. I needed to get the three species together behind something, and that something just happened to be their hatred of you. That doesn't mean you can't take advantage of this opportunity. And if, by chance, you make it through . . ."

Belani laughed, though there was no real humor in it. "We both know I won't survive this. Even if I'm not shot down by the Krahn, there's no way the Rajani would let me live."

James leaned forward toward the Sekani. "If you perform this duty and survive, I promise you I'll do what I can to help you. That's all I can do at this point."

Belani sat a moment looking at the floor. Finally, he looked up at James. "That's all I can ask for right now. Thank you."

"Don't thank me until after this is over," James said, standing up. "Now, unfortunately, you need to go back in your cell until I have everything worked out." He walked the Sekani back to the room downstairs. "Someone will be by soon to let you out and take you to the ship. I don't think it will be me. I have too many other things I have to do before this offensive begins."

"I understand," Belani said, bowing to him. "If we never meet again, I wish you long life and happiness." He walked into the dark cell, and James closed the door, making sure it locked.

James wasn't sure why he'd promised to speak for the Sekani if he survived. Perhaps after all the death he'd seen, he needed to be able to say that he'd at least saved one life, even if it was the life of a traitor.

◊

Ronak and Mariqa were settling down for the night, their spirited mating session having ended with him feeling somewhat unsatisfied, not to mention sore from the countless scratches inflicted by her claws. He could tell by the way she turned away from him soon after that she felt unfulfilled as well. The fire of their passion was burning low as they suffered defeat after defeat on Rajan. He'd thought that if he had come down to the planet, it would spur his warriors to fight harder and turn the tide of battle against the Rajani, but it hadn't happened. And now his relationship with his bloodmate was suffering because of it. There were times when he thought that he'd suffer any defeat as long as they were together. Then other times . . .

Perhaps we need some time apart, he thought. He also

wanted her away if there was an attack from the Rajani upon their base. Of course, if he told her his intentions, she would fly into a rage at any question of her ability to fight. Better to make it seem as if he were sending her away on an important mission. She would have to obey his orders. He was the Vasin, wasn't he? "I want you to take your ship and inspect the operations aboard the colony ship tomorrow," he said quietly from where he sat in the bed.

Mariqa turned to look at him, and for a moment he thought he detected a hurt look in her eyes, before it was quickly replaced by no expression at all. He was familiar with that look. She used it when she was angry and didn't want him to know it. "Yes, Mighty Qadira," she said, bowing her head slightly and turning away again.

He sat in silence for a long time, listening to her breathing and thinking about the best way to leave Rajan forever.

◊

James came in late from one of the countless meetings he had to attend to find Yvette still awake in their room. She was in bed, sitting up, as if she'd been waiting for him.

"You look tired," she said, smiling at him as he turned off the solar generator-powered light that the Rajani had provided for him and got into bed. She turned and was lying on her side facing away from him.

"I'm surprised you're still awake," he said, putting his arm around her and snuggling up close. They almost never had time to just talk anymore. They were both so busy that usually one of them was sleeping before the other got home.

"I was just thinking," she said. He couldn't see the tears that suddenly sprang to her eyes as she spoke, but he could hear the emotion in her voice.

"What about?" he asked. He'd already been sinking into sleep, but now felt a wave of apprehension.

"Us," she said.

Uh-oh, he thought. He opened his eyes. "What about us?" he asked.

"Is there an 'us'?" she replied. "I mean, really? If this war really ends someday, and we get back to Earth, then what?"

"I don't know what our future holds," he said quietly. "All I know is that if we're both alive when we get home, I want you to be a part of my life."

She turned and finally looked at him. He could see the glint of tears on her face. "Will we ever have a normal life after all of this? So much has happened since we first met . . ."

"I've had a normal life," he replied, gently wiping her face with his hand. "It's not that great without someone to share it with." He'd never really talked with her about his wife. He didn't know why, only that it almost seemed like a different lifetime.

"I just . . . I don't know," she said. "I guess I don't want to find out that we're only together because of circumstance, and not because we . . . care for each other. You know?"

"Well," he said, "it's not like I ever thought I'd meet some hot young thing who would think of me as something other than a creepy old man."

"Stop," she said quietly, slapping him on the arm. "I'm serious."

"So am I," he said, leaning forward and gently kissing her on the lips. "I've been a bachelor for a long time. The way things were headed, I expected to stay that way."

"When my mother was attacked, I never thought I would have any type of relationship with a man," she said. "It took me a long time before I trusted men. I even kept my father at more than arm's length. We only grew close again after I graduated from college and was on my own. But even then, it was always my choice on whether I would let anyone in. I didn't want to be hurt again. I guess I still don't."

"I have no intention of ever hurting you," he said. "But I can't guarantee anything, especially now, except that I'm yours. For as long as you want me. I'm yours." She laid her head on his chest, and he held her as they both fell asleep.

Chapter 7

It had been a while since James and Rauph had sat down to talk. Actually, when James thought about it, they hadn't really spoken together since before arriving on Rajan. So much had happened since then that James hadn't had a chance to speak with him until the opening presented itself, quite unexpectedly. James had sought out Bhakat, who was training with the Valderren, and had passed along his desire to speak to the Elders. The Elders then sent Rauph as their chosen representative. James was happy to invite the Rajani into his room when Rauph showed up at his door. James had only just returned from speaking with a group of Jirina troops, and was supposed to be getting ready to have dinner with Yvette, but he figured he had a little time to spare to sit down with Rauph.

Rauph seemed eager to talk as well as he walked over to a chair set across from James. James clicked on the translating device that was on the floor between them. He didn't really want Rauph to know how proficient he was becoming in speaking Talondarian Standard. It wasn't that he didn't trust Rauph. It was just that he didn't trust Rauph much.

"Please," James said, "sit down. Can I offer you some fernta? Water?"

"No," Rauph said, grimacing as he took the proffered chair. "I never cared much for fernta. Thank you."

"How are you feeling?" James asked, noticing the pained expression on Rauph's face.

"I wish everyone would stop asking me that question. Just because we're Elders doesn't mean we're old." He chuckled a moment before continuing. "Though I feel like it sometimes." He chuckled again and continued. "Bhakat tells me it was a close thing, there at the end. If he and Yvette hadn't found the medical equipment when they did, I wouldn't be here to complain about my ribs, which hurt every time the weather turns cold, I might add."

"I'm sorry," James said. "I broke a finger once, so I can't imagine what recovering from broken ribs must be like."

"Don't be sorry," Rauph said. "At least I'm here. And more importantly, you are here. Now, what was it you wanted to speak about?"

"The Resistance will be assaulting the Krahn base in two days," James said. "Ronak has come down to the planet's surface, and this may be our only chance to capture or kill him."

Rauph nodded sadly. "I had heard the rumors. I do wish there was another way to go about this. But I suppose this is why we brought you here in the first place."

"Yes, it was," James said. "And an assault like this will mean a great number of casualties, on both sides."

"Unfortunately, that is true," Rauph said, frowning.

"I'm forming special units," James said, plowing ahead. He was well aware of Rauph and the other Elders' stance when it came to this conflict. He didn't need to hear it again. "One of the units that I want is a medical unit that will take care of the Rajani, Sekani, and Jirina casualties during and after the fighting. We were able to find two Rajani physicians that volunteered to head up the units. I was hoping that the Elders would be willing to serve in these units as well."

Rauph sat for a moment, pondering James's request. "Although I may speak for the Elders, I cannot make this type of decision without their input. I'll take your request back and will let you know our decision. I'm afraid that's the best I can do at this point."

"That's enough," James said. *It will have to be,* he thought.

"Enough about fighting," Rauph said. "How are you doing? And the others? The only ones I ever see are Yvette and David. How are Kieren and Gianni faring in all this?"

"Everyone is well, as far as I know," James replied. "Sometimes days at a time go by when I don't see them. There always seems to be some pressing matter that keeps me busy. I'm always in one meeting or another these days."

"Like now?" Rauph said, smiling.

"Yes," James said, returning the smile. "But some meetings are more enjoyable than others, believe me."

"Oh, I know what you mean, truly I do," Rauph said. "It's all the Elders ever do, talk and more talk. It seems we're powerless to do anything but talk. And while we talk, the majority of the Rajani move away from the Kaa and its teachings. We are left with a choice: to either survive by fighting, or die clinging to our faith. It's no wonder most have chosen to live."

They sat in silence for a moment, each lost in their own thoughts. James couldn't imagine having to make that type of decision. Maybe it was his American upbringing—the sensibility that 'might makes right' and all of the other slogans of his childhood. He would have chosen to be a survivor every time, he knew. It wasn't in him to quit. Hopefully the Rajani, Jirina, and Sekani would turn out to be the same way once the fighting became heavy. If not, then the fighting wouldn't last long, at least.

"I want to know something," James said, after a while. "Why did you really choose the five of us? Was it just a coincidence that you chose five random people that ended up working out as well together as a team?"

Rauph thought for a moment. "You were the first Human we discovered, due to your exposure on the information telecast that we picked up emanating from your planet. Your news conference was broadcast on all of the stations. You seemed to be someone who was devoted to doing the right thing. We keyed in on your dwelling and researched the other Humans as much as we could in the time that we had to wait for the *Tukuli* to repair itself." He stopped speaking a moment to adjust in his chair, attempting to get in a more comfortable position. "We immediately discounted those individuals that were either too old or too young, and those who were mated or had younglings. We knew they probably wouldn't agree to leave others behind to take this journey. The other four that I eventually picked were narrowed down by our research and by observation."

"Observation?" James asked. "Just how long did you spend watching us?"

"You, not at all," Rauph replied. "We had your newsfeeds, after all. We were in orbit around your planet for approximately three of your Earth months before you were brought aboard the *Tukuli*."

"And how long were we aboard the ship before you woke us up?" James asked, leaning forward.

"We told you," Rauph said. "Approximately two Earth weeks. We had to do full physical examinations to make sure you were healthy, and that you were not carrying any viruses that could cause an outbreak of plague or something similar on Rajan. We didn't need to stop one disaster only to foster another in its place."

"And that took two weeks?" James asked, skeptical now.

"Well," Rauph said, "no, actually. But it did take two days."

"And the rest of the time you kept us asleep in order for repairs to finish, and then you woke us up and hurried us into a decision on whether to help you or not," James said.

Rauph sighed. "Yes. I couldn't take the chance that you would change your mind if we woke you too soon and you had too long to think about it while we were still within your solar system."

"That's what I thought," James said. "There's nothing we can do about it now, I guess. But I can tell you that I wouldn't have changed my mind. And I don't think any of the others would have, either."

"I know that now," Rauph said. "But at the time, we didn't know how you would react to us or the situation we placed you in. Or the question we posed to you once we woke you up. You must understand by now that there is no one else who would have helped us. Not the Galactic Alliance, and certainly not the ASPs. We were desperate to return to Rajan with someone or something that would aid our cause. Otherwise, we would have just come back here and joined our species and let the Krahn do what they would with us."

"So," James said, "the fact that all of us Humans worked out was just dumb luck."

"I guess so," Rauph said. "You're our saviors, whether we win this war or not. Without your presence here, the Krahn would have surely succeeded by now. They still may, but not without a high cost to them. For that, I am eternally grateful."

James stood up. Rauph's show of gratitude complicated things between them. "And yet you are still guilty of murdering two of my people for no reason."

"Yes," Rauph said, sadly. "It was so much easier when we only knew your race as an alien life-form. I don't expect you to ever forgive me for what was done, even if those Humans would have died anyway."

"You know that doesn't matter to us," James said. "The fact is, you were the cause of their deaths."

"I know," Rauph said. "And for that, I can only say I'm sorry so many times. If I could change what happened, I would." He stood up slowly. "I will take your request to the other Elders."

"Look," James said, holding his hand out to stop Rauph from leaving, "we've all killed other sentient life-forms because of this war. No one is innocent here. Except for maybe Kieren. I have no right to judge anyone. I can't carry any animosity toward you, when I might have done the same thing if I were in the same situation."

"You are a wise and forgiving Human," Rauph said. "I'm lucky beyond words that I found you out of all the Humans on your planet."

"Now don't go overboard," James said, smiling. "This doesn't mean we're going steady or anything."

"I have no idea what you just said. The meaning of your words eludes me," Rauph said, returning the smile. "But I understand the sentiment behind it, I think. Thank you, James."

◊

Kedar had asked Welemaan to meet with him to plan for their part in the coming attack on the Krahn. It was an interesting situation he found himself in. He and Welemaan had known each other long before the Krahn had attacked, but he would not have thought them to be friends, exactly. They'd been thrust together because of their mutual imprisonment at the hands of the Krahn. They had broken out of the Krahn prison together, only to be recaptured, and then had fought together afterward against the Krahn when James the Human had suddenly appeared in their midst. While their friendship had seemed to grow over the course of the fighting, their ideas on how to handle the war varied greatly from one another.

Welemaan was proud to be an Elder, and wanted things on Rajan to return to normal if they succeeded in defeating the Krahn. Kedar was practical enough to know that it would never be the same. The Sekani had tasted freedom, even if only on a limited basis. They would never go back to what they had been, and neither would the Jirina. James the Human had done his best to instill in them a sense of their own worth, and Kedar respected that. He worried sometimes about some of the things that Welemaan would talk about in private. Kedar did what he could to keep his friend in check, but as had been proven when Welemaan's strike team had returned from their mission, there was only so much that could be done to rein him in.

His train of thought was interrupted by a knock on the door of the meeting room where he was sitting. The door opened, and Welemaan walked in. "Sorry I'm late," he said, smiling.

Kedar returned the smile. He could just imagine the excuse Welemaan would come up with. "I suppose you were held up by something infinitely more important," he said.

"No, just something interesting," Welemaan said. "I was talking to a Sekani scout that had just returned from the Krahn airbase."

"Really?" Kedar asked, surprised. "I wasn't aware that we had sent any scouts that far south since the strike team disaster."

"Apparently Zanth did," Welemaan said. "Have to give it

to the little guy, he's a sharp one."

"Yes, I'm well aware of that," Kedar said. He'd spent enough time around the Sekani leader to know it would be a mistake to underestimate him. "And what did this Sekani scout have to say?"

Welemaan sat down before replying. "Seems the Krahn are still using the base, even though we know the exact location now. Kedar, I think we'll need to take that into account when we eventually attack their southern base."

"I agree," Kedar said. "We'll have to form a team to attack it—"

"No," Welemaan said, leaning forward toward him. "We need to lead a force of Rajani to attack it."

"Why?" Kedar asked.

"Because if we liberate any of their ships, we need to be in control of them," Welemaan answered. "None of this 'the ships belong to the Resistance' stuff that James the Human was spouting. We need to be in control of the ships when the fighting is over, Kedar."

"I doubt they'll be very happy with that," Kedar said. "If we're fighting this war together, then they're going to want to share in the spoils of our victory."

"I'll take care of that," Welemaan said. "It's really not important at the moment. What is important is what we do after the fighting on Rajan is done."

"What are you proposing?" Kedar asked. Welemaan's tone had taken on a darkness that Kedar had never heard before from his friend.

"I think we need to take the fight to them," Welemaan said.

"To who?" Kedar asked, confused.

"The Krahn," Welemaan said. "They must pay for what they've done here."

"You mean the Krahn home world? Are you serious? The Krahn have nothing to do with this," Kedar said.

"We don't know that," Welemaan said. "For all we know, this Ronak had his brother's full blessing in attacking Rajan. Gave him his own planet to rule, if you see my meaning."

"Welemaan," Kedar said after a moment, "I think we need to worry about rebuilding our own world after we win this fight. We're not going to have the resources to attack another planet. We'll be lucky to have the energy turned back on and clean water flowing again."

"How can you say that?" Welemaan said, standing up. "After what they did to us, to your family and mine. They must pay for this, Kedar."

"All I'm saying," Kedar said, attempting to mollify his friend, "is that we have to make sure Rajan is in a position of strength before we go attacking anyone." *And when that time comes,* he thought, *I'll have enough backing to make sure you're in no position to follow through with your plans.*

"Fine, we'll table this for now," Welemaan said. "But this isn't over, Kedar." He turned and walked out without even saying goodbye.

Kedar knew that Welemaan would bear watching now. He sighed, rubbing his eyes in fatigue. Hopefully all of this would end soon, and he could go back to just living his life without having to worry about everything and everyone else.

◊

Rauphangelaa left his meeting with Officer Dempsey and went directly home. He sat alone in deep thought about all that had happened since his return to Rajan. He'd known it would be difficult, had expected that there would probably be Rajani fighting alongside Officer Dempsey and the other Humans, but he hadn't thought at the time that so many Rajani would give up their belief in the Kaa. He, for one, would not abandon all he'd been taught. The Kaa was not just a way of life or a philosophy to be debated on its true meaning. It was so much more than that. It was a religion, a way of thinking about yourself and your role in the world, and in the universe as a whole. The rules that Ruvedalin taught all those years ago were not mere guidelines that could be bent to suit one's needs when it befitted them. They were meant to protect not only the Rajani, but others *from* the Rajani. As Keeper of the Stones, only he knew some very important details about Rajani history, and he knew what could happen if they returned fully to their war-like ways.

Ruvedalin's teachings had brought about a revolution in its time, and that revolution had not been a bloodless one. Rauph hadn't told any of that to the Humans when they had first woken up, lest it confuse them in their choice to help. Even many Rajani didn't know the full story of Ruvedalin. Ruvedalin's followers had been beaten, imprisoned, and sometimes even killed for their beliefs. Peace was not a concept the Elders of the time could abide. It was thought that their very way of life was in danger from Ruvedalin's words, and in a way, it was. Only after years of his preaching to the Rajani (and many of those spent in hiding from the authorities), was there finally a paradigm shift, one that Ruvedalin didn't live to see. He died of old age before his vision was fulfilled. But fulfilled it was, and that was why Rauph and the other Elders would set up their medical station miles behind the fighting, while their species, as well as the Sekani, Jirina, and Humans, fought the Krahn. They would sit and pray, and pray some more, and wait for the casualties to start flooding in. They would do their part in helping to save a society that may no longer want them after the fighting had finished.

Their way of life was once again being challenged.

Each of them could feel it, but none knew how to stop what the Krahn had set in motion. Despite what he'd told Officer Dempsey, most of the time the Elders sat in silence, none talking to their peers about trivial matters of state or leadership. They had no idea if they would ever rule again, even if the Krahn were defeated. Rauph was miserable, but not about this fact. He worried for his pupil, Bhakat. He worried about the Humans and the secret they carried, as well as what would become of them if they lived through this war. But mostly, he worried for the Rajani and for a future that seemed as dark as the depths of space. Rauph rose from his chair slowly. He hadn't felt well when he woke up that morning, and it didn't seem to be getting any better as the day wore on. He thought he must have eaten something that had upset his stomach.

Suddenly, he felt his chest squeeze tightly and sweat break on his brow. Pain radiated down his left arm, and he felt like he couldn't catch his breath. Then everything went black as he fell to the floor.

◊

Yvette was almost to the medical clinic when the nausea hit. She doubled over quickly, hoping that no one would see her as she threw up what little was in her stomach. After dry heaving for a minute, she stood up once again and began to walk. She really hated throwing up. It hadn't happened a lot recently, but once was too much, in her opinion. Maybe Bhakat would have something she could take to help quell the nausea a little. Of course, she would have to be careful. Who knew what an alien drug could do to the baby? She couldn't believe how much she'd started worrying about things like that. She was going to see Bhakat so he could test her to see how far along she was. She knew it couldn't be more than a couple of weeks. She'd only been experiencing symptoms for about a week. She didn't know a lot about pregnancy, though. She'd never had a reason to learn about it, knowing she couldn't get pregnant. Everything was new to her when it came to being a responsible mother.

Mother. That word caused her to smile, even though her mouth felt sour and her stomach was still rumbling, threatening mutiny yet again. She arrived at the clinic and found Bhakat waiting for her. As she followed him into the examination room, she was surprised to see he had a translating device set on a table near the bed.

"Have a seat," he said, pointing to the table. "Have you had any problems since the last time you were here?" he asked her. "Any bleeding or anything else that might be unusual?"

"No," she said. "What's with the translator?"

"I want to make sure that I understand everything you tell me fully, and also that you understand me," he answered. "I think this is too important to trust to my limited vocabulary."

Yvette smiled, knowing he was selling himself short. His English was very good, though he did have a strong accent. But she appreciated his sentiment. "I did vomit on the way here, but that seems to be normal these days."

"Yes, it's normal, but I want you to begin drinking more water," he said, making a note on a handheld tablet. "I'll talk to them about increasing your water ration. You're drinking for two now. I don't want you to become dehydrated."

"Okay," she said. "Do you have anything that will help with the nausea? I really hate feeling like this all the time."

"Unfortunately, nothing that I'd feel confident in giving you," Bhakat said. He walked over to the medibot and pushed a few buttons. "I want to take some vitals, if that's all right with you," he said.

"Sure," she said. "Should I lay down?"

"No need," he said. "I actually want to get your blood pressure while you're sitting, not lying down."

She sat while the machine took her statistics and wondered if she should have told James about the pregnancy the night before when they'd talked. *When I'm farther along,* she thought. At that point she felt like she would somehow jinx it if she told him. She knew it was irrational, but she still had a difficult time believing she was pregnant.

"You say you think you're only a few weeks?" Bhakat asked.

"Yes, I've only had morning sickness for a little over a week," she said.

"If you don't mind, I'd like to take a look at the fetus," he said.

"You can do that?" she asked, holding a hand to her stomach.

"Oh, yes," he said. "I need you to lie down on your back this time."

She did as he asked and watched as he hit a few buttons on the medibot. She saw a screen pop out of the side of the medical robot. She recognized it now from when they had rescued David from the Krahn. Bhakat placed the screen over her stomach.

"This won't hurt the baby, will it?" she asked, feeling a little jolt of tension between her shoulder blades.

"No," he said. "We use this machine on all of our own expectant mothers. If your fetus is as far along as I think, then it won't be harmed from a brief scan."

She nodded and then flinched as he placed a hand on her stomach. "Sorry," she said.

"My fault," he said. "I should have asked your permission; forgive me."

"No, that's not it," she said. "I'm just feeling . . .

apprehensive, I guess. About everything."

"Understandable," he said. "Most first-time mothers are the same way, from what I've seen. I didn't practice in this field, but I saw and heard enough from other doctors to know this is normal too. Just relax. This will only take a minute."

She watched as he pulled a small, round disk from the side of the monitor and attached it to her bare stomach. He touched the screen a few times, then smiled. *He's getting better at it,* she thought. *He's not doubting his medical training as much.* His bedside manner had improved from when they were together on the *Tukuli.*

Suddenly, the room was filled with a low thumping sound, a staccato beat that could only be one thing. "Is that . . . ?"

"Your baby's heartbeat, yes," he replied, smiling.

She felt tears begin streaming from her eyes as she listened to it. "Is it supposed to be that fast?" she asked, finally.

"Yes, that's a healthy heartbeat for a fetus at nine weeks," he said.

"Nine weeks?" she asked, surprised. "I'm that far along already?"

"According to my measurements," he said. "Of course, I could be a little off, having never had a Human patient before. But I think it's a pretty close guess. Everything seems to be just fine with your baby."

"Can you tell the gender?" she asked, not sure if she really wanted to know.

"Not this early," he replied. "Give it another nine weeks, and then we can take a look."

She was just about to thank him when the Rajani doctor she had met earlier came bursting through the doors. "Bhakat, my apologies for the interruption, but you need to come quickly."

"What is it, Andraal?" he asked, turning toward the other Rajani.

"It's Rauphangelaa."

"Oh my," Yvette said. "Go, Bhakat, I'm okay."

"My thanks," he said, squeezing her hand briefly. He hurriedly walked out, accompanied by Andraal.

Yvette sat and listened to the heartbeat for another minute before taking the sensor from her stomach. She couldn't worry about Rauphangelaa at the moment. She had to figure out how she was going to tell James.

◊

James wasted little time when he heard from Yvette that Rauph had suffered another heart attack. He walked to the medical clinic quickly and waited in the half-full waiting room, hoping to at least talk to Bhakat about Rauph's condition. The other occupants of the waiting room, all Rajani, nodded and smiled to him, and he returned their smiles, though he didn't recognize any of them.

A Rajani that he assumed worked there came out of one of the rooms and looked at him, expectantly. "I was wondering if you could tell me how Rauphangelaa is doing?" James asked.

"You are James the Human," the Rajani said, and James couldn't tell if he was asking or stating it.

"Yes," he said.

"It is an honor meeting you," the Rajani said, bowing slightly. "My name is Andraal. I'll let Bhakat know that you're here."

"Thank you," James said as the Rajani left him alone with his thoughts once again in the waiting room. It was only a few moments before Bhakat came out of the examination room and motioned for him to enter. James entered the room as the Rajani known as Andraal left. He nodded to the Rajani again, and then focused on the bed that took up one side of the room. Rauph had sensors attached to his body at head and chest, as well as a small device covering his nose that James assumed was feeding him oxygen. His eyes were closed, but James could see his chest rising, so at least he was still breathing.

"I informed Andraal to tell you to come back later," Bhakat said, gruffly. "Unfortunately, I was overruled."

James was surprised when Rauph opened his eyes, though he noticed that they didn't open very wide. "Rauph, how are you feeling?" he asked quietly.

"Old," Rauph replied, smiling briefly and closing his eyes again.

"Nonsense," James said, walking closer to the bed. He noticed, though, how weak Rauph seemed. He looked over at Bhakat a moment. The Rajani shook his head slowly. Damn, he thought, looking back at Rauph. "You need to get well soon. I can't be expected to handle all of this by myself."

For a moment James thought he'd fallen asleep, but then Rauph opened his eyes again. "Afraid you'll have to. I've already left instructions with Bhakat," he said, haltingly.

"He needs to rest now," Bhakat said, placing a hand on James's arm.

"Tumaani," Rauph suddenly said. "Julari, where are you?"

James turned to look at Bhakat, a question in his eyes. Bhakat just shook his head again and motioned toward the door. He walked out of the room. James took a step toward the door before Rauph spoke again.

"The Human is a killer," Rauph said, quietly. "Bhakat, we can't possibly bring him aboard this ship."

James turned back to look at him. "Who? Who is a killer?" he asked quickly, before Bhakat returned.

"We saw him. Saw the Human female die at his hands," Rauph said. Then, after another moment, "Perhaps you're right. But we must be on our guard."

"Who is it?" James asked again, not knowing if Rauph was referring to someone they had actually brought aboard the ship.

"Julari, why can't I find you?" Rauph said so softly that James had a difficult time hearing him over the sound the various monitors and breathing machines made in the room.

Suddenly, the door opened once more, and Bhakat entered. "Please, James," he said. "Rauphangelaa needs his rest."

James took one last look at the Rajani on the bed and turned back toward Bhakat. He finally nodded and walked to the door. "You and I need to talk," he said as he passed by Bhakat.

"I'm sorry," Bhakat said quietly, looking at Rauphangelaa. "I can't leave his side right now."

"I understand," James said. "But you need to come see me as soon as you can, all right?"

Bhakat nodded, and then closed the door behind James as he once again entered the waiting room area. James was disappointed, but vowed that he would return soon to speak with Bhakat about Rauph's words, if Bhakat failed to keep his promise. If there was a killer among them, he needed to know who it was, though he had a feeling that if it was any of them, he needed to keep a closer eye on Gianni. His cop instincts had warned him from the very beginning about Gianni, and they were seldom wrong. Although the man had seemingly changed since arriving on Rajan, that didn't mean that James would underestimate him or assume that he'd actually changed for the better.

◊

Tumaani had heard that Rauphangelaa had a heart attack aboard his ship after the Krahn invasion, but he'd hoped that his friend was better now. Rauphangelaa certainly hadn't acted sick to Tumaani in their time back together on Rajan. He had seemed feistier than ever. Instead, the Keeper of the Stones was close to death now. It wasn't fair. After all they'd gone through against the Krahn, for Rauphangelaa to not see the end would be a tragedy. What would be worse than that, he knew, was if he didn't get a chance to say goodbye. His duties had so far kept him too busy to see his friend, but he'd finally told everyone he was leaving to see Rauphangelaa—everything else could wait.

He arrived at the medical clinic to find Bhakat kneeling and praying at Rauphangelaa's bedside. "May I join you?" he asked, quietly. He looked at his friend, now hooked up to a machine that provided oxygen to him and other various sensors hooked up to his head and chest. He felt tears come to his eyes.

Bhakat looked up at him as if half asleep. "Oh, of course, Tumaani." He stood up, and Tumaani could see that his first impression wasn't far off. Bhakat looked like he hadn't slept in some time. "I'll leave the two of you alone. I'll just be in the other room," Bhakat said, bowing and walking out.

Tumaani knelt down gingerly on the floor next to Rauphangelaa's bed. His hip had started giving him problems lately. *Maybe I am getting old,* he thought, looking at his friend. Tears sprang to his eyes once again. Rauphangelaa and he had been friends for a long time. There had been a period of time when they were on not-so-friendly terms because of a female, but that time had passed, and over the years, their friendship had become stronger for it. Yes, they had their disagreements, but that's how it was with friends, he supposed.

"Tumaani," Rauphangelaa said querulously.

Tumaani looked up to see that his friend's eyes were open and looking at him. "Rauphangelaa," he said, quietly.

"Disks . . . Bhakat has them," Rauphangelaa said, in a halting voice. "You . . . are now . . .Keeper . . . Stones." Rauphangelaa's eyes closed, and Tumaani didn't need to hear the medibot's alarm to know that his friend was gone. He bowed his head and felt the hot tears rolling down his cheeks as Bhakat came rushing in through the doorway.

Chapter 8

Ries breathed a sigh of relief when his pilot finally informed him that they had left the Mandakan System. He went to check on their guest. He found that the Talondarian prince was still unconscious in the room that Punjor had placed him in. He was turning to leave when he saw Jerboxh walking down the corridor toward him, his tail swiping back and forth as if it wanted to slice the walls in two.

"Return to the bridge," Ries said sternly.

The pilot just kept walking toward him, a scowl on his face. "Are you a lunatic, or just incredibly stupid!"

Ries was surprised by the vehemence. "What did you say to me?"

"I guess it's the latter, then," Jerboxh said, stopping in front of him. "What do you think is going to happen when the Talondarian King discovers that his son has gone missing?"

"It's not your concern," Ries said coldly, turning away from him.

Jerboxh reached a hand over and grasped Ries's lower left arm, his claws digging painfully into the forearm. "Don't you dare turn away from me," he hissed.

"Who do you think you are, Pilot?" Ries asked, beginning to really grow angry.

"I'm the GI agent assigned to watch you and make sure you don't do anything abnormally stupid," Jerboxh said. "Obviously, I've failed in that task."

Ries stopped a moment, wondering if he was telling the truth. *Would GI have sent someone to watch him?* After thinking another moment, he realized that he shouldn't have been surprised. They wouldn't just trust him again after the agent who recruited him turned out to have his own objectives. "Then why tell me?"

"Because we're both going to be dead very soon," Jerboxh exclaimed loudly. "It probably doesn't matter if you know, at this point."

"Don't be so dramatic," Ries said. "All they know is that he's disappeared. They'll have no leads. The Carterfan knows what he's doing."

"You're referring to Zazzil, I assume?" Jerboxh asked. "You're trusting our fate to a major crime lord? That's just great. Did it ever occur to you that he might be setting you up? You're a scapegoat if the king ever finds out where his son went missing."

"Let me worry about Zazzil," Ries said. "I haven't lived this long by trusting everyone, especially, as you say, major crime lords. I have the situation under control." He acted as calm as possible, but he knew Zazzil wasn't above this kind of treachery.

Just then, an alarm began to sound. For a moment, Ries thought it was a proximity alarm. Then it dawned on him what it actually was: the medical machine that he'd attached the prince to after they'd placed him on the ship. The alarm meant that the Talondarian's heart had stopped.

◊

Belani wasn't sure how long he'd sat in the dark cell before someone came for him, but he felt that it couldn't have been longer than a full day, at the most. Once again, the door opened, spilling light into his cell, except that this time it didn't feel like a revelation of his doom but like the dawn of a new life, no matter how short it might turn out to be. It took far less time for his eyes to adjust to the light, so it wasn't long before he saw two figures waiting for him outside the doorway. He stood and walked to the opening. His heart sank as he saw that one of the figures was Welemaan. The other, surprisingly, was Yvette of the Humans.

"Hello, traitor," Welemaan sneered at him. The Rajani was carrying the translating device that James had brought the previous day. "Ready to die?"

"That's enough," Yvette said. "You're here to escort him to the ship, not provide commentary. And I'm here to make sure he makes it to the ship safely."

"If it was up to me, he wouldn't," Welemaan said.

"Well, I guess it's a good thing that it's not up to you, then," Yvette said. "Do I have to ask Kedar to replace you on this little job he's assigned you to?"

"No," Welemaan said. "No, I know my duty here, Human. Though I may not like it, I will perform it."

"Good," Yvette said, smiling. "Then we shouldn't have any problems. Let's go."

Belani could see that her smile never reached her eyes. He thought it was interesting that James, who seemed so even-tempered and understanding, could have paired up with someone so cold and deadly. He'd heard stories about her after she'd arrived on Rajan, of the death and destruction she'd caused amongst the Krahn. He was just grateful she was on their side. They walked in silence until Yvette led them to another nondescript house. She walked up to the door.

"What's this?" Welemaan asked.

"A quick detour ordered by James," Yvette said. "Wait out here." She grabbed the translating device from his hand and led Belani through the front door of the dwelling. He followed her down a hallway to a closed door. She opened it and stepped aside.

Inside, he found a miracle.

There was a tub full of hot water with a bar of crude soap set on a long table next to it. Also on the table was a clean towel and change of clothing.

"James said you'd need this," Yvette told him. "And he was right." She had a strange expression on her face, with the muscles around her nose contracted. "You have ten minutes, I suggest you use them. I'll be outside."

After ten luxurious minutes, he opened the door to the house and walked outside. It may have been the last bath of his life, but it would forever be the best one he'd ever had.

"Shall we?" Yvette said, turning to walk away. Welemaan didn't say a word, but his expression remained unchanged as he turned to follow her. Belani knew he wouldn't be happy that a prisoner had received such preferential treatment.

Finally, after a few twists and turns through the streets, they made it to their destination. It had once been the Rajani prison. Belani had to smile at the irony. He could see small guard outposts around the prison walls that were camouflaged from the sky. No ships passing over this position would see them. He guessed that this was where they'd hidden the stolen Krahn ship. They passed three Sekani guards at the entrance to the prison. They all sneered at him, but kept their words to themselves in front of the Human female. Belani was glad that James had sent her as his security escort. She had a reputation for being deadly in a fight and quick to anger.

They walked through the prison building and out into the

courtyard. Belani had heard that the Krahn had kept Rajani and Jirina prisoners there for a time, but there was now no evidence to suggest it had happened at all. The courtyard was deserted now, the only thing inside it a large camouflage tarp covering the stolen ship. The three made their way to the tarp, Welemaan keeping an eye on the sky the entire time, and walked under the edge. The tarp had been staked down on all four corners, but left enough room to walk under if you were low to the ground like Belani. The other two had to crouch. Belani was surprised to find that the ship's hatch was open already, and two Sekani were inside, prepping the ship for flight.

He'd been in severe emotional distress the last time he'd been on the ship, but he remembered that it was equipped for a pilot and co-pilot, with two benches in the back area for crew members or troops. He wasn't familiar with the particular model; more than likely it had been pirated somewhere out in space and brought aboard the colony ship for repairs and then equipped with two guns in the front and one in the back. The controls were set into the column in front of the pilot, with a trigger attached to the steering yoke. It wasn't a large ship like the Talondarian models the Rajani favored, but for what he needed it to do, it would suffice. The two Sekani nodded to Welemaan and left without speaking or even looking at him.

"I'll leave you two here," Yvette said. "Good luck," she added, looking at him.

"Your translator," Welemaan said, holding it out to her.

"Keep it with you," Yvette replied, smiling. This time the smile was genuine. "You might still need it." She walked away with a wave of her hand as she turned her back on them.

"Well," Belani said, "I think you can turn it off, at least." He turned and sat down in the pilot's chair and started to familiarize himself with the controls.

Welemaan waited a moment before setting the device down and clicking it off. "I suppose you're enjoying this," he said.

Belani ignored him. The Rajani had been the one who'd shot the Krahn who had been about to kill him. He was also the one who'd struck him a few times on the trip back to the Resistance stronghold, when he'd found out that Belani had betrayed them. Belani had nothing to say to the oppressor.

"All right," Welemaan said, sitting down in the co-pilot's chair. The chair was almost too small for his large frame. "Enough small talk. Ship is fueled and ready. You should have enough to last eight to ten hours, as long as you don't perform any outrageous maneuvers out there. Target base has been input into the ship's telemetry. You shouldn't have any trouble finding it. There are a few rounds left in each gun, but not enough for a sustained fight. Your best chance is to run and draw them off from our position."

"And don't do anything stupid, like trying to attack the Krahn colony ship," a voice said from the open hatch. They both turned to see James the Human standing outside the ship with his head poking inside.

"Your Talondarian Standard is improving, James," Welemaan said.

James walked over and turned on the translator. "Not as much as I would like, but it's getting there."

"I finished briefing him on the ship, and even managed not to strangle him with my bare hands," Welemaan said, standing. "The rest is up to you."

"Thank you, Welemaan," James said, standing aside so that the big Rajani could pass by in the cramped quarters.

Welemaan nodded to the Human and walked to the hatch before turning back. "I wish you luck, traitor, only because we need all the help we can get in this fight. But don't expect a hero's welcome if you survive this." He turned and left.

"My best friend," Belani said, turning to look at James.

"If that's your friend," James said, "I'd hate to see how your enemies treat you." They both laughed before James became serious again. "All we need is time," he continued. "Don't try to be a hero. We just need time to stage our assault on the Krahn base without having to worry about a counterattack coming from the sky. I need you to fly in there and draw away as many of their ships as you can. Our intelligence tells us that they've been running low on fuel, so they've been limiting the number of ships flying at once. Hopefully, there will be only two or three in the air to contend with at first, but it could increase to as many as ten once we've lost the element of surprise."

"You're full of good news," Belani said. "When do I leave?"

"Tomorrow morning," James replied. "I want you to get a good dinner, a good night's rest, and a hearty breakfast before you fly. No guardo, I promise. I've directed them to supply you with everything here. You'll be safer staying on the ship tonight."

Belani nodded. He was aware of the danger of showing his face outside the prison.

"You're on your own from here," James said, extending his hand.

Belani wasn't sure what the gesture meant, so he just stuck out his own hand toward the Human. James grasped it and squeezed, though not painfully.

"Good luck," James said. "Hopefully we'll meet again."

Not if everything goes as planned, Belani thought, smiling sadly. "Thank you, James. For everything. I'm truly grateful."

The Human squeezed his hand again, then left him alone

on the ship.

◊

Ries ran into the prince's room, Jerboxh close behind, to find the prince sitting up, the heart monitor clutched in his hand. The expression on his face said that he wasn't amused. "Where am I?" he asked, wincing in pain as he attempted to get out of the bed.

"That's not information you need to know," Ries said, approaching the bed. He reached out to push the prince down onto his back. He was surprised when the prince swung his hand and connected with Ries's face. The sting to his ego was more than the force of the blow. The prince was still very weak from his earlier interrogation, but he'd still struck Ries, and in the presence of a fellow agent.

"Well, that will be enough of that," Ries said. He pulled his stun gun out and hit the prince with a jolt. The prince instantly fell back onto the bed. Ries turned to look at Jerboxh. "Thank you so much for your assistance," he said. "By the way, what level are you?"

"One," Jerboxh answered, sullenly.

"Good," Ries said. "Then tie this sack of garbage up tight, and make sure he won't get loose again. That's an order." Technically, Ries knew that he needed to be at least a fourth level agent to give orders, but on any field mission, the GI codex stated any superior agent must be obeyed.

Jerboxh slowly approached the bed and began to place the prince's arms in the restraints that were attached to the bed. His tail twitched incessantly as he grumbled to himself. Ries smiled and left the room, taking simple pleasure from the pilot's unhappiness.

◊

Kieren was more excited than at any other time since she'd arrived on Rajan. Except, perhaps, when Gianni had asked her to dinner that first time, but even then, her excitement had been tempered by uncertainty. The funny part about that night was they hadn't eaten until the next morning. But now, she had a spectacular secret, and there was only one person she wanted to share it with.

She found him right where she expected him to be that early in the morning. "Get up, sleepyhead," she said, jumping on his cot.

"What?" Gianni mumbled, not moving.

"Time to get up," Kieren said cheerfully. "There's something I want to show you."

"C'mon, Kieren," Gianni said, still not moving. "Do you know how late I was out with the Sekani? Do you know what kind of hangover fernta gives you?"

"Your fault for partying with the locals," Kieren said. She knew that he'd been celebrating with the Sekani males because they were all going to go into battle within the next day or so. Many of them would die soon, but for those who lived, they would possibly see the liberation of their planet, and of their species.

Kieren was surprised at the change that had come over Gianni in the time since they had come to Rajan. He hardly ever reverted to what she thought of as his 'tough guy' persona anymore. He seemed more at ease with everything now. She would like to have thought it was her influence on him, but she knew that this kind of change could only have come about from his own choice. A choice he made to become the man she had eventually fallen in love with.

He was also very popular with the Sekani warriors, as evidenced by the way they kept plying him with fernta the night before. She had gone to bed early; she was a morning person and hardly ever stayed up late, even on Rajan. But none of that was important, she knew, shaking him again.

"Please, Gianni," she said. "There's something I want you to see."

"Okay, okay," Gianni said, slowly sitting up. "Where is it? Oh, God, you don't suppose they have aspirin here, do you?" he asked, holding his head in his hands.

"Aspirin comes from the bark of a tree that's native to Earth," Kieren said, before adding, "you big baby," under her breath. She handed him a bottle of water. "Here, this will help. Get dressed."

After a few more minutes of complaining and moaning about his head and his stomach and everything in between, he was finally dressed.

"All right," he said. "Where is it?" He was looking confusedly at her hands, as if whatever she wanted to show him couldn't possibly be anywhere else but in her grasp at the moment.

"You have to come with me," she said. "It's not far . . . by air."

"Air!" he asked. "Please don't tell me you've been flying off somewhere without telling anyone."

They walked out of the gates of the Sekani compound, nodding and smiling to the guards. The two Sekani looked a little peaked themselves, but they had nothing but smiles for the Humans.

"It's relatively safe," Kieren said, continuing their conversation. She pointed the way they were heading. "I just needed to . . . get away, I guess, from all of this devastation. I mean, I thought it was bad in Detroit, with all of those abandoned, run-down buildings and everything. But here, you wake up and all you're faced with is destruction as far as you can see."

By this time they had walked approximately two hundred yards north of the Sekani compound. They continued walking until the rubble from the buildings began to thin out.

It was a beautiful, fall-like day, though warmer than either of them was used to back on Earth. It was slightly breezy, but the sun was shining, and the flying creatures (she still couldn't bring herself to call them birds—they were just too strange looking) were calling out to each other in their high alien voices.

"This should be far enough," she said, looking around.

"Far enough for what?" Gianni asked.

Kieren powered up, and Gianni instinctively did as well, looking around for danger. She walked around behind him and put her arms under his, interlocking her fingers around his chest. Where their energy fields touched, the energy flared and mingled together. She concentrated, and they slowly began to rise. They picked up speed as they reached twenty feet in the air and began to fly straight north. Soon the buildings disappeared altogether as they reached the grasslands north of the city. There were a few farms, but no signs of the Krahn or anyone else.

They continued until they reached a cliff overlooking a small bay that jutted northward into the land. They set down softly and dropped their energy fields. The cliff was almost two hundred feet above a small, sandy beach. Large flying creatures, ones they had never seen before, were nested on the rocks of the cliff face and flying down over the water to catch whatever happened to be swimming by far below. There were whale-like animals swimming in the bay; a large family unit, from what they could see. They could also see on further inspection that the creatures looked more reptilian than whales, though they, too, seemed to breathe air, as evidenced by their blowholes.

"Isn't it beautiful?" Kieren asked, smiling.

Gianni had grown up in a large city. He'd never been

camping and was more comfortable smelling car fumes than bonfires, and hearing the subway roll by than hearing crickets chirping at night. But he had to agree with her. "It's special," he said. "Your special place."

"I'm sharing it with you," she said, turning to look at him. "That makes it our special place."

He stepped forward and embraced her, smelling her fresh scent, letting it permeate his senses. "I guess it does," he said softly.

Kieren turned to look back down at the water, her arm still around him. "I love you," she said quietly.

Gianni was quiet for a moment.

"I'm sorry," Kieren said, now looking at him and pulling her arm away. "I shouldn't have said that. Not now."

"Stop," Gianni said, holding a finger to her lips. "It just . . . took me by surprise, that's all. I . . . didn't think you'd ever feel the same way about me as I do about you." He cupped her chin in his hand. "Kieren, I love you, so much." He leaned in and kissed her, cradling her head in his hands.

They found a grassy spot under a small tree and made love in the sunshine of an alien world. After, as they lay together listening to the sounds of wind and surf and calling animals, Gianni turned his head to look into her eyes. "Thank you for this," he said, smiling.

It was the most peaceful place he'd ever seen, and he felt it well up deep inside of him. He hoped it would last through the coming storm.

◊

Ries had just finished his dinner when Jerboxh's voice came over the ship's communication system. "Ries, Prince Creon wants to talk to you in his room."

Ries smiled and drank the last of his kolan. He made his way down to the prince's room. As he drew closer, he heard the prince and Jerboxh speaking. Just as he was about to walk into the room, Jerboxh walked out. "What does he want?" he asked the surly agent.

"I think he might be ready to talk," Jerboxh said. "Maybe if you used a little tact instead of torturing him, he'd actually tell you something important."

"Not my style," Ries said. "Oh, and I've run out of kolan in my room. Replenish the supply from the stores you brought aboard from the port."

"Sorry," Jerboxh said, smiling. "We left too quickly. You were in too much of a hurry, and the kolan was never delivered." The Sh'kallian laughed and walked down the corridor, away from Ries. Ries just gritted his mandibles, knowing that the pilot was kidding. At least, he hoped that the pilot was just kidding.

He walked into the prince's room to find the Talondarian still lying on his back, though alert. "Are you willing to answer my questions now?" he asked the prince.

"As long as you don't hit me with your pain inducer again," Creon replied. "I'm growing tired of it."

"Good," Ries said. He pulled a chair over next to the bed and sat down. "What is the name of T'van's Sekani contact on Rajan?"

"I assume you're going to kill me once I've told you what I know," the prince said. "And if that's the case, then why should I tell you anything?"

Despite himself, Ries was beginning to like the Talondarian prince. He'd proven to be far tougher than Ries thought he would be. Ries had expected a soft, spoiled child who would fold at the first hint of pain. And yet, he continued to defy Ries's wishes at every turn. It was almost a pity he would have to die soon. Just then, his antennae started to twitch. Something was wrong. He turned just in time to block the blow from the chair with his upper left arm. Jerboxh growled in frustration and leaped back, still holding the chair in front of him. Ries stood quickly and crouched down, pulling out his stun gun in the process.

"How much did he promise to pay you?" he asked the pilot. "You should know by now that even if you were to get away, killing a GI agent is frowned upon. You wouldn't live long enough to spend it."

"Creon also offered me asylum on Talondaria," Jerboxh replied, beginning to move to his left.

Blast! Ries thought. He could see that talking wasn't going to get him anywhere.

"The offer stands for you, too, Agent Van," Creon said from the bed. "My father would be more than willing to set both of you up comfortably if you return me safely to Talondaria."

"You shut up," Ries said, not looking at the prince. He knew that concentrating on Jerboxh was the difference between living and dying on the ship. He intended to live.

Jerboxh lunged forward with the chair, and Ries grabbed two of the chair legs with his bottom hands, while simultaneously reaching over the top with the stun gun in an attempt to hit him. The Sh'kallian dodged the blow, but held on to the chair.

"I could use a little help," Jerboxh said, and suddenly Ries was in pain. He gasped as the jolt went from his upper left shoulder, down his arm, and across his back. He fell to his knees.

Blast, he thought weakly. He hadn't checked the prince's restraints when he'd entered, assuming that Jerboxh had followed his orders. *Stupid,* he thought, just before another jolt of pain went through his head, and everything turned black.

Chapter 9

Tumaani was still in shock at the death of his friend and rival Rauphangelaa. He was sitting in his room, looking at the small data disk that Rauph had left for him. He knew he would have to look at the information contained on the disk, but at the same time, he dreaded what he would find. He remembered when Rauphangelaa had been appointed as Keeper of the Stones. When Tumaani had seen him after the ceremony, Rauphangelaa had changed. He'd seemed tenser, more secretive, as if the knowledge he'd received had placed a great weight on his shoulders, and he was struggling to hold it up on his own.

The Keeper of the Stones was the only one who knew certain information about the Johar Stones, Tumaani knew. It was information that they took to the grave. Information, he assumed, that was contained on the disk he held in his hand that very moment. Rauph had taken his responsibility seriously. Tumaani had asked him a few times if there was anything he could do to ease his friend's burden, but Rauphangelaa had refused to confide in anyone. It had begun to create a rift in their friendship.

Although they had been rivals for the affection of Julari, who had ultimately become Rauphangelaa's first and only mate, it hadn't become an issue between them. She had chosen Rauphangelaa, and Tumaani had respected her choice and had even bore witness at their union ceremony. But after his appointment as Keeper of the Stones, their relationship had deteriorated swiftly. Tumaani could admit now that part of it had been a certain sense of jealousy he'd felt at the time for not being selected for such an important post himself. He'd resented the fact that Rauphangelaa was more respected by the other Elders, or so it had seemed then. There was also the fact that Rauphangelaa had not trusted him enough to share the burden of knowledge.

They had quarreled, and both had said things that they would later regret. They had eventually both apologized to each other, though their relationship was irrevocably altered. Tumaani, by then, had been appointed as Keeper of the Past, and although he and Rauphangelaa worked together closely due to their posts, it was purely a professional business relationship for a number of years. And now Rauphangelaa was gone. He had chosen Tumaani as his successor as Keeper of the Stones, although it seemed that there were no longer any Stones to keep. Tumaani wasn't sure he'd been chosen because Rauphangelaa had thought him the best choice for the post, or if it was a last gesture of friendship.

Either way, Tumaani knew he would eventually have to read the data on the disk. He sighed as he stood and placed the disk in a pocket of his robe. He would have to go to the central computer that they had recently liberated from the Krahn. *Might as well get it over with,* he thought, sadly. After all this time wanting to know the secret of the Stones, he wasn't sure now that he wanted to know anything at all. Perhaps the information should just be buried along with his friend. It seemed to bring nothing but heartache.

◊

Kieren woke to the sound of knocking at her door. She

opened her eyes blearily to see the sleeping form of Gianni lying next to her. She smiled, watching him breathe slowly, then got out of bed and quickly got dressed. When she opened the door, she was surprised to see that it was Yvette. Yvette's smile of greeting turned to wide-eyed surprise when she saw who else was sleeping in Kieren's room. Kieren stepped outside and closed the door. She could feel her face growing red in embarrassment.

"So, I guess you guys made up?" Yvette said, her smile returning.

"Yeah," Kieren said, smiling. She was surprised when Yvette stepped forward and gave her a hug.

"Good for you," Yvette said quietly.

"What's wrong?" Kieren asked, pulling away to look at her friend's face. "Did you get in a fight with James?"

"No, that's not it," Yvette said. Then she burst into tears.

Kieren was in shock for a moment, not just because Yvette was crying, but because it was Yvette. She was the toughest woman Kieren had ever met, besides some of her college professors. For her to cry, something must really be wrong. She looked around for a moment, looking for a place to sit, and finally decided to just sit right where they were. She and Yvette sat down, and Yvette began to wipe her face on her shirt as she calmed down. Kieren waited a moment, then reached over and held Yvette's hand, unsure if the gesture would cause the other woman to pull away. Yvette had never seemed like the touchy-feely kind of person. She was once again surprised when Yvette held her hand tightly and smiled at her in gratitude.

"I'm sorry," Yvette said. "I didn't mean to make a scene."

"It's okay," Kieren said. "What's wrong?"

"My hormones are all screwed up," Yvette said.

"Why . . . ?" Kieren began to say, then a thought struck

her, and it was her turn to look in wide-eyed surprise. "Are you . . . ?"

Yvette smiled and nodded, then started crying again. Kieren leaned forward and gave her a hug. "I'd say congratulations, but I'm not sure if that's the right word, by your reaction."

"No, I'm happy," Yvette said. "More than you could know. I didn't think I could get pregnant. It's a miracle that I did. It's just that, I don't know how to tell James."

"Does he not want a baby?" Kieren asked. She wasn't sure what the problem could be.

"I don't know," Yvette replied. "That's why this is so hard. I'm not sure what his reaction will be. I don't know if you know, but his wife died not long after they were married. She was pregnant at the time."

"Oh my God," Kieren said. She hadn't known that about James, but she supposed it explained a few things about him.

"It was a long time ago, but still . . ." Yvette said. "And he's got so much he's already dealing with now. I don't want him to be distracted. He's too important to the Resistance."

"You don't really think he'd be mad or something?" Kieren asked. James didn't seem like the kind of person who would react that way, but Yvette knew him better than anyone else on the planet.

"No," Yvette said, looking down at the ground between her crossed legs and playing with some pebbles. "I don't know. I just, I guess I just don't want him to reject us."

"Do you love him?" Kieren asked.

"Yes," Yvette said, looking up at her and smiling.

"Does he love you?" Kieren asked.

"I think he does," Yvette said, looking back at the ground. "We've never really said it."

"Oh," Kieren said. She could see now why Yvette was

hesitant to talk to him about the pregnancy. "Do you, I mean, do you want the baby?"

Yvette looked at her, a look of surprise on her face. Then she smiled. "Yes," she said. "More than anything else."

"Then tell him," Kieren said. "He needs to know. And if I know James, it will make him very happy."

"Will you be with me?" Yvette asked.

"Oh, um, sure, if you really want me to," Kieren said. "Now?"

"No," Yvette responded. "Like I said, he's busy right now. But I'd like it if you were there. Just in case things go wrong."

"It won't," Kieren said. "I promise. You'll see."

Just then, the door opened to Kieren's room, and Gianni walked out, still rubbing the sleep from his eyes. He saw Yvette and stopped. "Uh, hi, Yvette."

"Hello, Gianni," she said, standing up. "We're done here, I think. Good seeing you." She turned to Kieren, who was also getting to her feet. "Thank you, Kieren."

"No problem," Kieren said, and gave her another hug, which Yvette returned.

As Yvette walked away, Gianni put an arm around Kieren's shoulders. "What was that all about?" he asked.

"Girl stuff," she said. "Don't worry, everything's fine. Or at least, it will be very soon." She smiled as she watched her friend walk away.

◊

Tumaani made his way from his house to the building housing the Rajani central computer. It began to sprinkle as he'd stepped out the front door of his house, and by the time he'd made it to the central computer building, it was a full downpour, the thick, gray clouds opening up above him. *The rainy season had to begin on my walk,* he thought. He wished his Elder's robe had a hood, but at least it kept the rest of him relatively dry.

There were several armed Rajani guards outside the building when he arrived. He nodded to them as he passed. They didn't impede his progress. They all knew who he was. He walked into the building and down the corridor to a set of stairs that led to the basement, shaking the water from his head as he did so. He nodded to the Rajani standing guard at the door, though he didn't recognize him, and walked into the computer room. He was surprised to see that Kedar was there.

The large Rajani stood as he entered. "Good morning, Tumaani. I hope your rest was peaceful," he said.

"And yours as well," Tumaani said. "If I'm interrupting, I can return at a later time."

"No, no," Kedar said. "I was just about finished with my research." He reached down and closed whatever had been on the screen display.

"May I ask what you were researching so early in the morning?" Tumaani asked, curious.

"I was only attempting to learn more about the Krahn Horde," Kedar replied. "Anything at all that we could use to defeat them in battle, but I'm afraid there's not much in the computer's data banks that will help, and our communication signal is still being jammed by their blasted colony ship."

"I see," Tumaani said. He hated the fact that some of the Rajani had chosen to forsake the Kaa and join in the fight against the Krahn, but there was nothing he could do about it at the moment. "If you'll excuse me, then, I need to use the computer. In private."

"I understand," Kedar said, standing up. "I'll leave word that you're not to be disturbed, Keeper."

"Thank you," Tumaani said. He waited until Kedar had left and the door had closed before he pulled the small data disk out of his pocket. He sat down in the chair and inserted the disk into the computer's interface device. The screen quickly displayed five data files in numbered order. He opened the first and began to read.

My name is Daltori. I am one of approximately fifty thousand Rajani who have been forced to leave our beloved planet by the Galactic Alliance consortium. Allow me to be more specific: forced to leave by the Talondarian Empire. But then, they might as well be the same thing these accursed days. The Talondarians are in total control of the Alliance now, may their sun turn black.

Most of the males forced to leave are either too young or too old. Fortunately, there are also breeding-age females. All of the females are leaving, actually. Our species will live on through them, through my own pregnant mate. My medical condition would not allow me to become a Stone Soldier myself, unfortunately. Yet I have been placed in a position of leadership aboard this vessel as we head to the unknown. We did not yield our planet without a fight; but in the end, with the threat of total planetary annihilation, we were forced to surrender. Our Stone Soldiers battled valiantly, but were forced to return to Rajan. In essence, they will be exiled on their own planet, doomed to live there with no otherworldly contact, and no access to ships or any other advanced technology, and of course, no females.

In the negotiations that followed our defeat, the Talondarians agreed to some concessions in an effort to come to an accord with our government. Aboard our ship we carry not only Rajani, but our servant species the Jirina, as well as a number of the recently conquered Sekani. They are to go with us to help ease our exile on our new world. The Rajani have agreed that all unaltered members of the species shall leave for the planet designated A2242. All of our Stone Soldiers shall remain on Rajan with no available means of interstellar travel;

they cannot leave the planet again. All Johar Stones must also remain on Rajan.

While the Talondarians 'graciously' allowed us to keep our servants, none will remain with the male Stone Soldiers on the planet. They will be alone, unable to contact the outside galaxy and unable to leave the planet for which they fought for so long. May Golgar damn the Talondarians forever, and may their empire crumble into the Sea of Fire. And yet there is still hope for our species, however faint it may be. I have seen to that. I was given six Johar Stones by Tobraani, First in Command of the Stone Soldiers. I have been entrusted with this duty. I and I alone know this secret. I am now known as the Keeper of the Stones, and the fate of us all lies with me.

We shall rise again, and to greater heights than ever before. This I do swear by the blood of the Talondarians.

Daltori-tuc-Nephtalti
First Keeper of the Stones
Standard Year 10738

Tumaani sat back in his chair, stunned by what he'd just read. Could it be true? If so, it was no wonder that previous Keepers had wanted to keep this a secret. As Keeper of the Past, his records only went back to 10945, which would be close to two hundred years after the date on the log he'd just read. Conflicting emotions battled in his mind. He felt empathy for Rauphangelaa, at the knowledge that he'd been forced to keep to himself over so many years. He felt anger, knowing now that he and the rest of his species had been living on a planet that was not their own and had not even known it. The war of emotions was like a knot in his stomach, and he felt a wave of nausea pass over him. For a moment all he could do was close his eyes and sit, waiting for the feeling to pass.

He eventually opened his eyes again and quickly closed

the log and just as reluctantly opened the second one. He began to read once again.

It is a great day for our species and for our planet. Our Talondarian oppressors are finally leaving Rajan. All we have ever wanted was to be left in peace and solitude, and now, finally, the day has come. But as we all rejoice in our newfound freedom, let us also remember in our hearts and minds the sacrifices we have made along the way. Remember those first brave Rajani that came to this planet, and the many that died so that our species could live, such as my beloved father, may Golgar watch over him.

It could not have been easy to survive on a planet so different from our home world, if stories passed down are true. I was born aboard the spacecraft on its way from our old world to this one. Now I am the oldest, and so have taken the title of Elder. I alone am the last remaining survivor of those who made the trip across space to this place. It is a harsh world, but we have prevailed. And we are now out from under the yoke of the Talondarian oppression. Sadly, we have only been free for a few months, and already there is unrest amongst our species. The upstart followers of Ruvedalen have started spreading their beliefs, unfettered, throughout the land.

This movement must be stopped in its infancy. As Keeper of the Stones, it is my duty, unfortunately, to remind us all of what we have lost, but also what we must regain. Golgar be praised, with his help we will crush this insidious threat from within and then restore to glory the Rajani Empire.

Zeralta-tuc-Daltori
Keeper of the Stones
Standard Year 10805

Without stopping to think about what he had just read, Tumaani closed the log and immediately opened the third log.

All ties to our former lives are now gone, and I, for one, am thankful. Our last battle has been fought, though the blood that has been spilled may not wash away for a thousand years. It will never leave my own hands, of that I am certain.

Was it necessary? There are some days that I am sure that it was; but others when I look in the mirror and all I see is a killer dressed as a Priest.

I have not cut my hair in twenty years. It has grown quite long. I should get it cut, now that the battles are over, but my friend Habalas said no, I should keep it this length as a symbol of the length of our struggle to free Rajan from those who would have brought ruin to our civilization with their aggression, their anger, and their war-like ways.

We needed a better way, and were lucky to find allies in our Talondarian brethren. Without their aid, our revolution would have been surely lost.

There is still so much work to be done, but for today, we celebrate, knowing that our younglings will live in a better world than their Elders. As a last act of freedom, I will find somewhere safe to hide these abominations called Johar Stones. Just having them in my possession sickens me, knowing the terror and death that they represent. Now is the time for peace, and I have changed my title accordingly. No longer will there be a Keeper of the Stones. This I swear.

Malovin-tuc-Talabi
Keeper of the ~~Stones~~ Past
Standard Year 10827

Tumaani sat back again, the feeling of nausea ready to overwhelm his senses once again. If this information was true, then it was no wonder Rauphangelaa had felt so burdened with it. He could finally understand why Rauphangelaa had never told anyone, not even his closest friend. No one else must ever know about it. The future of their species depended on it.

He opened the fourth log, and was surprised to see that it had been created by Rauphangelaa.

Tumaani, my friend,

I apologize for not telling you the truth long ago, and that I could not tell you until now. If you're reading this, then it means that I'm dead, a possibility that I'm well aware of, with my prior medical problems, which is why I'm creating this log. I've informed my former Pledge, Bhakat, to deliver this data disk to you in the event that I cannot do it myself before the end.

If you've read the files enclosed herein in order, then you know now why I couldn't tell you the secrets they contain. I apologize again for the burden I've placed on you as Keeper of the Stones. You now know the truth of our past, and must keep it secret, lest our civilization turn away completely from the teachings of Ruvedalin. Your burden has been made somewhat easier to bear by the fact that all of the Stones in my possession have now been implanted. There are no more for you to keep safe.

I've sat and wondered during my trip to find the Humans if it wasn't fate that they were the ones I found on my search for help. They are an amazing species. I only hope that the Stones do not cause them to make the same mistakes as our own species has made. I pray that the Rajani never learn of their imprisoned brethren on our home planet.

You've read the three data files on this disk, and they contain information that it will be difficult to process, I know, but there is one more piece of information that you need to know. The fifth, and final document on this disk details everything known about the Johar Stones. They are not what most think they are, and the Humans, as far as I know, also do not know their true properties. I leave it to your discretion to tell them. I'd struggled with the choice, but now it's yours, and for that, I apologize.

Goodbye, my friend. I truly hope the best for you and hope that you can make our planet whole once again after all of this fighting is over. I pray every day for peace.
Rauphangelaa-tuc-Nebraani
Keeper of the Stones
Standard Year 12763

Tumaani felt tears spring to his eyes as he sat and thought about the way he'd treated Rauphangelaa after he'd become Keeper of the Stones. He thought about his petty feelings of jealousy and envy at the time. No, that was untrue, he realized. Those feelings had still been just below the surface when Rauphangelaa had returned from his trip to find the help they all so desperately needed. And now it was too late to apologize for them. Rauphangelaa was gone. Tumaani dropped to his knees, his sobbing echoing off the walls of the computer chamber.

◊

Yvette felt better after speaking with Kieren. It had felt good to talk to another woman. She was also happy to see that Kieren and Gianni were finally together. Maybe she wouldn't be the only one expecting in the future. She looked up, feeling the first drops of the rain that had been threatening to fall all morning. She picked up her pace as it began to come down harder. It was cold, and she wasn't dressed for it. As she neared the Rajani section of the city, she finally gave up her effort to hurry. She was soaked by the increasingly heavy rainfall. As she walked, she was reminded of the last time she'd been on Earth. It had been raining that day, as well. She was suddenly choked with emotions as she wondered how her father was dealing with her disappearance. If she ever returned to see him again, how could she ever tell him the truth? Her father was a practical man. Even if she showed him her powers, there was no telling if he'd believe her story about being abducted by aliens and taken millions of light years away. More than likely he'd think she was part of some government experiment or something similar that was at least familiar to his sensibilities. And the pregnancy would certainly take some explaining on her part. Doubts began to creep in again when she thought of James. Would they still be together to tell her father about the baby? Would she have to raise the child all by herself? Just then she noticed that she was close to her room. She ran the last few hundred yards, glad that she wasn't too far along. She could still run, and it felt good to cut loose a little. She hadn't been back to her quarters in some time, having spent all of her nights at James's place. After so long it no longer felt like it was hers; like she was visiting a place that she used to live. She was surprised to find Welemaan waiting for her. The tall Rajani was leaning against the side of the building as if unbothered by the rain, and perhaps he wasn't. Yvette had heard that he was practically raised aboard ships that his father owned. A little rain wouldn't compare to the constant spray from a choppy ocean.

"Hello, Welemaan," she said as she approached.

"I was hoping you would come back soon," he said, smiling. "I had hoped to catch you before you left this morning, but no luck. You must have had an early appointment."

Yvette smiled back at him, but didn't mention that she mostly spent her nights at James's quarters. It was none of his business. "What can I do for you?" she asked as she opened her door.

"Well, you can invite me in out of the rain, to begin with," he replied, his smile still intact.

Yvette had known her share of politicians in her time, including her father. She had no problem spotting one now. The Rajani wanted something, and presumably it was something that he was unwilling to ask James for, so he'd come to her. She'd have to invite him in to find out what it was. "Come in," she said as she walked through the doorway and left the door open for him.

Her room looked the same as it had when last she'd left it. There was a small pile of dirty clothes next to the bed, which wasn't made. Besides that, there wasn't anything else that she'd have to take to James's to make the move there permanent. She sat down on her bed and looked at Welemaan. Her eyes still felt puffy from crying earlier, and she needed to change out of her wet clothes. She was in no mood for political games.

"You seem like a practical individual," Welemaan said, shaking himself off. He looked up to see her staring at him intently. "Which is why I was hoping to speak with you about what your plans are after we've won this war."

"Ha," she said. "I think you're getting a little ahead of yourself. There's still a rather large battle or two to go before we know if our side will come out on top in this."

"I'm optimistic," he replied, dryly. "May I?" he asked, pointing to the chair, which was the only other piece of furniture in the room.

She nodded. "Feel free."

"Thank you," he said. "You wouldn't happen to have any fernta around?"

"No, sorry," she said, unsure if she'd offer it even if she did have it. The drink was traditionally used between friends, and the big Rajani didn't qualify. "I can't stand the stuff."

"No harm in asking," he said, leaning forward in his chair. "Back to my earlier point, what are you and the other Humans planning on doing after this war ends? You are more than welcome to stay and help rebuild."

"Rauph didn't ask us to rebuild, he asked us to fight his

war for him," she said, unsmiling. "I plan on leaving as soon as possible, and as far as I know, so do James and the others."

"If you don't mind my saying so, that seems a bit uncharitable on your part," he said, frowning. "We'll need just as much, if not more, help rebuilding as we did fighting the Krahn."

"I'm sorry if that's how you feel about it, and I've only expressed my personal feelings on the matter," she said, standing up. She was suddenly feeling very nauseated again. The room was small and stuffy, with no air flow. "If you want an official answer from all of us, you'll need to talk to James. He's our leader. Now if you'll excuse me, I need to clean up this mess and then go out on patrol."

"Thank you for your time," he said gruffly. "Sorry to have wasted it." He walked toward the door before turning back to her. "Maybe if you lost something important to you in this fight, you'd understand how the Rajani have suffered."

She powered up and walked toward him. "Are you threatening me or the others, Welemaan?" she asked him coldly.

"No," he said. "I misspoke, and I apologize. I was only thinking that if you knew the hardship that we've already been through, maybe you'd know how much we still need you."

"I think it's time for you to go," she said, staying powered up. He nodded briefly, and then walked out the door. She waited a moment more to make sure that he was gone before dropping her power field. She quickly walked to the corner of the room and threw up her protein bar from breakfast. "Damn," she said quietly. She was glad that she'd been able to hold out until the Rajani had left. Showing weakness in front of a politician like Welemaan would have been a mistake. She'd have to talk to James about the Rajani before too long, but at the moment she just wanted to lie down and rest. Then she locked the door, something she had not thought of doing before. Better to not take chances that the angry Rajani would return to find her sleeping.

Chapter 10

James had put out word to the Resistance troops to get as much rest as possible during the week before the offensive. That included his Human companions. He didn't want to start the mission out wrong from the beginning because everyone was tired, when they should be wide awake for their march to the south and the subsequent fight it would bring. He'd tried to instill in them all a sense of strategy and give them a plan for the operation, but he had his doubts about whether it would hold up when the fighting became heavy. There was only so much he could do, he knew. They hadn't had time for proper training, and most of them were used to survival tactics—hit and run, not attacking a large, hardened target.

He'd also done his best to separate some troops out into specialized units. These units had trained exclusively in their individual duties, such as the medical unit that would set up a triage center and field hospital using the equipment that was left over from the destroyed medical clinics. Bhakat had begun to restore the clinics where he could, but many of them were damaged beyond repair. Many of the Rajani Elders who had refused to be involved in the fighting were willing to staff the field hospital, which James was grateful for—it would free up the Valderren for the actual assault.

A few of the Elders had been galvanized into action after Rauph's death. James had told Tumaani of his conversation with Rauph about the field hospitals, and Tumaani had spread the word to the other Elders.

There was also a unit devoted to demolition. They had whatever explosives they could carry, and would use them to blast a hole or two in the wall around the Krahn compound, a wall that the Krahn had erected from pieces of Rajani buildings in the time they had occupied the area. James was happy that they had begun to receive good intelligence from the spies they'd sent south after hearing of the failure of the strike teams. Most of the rest of the troops would be simply *ground pounders*—infantry troops whose only purpose would be to fight, and die, if need be.

James had let the 'juniors' sort out amongst themselves a command hierarchy, with himself as overall battle commander. Zanth, Kedar, and Mazal reported directly to him. They relayed his orders to their lieutenants, who then ordered their troops. He had told the leaders they needed to stay in the rear, but they had all protested, refusing to stay out of the thick of the action. James had argued the point with all three of them for what seemed like hours, but they had all remained steadfast in their convictions. Finally, he'd relented. He was, after all, only there as an advisor, technically speaking. This really would be an all-or-nothing offensive. If they were defeated here, they might never get another chance at ending the war. And if any of the leaders were to get killed, it could turn ugly if the power vacuum wasn't filled quickly and efficiently, and most importantly, with the right individual.

James was finishing up a final afternoon briefing with his team and the junior leaders. It was all a go now; there would be no turning back. Either they would win this war soon and he and the other Humans would be able to return home, or they would fail and be stuck on Rajan for the rest of their lives, however long or short that would turn out to be.

As all of the Humans were walking out the door of the headquarters building, perhaps for the last time, Yvette walked up next to him and squeezed his hand reassuringly. "It's a good plan. Don't worry," she said, smiling up at him.

"Oh, you know me," James said. "I'll worry until it's over." And she did know him, he realized. He'd spent most of the last year with her, except for the time they'd been separated after they first arrived on Rajan. And now there was a chance he might lose her within the next couple of days, if things went badly with the offensive. "Can I talk to all of you for a moment?" he said, stopping before he walked through the door.

"What's up?" Gianni asked. "We're not about to get some sappy speech, are we?" All of the others stopped as well and faced James.

"I just want to know how you're all feeling about this," James said, ignoring Gianni's sarcasm. "We really haven't had a chance to talk in a while as a group." It was true, with everyone spending time with their alien units most of the time, they hadn't really had a chance to just have a meeting or even hang out, as they had done aboard the *Tukuli*.

"What's to talk about?" David asked. "Either we'll win or we won't."

"There's more to it than that," Kieren said. "C'mon, David, don't you want to go home?"

"I don't know if there is a home to go back to at this point," David replied, and walked out the door without a backward glance.

"Yvette," James said, "keep an eye on him out there, will you?"

"If I can," Yvette replied, frowning. "But you know as well as I how difficult that can be."

"Yeah," James said. He was still thinking about the conversation he'd had with Rauph. Perhaps Gianni wasn't the one Rauph had been talking about. He just couldn't be sure anymore. They'd all changed since they'd arrived on Rajan.

"Don't worry, Big J," Gianni said, smiling. "We all know what we're doing."

All James could do was smile at the nickname. It reminded him of a simpler time, before they'd all become so mired in the damn war that they hardly ever spent time together socially. "Well, just make sure you look after each other," he said. "Good luck out there, and be careful. Remember, this isn't our war to win. We're here to help the Rajani, but that doesn't mean we have to die for them."

◊

Sendok had done as the Human had said; he'd gone the long way to head back to Nestbase One. He'd headed west shortly after his captor had left him on the cliffs overlooking the ocean. He'd traveled back close to the edge of the desert in a bid to go undiscovered by the Rajani or any of the alien Humans who fought for them. He needed to tell Ronak that the Rajani were planning to attack soon. They had to either fortify Nestbase One or abandon it altogether. There wouldn't be a lot of time to make the decision; it had taken him a few days to make the journey. He felt weak as he looked up at the merciless Rajani sun. His skin felt hot and dry to the touch, and he hardly had any spit in his mouth, but he was determined to return to warn Ronak. He also intended to make sure he wouldn't be left behind.

He cautiously made his way east as he reached an area that he recognized. He didn't want to get shot because some idiot warrior became trigger-happy. Now was not the time to go barreling into a checkpoint. He walked slowly toward a section of the city that he knew was occupied by at least one unit, and saw some warriors gathered around a large chunk of rock. His spirits rose as he walked toward them. He'd made it back. As he came nearer, some of the warriors saw him and raised their weapons before quickly lowering them toward the ground once again. He picked up his pace as he approached them, his plumage raised.

"Get me some water," he ordered. One of the warriors, Uglok, pulled out a small canteen and handed it to him. Sendok drank, being careful not to swallow too fast lest he immediately throw it back up again. "I need to get to Nestbase One," he said after he'd drunk his fill and handed the canteen back. "Two of you will accompany me, and the rest will stay here. Keep your eyes open. The Rajani are coming."

◊

Belani didn't know why James the Human had helped him so much after what had happened with the strike teams. He was just happy that he had. As promised, he was able to get a decent night's sleep and had a hearty breakfast of cooked dran eggs and pulko steak with thick bread to top it off. When it came time to go, he was ready. He hadn't spoken with anyone since James had left the night before, but he was fine with that. There was no one else he wanted to talk to at this point. He had woken up at peace with the fact that he would die that day. He closed the hatch on the ship, sat down in the pilot's chair, and buckled the safety harness across his chest. He hit the ignition switch and heard the lift vents begin to fire up.

The ship rose slowly from the ground. He was on his way, and his heart soared at being able to fly again, even if it was only the ugly, combustible fuel-engine-powered Krahn ship he was now in, and not one of the Talondarian models with the quieter fusion engines that he'd piloted before the invasion. He ascended up to a thousand feet and checked the ship's computer for his heading. He saw that Rajani, Jirina, and Sekani troops were amassed just south of the prison, readying for their march to the Krahn base. He silently wished them luck and continued on his way, switching the engines over to the backburners. He'd be seeing many of them soon on the Great Hunt, if the Goddess allowed.

The first Krahn ship he encountered was a small scout ship, only large enough to hold a pilot and fuel. He hit it hard and fast with his forward guns, hoping that it didn't have time to report anything to the Krahn base or colony ship. He continued on his way, the Krahn ship a smoking ruin on the ground behind him. He'd been lucky, he knew. The Krahn weren't looking for the enemy in the air, but that wouldn't last long. He continued on his course south toward the Krahn base. A thought came to his mind, and smiling, he changed his heading.

The Krahn airfield was bustling with activity that morning as they refueled ships that had been on patrol the night before or made the trip from the colony ship to the surface of Rajan. Belani flew in with a scream of engines and strafed the vehicles on the ground. He wanted to inflict as much damage as possible, to both the ships and the fueling facilities. He came around and performed one more strafing run before heading east to the Krahn base. The Krahn at the airfield were left scrambling, with four of the six ships in various states of destruction, and chaos reigning among the fuel tanks, most of them on fire. Soon they began to explode, sending red-hot shrapnel out for hundreds of feet around them, and cutting down fleeing Krahn warriors in their tracks.

The element of surprise was now lost, Belani knew, and they would be waiting for him over the base, but he'd at least reduced the number of ships that could attack both him and the troops that would be arriving from the north later that day.

The plan was for the Rajani, Jirina, and Sekani troops to arrive at sunset. Both the Rajani and Sekani had good nocturnal vision; the Krahn, a little less so, and the Jirina and Humans about the same, which was to say, almost none at all. The tactical advantage was minimal, but they needed all the help they could get. Belani's task was to draw off as many ships as he could toward the Desert of Ambraa to the west. He checked his weapon count and saw that he'd used more than half of the limited rounds that he had started out with that morning in his forward guns. It wouldn't take long to completely run out. The ship's navigation computer informed him that he'd almost reached his destination.

Suddenly his ship's proximity alarm started blaring as a Krahn ship that was twice the size of his own swooped down from above him. Belani banked hard left to avoid fire and noticed that there were two more ships behind the larger one, coming in from somewhere in orbit above the planet. He headed straight toward the Krahn base. He needed to see if there were any other ships above the base. His ship was small and maneuvered pretty well. He thought he would be able to outmaneuver the larger ship, but once the smaller ships arrived, he would have to beat a quick retreat.

Belani saw the large estate laid out before him and the mass of Krahn troops stationed around it. He also saw that there were two more ships hovering above it. That made seven ships, counting the two operable ones still at the airfield. Well, he thought, at least it wasn't ten, as James had told him. He considered his strategy for a moment. He could attack the two ships above the base, but he would quickly run out of ammunition. His best bet would be to try to exhaust the other ships' fuel supplies by taking them on a chase. More than likely he had more fuel than the other ships, unless they had refueled before his attack on the airfield. He felt the impact as three rounds hit his ship. He'd let the original larger ship get too close. He checked his computer—minimal damage to the left rear panel.

Belani made his decision. He sent his ship into a dive, straight toward the two ships above the base, and fired a few rounds just to get their attention. He also fired some out of the gun on the rear of his ship, which struck the large ship behind him. Hoping they would take the bait, he banked and headed west. He watched on his ship's computer as the original large ship stayed over the base. Maybe he'd gotten lucky and damaged it. The two ships that were over the base gave chase. He throttled back on his engines, not wanting them to lose interest. When his ship's proximity alarm sounded again, he revved up and took off once more. He saw on his computer that one of the ships from above had broken off to give chase, while the other one took up position over the base. He swore, but continued on. At least he'd draw three of them away for as long as he could. He would fly until his fuel tank ran empty or he was shot down.

◊

Bhakat and Yvette were preparing for the fight ahead. Bhakat found himself in a strange predicament. While the other Rajani seemed happy enough to have him around to fight, he also had the feeling that they would be just as happy if he wasn't around the rest of the time. He spent most of his time alone or with Yvette, when he wasn't carrying messages between the Valderren and the Elders. He'd done what he could to set up medical clinics in the northern areas of Melaanse, but now that they were established and running as efficiently as possible given the circumstances, he found that he felt somewhat out of place in Rajani society. It wasn't that he felt shunned or even ignored, it was that he always had the feeling that his fellow Rajani would sigh with relief whenever he left their presence.

Yvette, on the other hand, was the most self-confident being he had ever met. She dealt with problems without letting the stress of the situation get to her, even when she'd discovered that she was pregnant. He envied her sometimes, wondering if he cared too much about what the Elders thought of him. He smiled at her as she bid him goodbye and good luck, and gave him a hug, which he returned. He waved at her as she left. He'd have to report to Kedar soon, he knew, but he was enjoying what little quiet time he had left before the fight.

The reason he'd wanted to become a doctor when he was younger was to help his fellow Rajani. Yet, after a few years of training and then practicing what he had learned, he'd begun to feel lost. While his studies had gone as planned, the pressure of responsibility at times made him think he'd chosen the wrong vocation. His crisis was not so much in his self-confidence, but as a deeper belief that he wasn't making any sort of difference. The first time one of his patients had died, he'd gone to his house and cried the rest of the night, vowing to himself that it wouldn't happen again. He wouldn't allow it. But, of course, it did soon enough.

He'd talked to Rauphangelaa, who had known his own father before he died. Rauphangelaa had explained to him what it meant to study Ruvedalin's teachings and to devote his life to peace. He'd then pledged to Rauphangelaa's house in hopes that the Kaa brought the answers to the questions he had. And now, he felt like a failure once again. He had broken the most sacred law on Rajan by implanting himself with a Johar Stone. Not only that, but he identified more with the Valderren now than the Elders. His sense of betrayal was palpable at times, as he spoke to Tumaani or the other Elders since Rauphangelaa had died. He remembered the disappointment in his former Master's eyes when Rauphangelaa had first learned that Bhakat had implanted himself with a Stone. His sense of shame had been almost overwhelming.

Then Tumaani had asked him to stay with the Elders during the upcoming assault on the Krahn main headquarters. Tumaani had tried to persuade him that his medical training was needed more than his ability to fight. Bhakat knew in his heart it wasn't true. He had explained to Tumaani that his powers could help end the war quicker, and that would save many more Rajani lives than if he was treating injured troops. He remembered the last time he'd talked to Rauphangelaa, as his former Master lay dying. He'd asked for forgiveness while kneeling at Rauphangelaa's bedside. Rauphangelaa had either been too weak or still unwilling to give it, because he'd died before absolving his former pledge. After he'd slipped away, Bhakat had sat in the dark for a long time by himself. He was alone once more. He knew that if he lived to see the end of the war, he would still die—Rajani law demanded it— but he was willing to make that sacrifice if it meant he could save his species. Saving himself seemed like asking too much.

Chapter 11

Ronak sat on his throne and fumed as his counselors presented him with intelligence reports day after day that showed not only were they no closer to finding the Johar Stones, but the Rajani had begun to form a potent insurgency and were beginning to gain leverage in the northern part of the city. On top of that, their airfield had just incurred serious damage from an attack of one ship. One ship! While this made him angry, what secretly made him want to kill every living thing in the room was the knowledge that his efforts in fighting the Rajani insurgency had proved inadequate. They seemed to be losing worse than when his idiot cousin was in charge. To make matters worse, his cousin Sendok had disappeared after an attack on his checkpoint and was presumed dead. The list of even semi-competent commanders was growing thin.

"Where is my cousin, Toruq?" he finally asked, sighing.

"I believe he's on guard duty in the cellar, as he's been since your arrival, mighty Ronak," Kalik answered.

"Bring him before me," Ronak said. He knew that this was going to be difficult to do, but he needed to do it.

When Toruq finally arrived, Ronak was dozing on his throne. Kalik cleared his throat loudly. Ronak slowly opened his eyes. "Good," he said, sitting up straight on his throne.

"What can you tell me about the Sekani prisoner you're guarding in the basement?"

Toruq bowed. "He's the one I told you about before, mighty Ronak. He was captured along with one of the alien creatures that you've been searching for since arriving on Rajan."

"A creature," Ronak sniffed in disgust, "that has since escaped your custody."

"Yes," Toruq said. "I was hoping the Sekani would provide intelligence on the whereabouts of the creatures, but as yet, he has not divulged anything, despite my best efforts."

"Your best efforts." Ronak sniffed contemptuously. He'd had middling grades in military school at best, but Toruq was the only one he knew with even worse grades. "Why am I not surprised that your best efforts have ended in failure?" His counselors laughed at this quip, not because they found Ronak to be funny in any way, but they knew that Ronak was more dangerous when he was in a serious mood. It was better to keep him happy. "Enough," Ronak said, and the room grew quiet. "You can leave him to rot for all I care. The important thing now is to find these creatures that the Rajani have brought to help them. Find them, and you find the Stones. Now, get out of my sight. You're reinstated, and only because you're the best of a bad lot. Don't fail me again, or I'll have Mariqa feed you to her plants, one piece at a time."

"Yes, Mighty Ronak, Merciful Ronak," Toruq said, bowing as he backed away from the throne.

"Do you think this wise?" Kalik asked after Toruq had left.

"He'll try twice as hard, or he'll be dead," Ronak said with a dismissive wave of his hand. He was becoming adept at acting the part of the tyrannical ruler. "Either way, he's no longer my problem. I'm returning to my colony ship."

"I would advise against that at the moment," Kalik said. "We've already had one attack on our airfield by a ship of unknown origin. We don't know yet if there are any others. It's safer right now for you to stay here."

"Should I cower in this hole, afraid to act freely?" Ronak asked. "Never! I tell you, I will not become a beast trapped in its own lair, waiting for the hunter to mercifully end its life."

"Well said, bloodmate," Mariqa said as she entered the throne room. "The enemy ship attempted to attack this base just as my ship and our escort were coming back from the colony ship. I sent three ships in pursuit of it. They should have no problem defeating it." Mariqa sat down on the top step of the dais. Even she was not permitted to sit on the same level as the High Vasin.

"Good," Ronak said. "Bring me word when the ship is destroyed." One of his counselors scurried away toward the communication center as Ronak turned to Kalik. "Meanwhile, I believe it's time to show the Rajani who's still in charge on this planet."

"What do you wish to be done, Mighty Ronak?" Kalik asked.

"An aerial assault of the northern section of the city," Ronak said. "You know that's where they are as well as I do, Kalik. I want it leveled. No mercy shall be shown to the enemies of Ronak. Send all ships."

"But Ronak—" Kalik began.

"But nothing," Ronak interrupted him. "Do as I command, or you'll face the same fate as the Rajani."

"Yes, Mighty Ronak," Kalik said, bowing stiffly before his liege.

Ronak waited until Kalik had left the throne room before speaking. "I told you to stay on the colony ship," he said quietly.

Mariqa looked at him before dropping her eyes. "I could not bear your absence," she finally said. "Please don't send me away again, bloodmate."

Ronak was surprised by her reticence. It wasn't in her personality to be passive. "The incident with the insurgent ship is exactly the reason I wanted you safely on the colony ship," he said, standing up and walking to where she still sat on the top step. "The Rajani are becoming bolder in their attacks."

She stood up quickly, her anger flashing in her eyes. Ronak knew that if she possessed plumage, it would have been raised. "I don't fear them," she said.

"But I fear for you," he said, gently placing his hands on her shoulders. "When I thought you were lost back on Krahn, I almost gave up. I can't lose you." He watched her expression soften. He was about to tell her his plan for leaving later that night, when the doors to the throne room burst open. Ronak turned to scream at whoever it was who had interrupted him. He stopped short when he saw that it was Sendok. The commander was dusty and bloodied.

"Mighty Vasin," Sendok said, staggering to the foot of the steps before bowing.

"And where, exactly, have you been?" Ronak asked, crossing his arms.

"I was captured by one of the Human warriors brought here by the Rajani," Sendok said.

"Hu-man?" Mariqa asked.

"Yes," Sendok answered. "That's what they call themselves. The one that captured me was the same one I had captured earlier and given over to Toruq."

"Quite a coincidence," Ronak said, returning to his throne and sitting.

"What are you implying, Cousin?" Sendok asked, looking

up.

"How was it that you were captured, and yet managed to escape?" Ronak asked. "The Rajani don't let their prisoners live."

"As I've said," Sendok replied, "it wasn't a Rajani who held me captive. This Human sent me with a message for you."

"Oh? And what is that?" Ronak asked.

"That they're coming," Sendok said. "They're coming soon, and—"

"We already know that, you fool," Mariqa said. "Our refueling station has already been attacked."

"Enough, bloodmate," Ronak said, smiling. "I welcome your return, Cousin. Unfortunately, you won't be returning to your leadership duties. I've just given your job back to Toruq. At least he hasn't disappeared on me without a good explanation. You'll have to report to your unit as a warrior. We'll have you clipped when the time is appropriate."

"But, Ronak—" Sendok began.

"How dare you address him so casually, Warrior," Mariqa spat at him. "Now be gone from his sight."

Ronak watched as his cousin bowed silently and walked from the throne room. Sendok's news only confirmed what he already knew. It was time to leave.

◊

The first wave of the Resistance reached the outer Krahn defenses just as the sun was beginning to set. They hadn't made great time marching south through Melaanse, but they weren't too far behind schedule, either. The Krahn were caught unawares, and their relatively small numbers were easily overcome by the mass of Rajani, Sekani, and Jirina. No prisoners were taken, as usual. The Krahn weapons were added to the limited number that the Resistance possessed.

Most of the troops were armed with whatever they could find—pieces of board with nails protruding from them, large knives, and even sharp rocks.

The Resistance troops pressed forward to the south, spreading out their ranks so that no Krahn were missed. They moved swiftly, knowing that the element of surprise wouldn't last long. By midnight the Resistance had made their way to the center of Melaanse and had met stiffer opposition from the Krahn. Casualties began to flow into the triage center that the Elders had set up as the troops continued south, most of them brought in by designated medics embedded with each of the species.

By four o'clock in the morning, they'd set up on the outskirts of both the Krahn base and the airfield. James had sent a message directing Kedar and Welemaan to take their contingent of Valderren and attack the airfield, with hopes that they could take it out so that no more ships could take off or land. James said the signal to attack would come shortly by messenger, when the Sekani and Jirina were in position.

Welemaan was familiar with the area, and set up the troops to attack in a pincer movement that would catch the Krahn in the crossfire, while taking advantage of the natural topography of the land to minimize Rajani casualties. They would meet back with the main body for the assault on the base after securing the entire area around the airfield. Kedar's troops, which included all of his lieutenants and Bhakat, set up in their positions and waited for the signal to attack.

◊

Belani knew he was in trouble when the red indicator light for one of his ship's engines wouldn't turn off. He'd led quite a chase from the Krahn headquarters west out over the Desert of Ambraa, but now it seemed the chase had come to its inevitable end.

Little was known about the desert. Exploring the planet was forbidden under Rajani law. Exploring the planet, the Rajani Elders believed, was too much like exploring the universe, if only on a smaller scale. Either way, it led to more exploration, and eventually, a desire to own the places you've explored, no matter who or what may have been there previously. All that was really known about the desert was that it was virtually uninhabitable and filled with creatures that could kill quickly and efficiently. Luckily, the Rajani had discovered that most of the creatures, like the kleng beast, only lived in places where they could move easily through the loose sand. The Rajani made sure to keep their livestock in areas with firm soil. He'd heard that the Human named David and Janan'kela had landed in the outermost part of the desert when their escape pod came down. If they had landed any deeper into the desert, they probably would have died before reaching the grasslands, even with the Human's Johar Stone-augmented speed.

Belani had led the Krahn ships as far as he could and still make it back safely with the amount of fuel he had left. One of the Krahn ships had already gone down, presumably running out of fuel. The other two had tried their best to maneuver so that Belani's ship was caught between them, but so far he'd been able to escape their crossfire. If he had only been trying to get away from them, he would've been free long before, but he had done what he could to keep their interest in him so that they wouldn't return to their base in Melaanse. He set a southeastern heading and hoped he could make them travel too far from their base to be able to return before either they shot him down or his ship failed for good.

Suddenly, his ship's sensors showed that a second Krahn ship was going down in the predawn light over the desert. Then his own engine cut out, leaving him with only one, and no chance of outrunning the last Krahn ship. His luck had finally run out. His proximity alarm went off as the Krahn rapidly caught up to him. He fired the remaining rounds left in his rear gun, some hitting the other ship, but most missing. He felt the impact on his own ship as the Krahn opened fire. Smoke began to fill the cabin as the remaining engine's indicator light came on. When everything on the control panel lit up all at once and then went dark again, he knew the ship was going down. His altimeter showed that he was at a thousand feet and falling fast. More shudders racked the ship as the Krahn poured on their firing.

At four hundred feet above the ground, the first damaged engine exploded. He fought the steering yoke as the ship went into a spin. He lowered the landing gear to try to stabilize the ship in the air. In a last-ditch effort, as the ship was only a few dozen feet above the desert floor, he pulled up hard as the ship hurtled toward the rolling sand dunes below. The maneuver proved too much for his system, as the g-forces caused him to black out, and he knew no more after that.

◊

When the signal to attack the airfield finally came, the Rajani troops were surprised to find that there was little resistance and a great deal of destruction already to the ships and facilities. After defeating the limited number of Krahn left at the airfield, Kedar, Welemaan, and Bhakat gathered to discuss the state of events.

"It looks as though our job here was done for us," Kedar said, smiling. He wiped a large hand over his newly shorn skull. The Valderren had adopted a new look, shaving off their normally long, flowing locks of hair to symbolize their break from the teachings of the Kaa.

"It would appear so," Bhakat said. He hadn't cut his hair, still torn as to his loyalties. He didn't really care about the inside politics going on between the two Rajani factions. "Was it Belani the Sekani?"

"Don't mention that name to me," Welemaan said with a sneer. He'd kept his hair in a Ralek, now that it had grown out to an acceptable length.

"If he did this," Kedar said, "then as far as I'm concerned, he's at least earned my gratitude, if not my forgiveness."

"Bah," Welemaan said, frowning. "What's your plan now?"

"Leave a dozen troops here to secure the airfield and log the state of any ships. They may prove useful in the future if that cannot be quickly repaired now," Kedar replied, sobering up once again. "I fear we can spare no more than that. The rest of us will move toward the Krahn base to the east."

"I agree," Bhakat said. "We're wasted here."

"Bhakat," Kedar said, "I need you to take the point. If they're waiting for us, I'd rather they fired on you first, and gave us a little warning."

"No offense," Welemaan said, laughing sarcastically.

Bhakat smiled. He didn't mind going first, if it would help to save lives. Being a decoy wasn't hard when he was impervious against just about anything the Krahn could throw at him. "Let's go," he said, powering up once more.

They headed east toward the Krahn base.

◊

Kieren and Gianni had gone into battle along with the Sekani contingent. The Sekani were sent to the east of the Krahn base to make sure the Krahn didn't escape by sea, improbable as it would seem. They'd met resistance before they could reach the ocean, and were now at a standstill because of a Krahn ship flying overhead, pinning them in place.

"We need to keep moving!" a Sekani yelled toward Kieren

and Gianni as the ship flew toward their position once again. Rounds exploded around them as they hid behind rocks and debris.

"Gianni, can't you do anything?" Kieren asked.

Gianni stood and closed his eyes. Suddenly, a force field appeared in front of the ship as it flew in for another strafing run. The ship flew straight into the field and exploded in a fiery ball of scrap metal. The Sekani cheered and cried out his name.

"It actually worked," he said to Kieren. "Wasn't sure if the force field would be strong enough to stop the ship."

"Don't get a big head," Kieren said, sounding a lot like James.

After the ship was destroyed, Kieren sought out Zanth, finding him crouched behind a large piece of building as bullets flew past them. "James said to wait for the signal to press forward."

"They're weakening," Zanth replied. "We must press the advantage now. We need to at least reach the coast so they can't circle around behind us."

A Krahn popped up from behind a boulder-sized piece of rubble, and Zanth shot it in the face, the back of its head exploding in a cloud of blood, brains, and bone. Another Krahn stood up and shot at them. Zanth suddenly screamed in pain as a blossom of red appeared on his arm near his shoulder. He fell down, gripping his arm and screaming.

"Damn it!" Kieren yelled. She bent over Zanth and picked him up, carrying him over behind a large piece of building. She didn't see a Krahn warrior who was about to attack her as she laid Zanth back down on the ground. The Krahn jumped at her, just as Kieren heard Yvette's voice.

"Kieren, down!"

Kieren turned and was knocked down by the Krahn. It

straddled her, trying to claw through her energy field. "That. Is. Enough!" she yelled. She punched it in the face, knocking it off her. They both stood slowly. It hissed as it reached out its claws toward her. She kicked it between the legs and then punched it with a double-handed fist, knocking it down. As it began to stand up again, a yellow spear suddenly went through the side of its head.

Yvette walked up to her as she pulled back her spear. "Hmm. Males of any species all seem the same."

Kieren was breathing hard, her hands on her knees. She looked up at Yvette and smiled. "Wouldn't want it any other way." They gave each other a high five, their power suits flashing at the contact.

"Are you two done now?" Gianni asked, walking over to their position as Kieren went back to where Zanth lay on the ground. She found that he'd passed out in the time she spent fighting the Krahn warrior. "Yvette, I thought you were supposed to be helping James out with the Jirina farther to the west."

"She was," James said, walking up to where the others were standing. "We ran into a problem getting through. We've had to travel farther east in hopes we can squeeze through this way. There's a large building in front of us that we'll have to go around. We don't have time to try to demolish it."

"Risky gamble," Gianni said.

"Yes, I know, but it was either that or move farther to the west," James said. "And that way we ran the risk of running into our own troops coming from the Krahn airfield. I didn't want to take the chance of having a friendly fire incident."

"How is Zanth?" Yvette asked.

"He seems to be okay, but he's unconscious now," Kieren replied, bending over to look at the Sekani. "Luckily, he was hit with a laser round, and it seems to have cauterized the wound. It's hardly bleeding."

"Someone has to take him to the med center," James said, looking at all of them. "Who will it be?"

"Kieren," Gianni said.

Kieren squared off to face him. "No way, Gianni. Zanth is my friend, but there is no way I'm passing on this."

"Kieren, look—" Gianni began.

"No, you look," Kieren interrupted him. "We're a team. We should stick together."

Just then David ran up to their position in a blur of blue light. "What's going on?"

"Zanth has been injured," James said.

"David, how long would it take to get him back to the main medical center?" Yvette asked.

"Twenty minutes, max," he replied.

James pointed over his shoulder at the fighting. "I'll give you fifteen. We'll try to push through this."

David picked up Zanth. "If I'm not back when you attack the base—"

"We'll keep an eye out for Janan," James said. "Don't worry."

"Who's worried?" David deadpanned, before taking off in a blur.

"Now," James said, "I think we need to regroup. Zanth's injury has left us with a problem," he said as he smiled at Yvette. "We need to have a short conference with the Sekani lieutenants and the Jirina as well. I need you guys to go and inform them that we'll meet at the large fountain we passed on our way here. Tell the troops to hold their positions for the moment. Hopefully this doesn't kill our momentum."

"We'll let the Sekani know," Kieren said. She and Gianni hurried off.

"Guess that leaves me with the Jirina," Yvette said, already turning to walk in their direction.

"Be careful," James said, wishing he could give her a kiss through their power fields.

Chapter 12

Ronak chewed lazily on the haunch of a Sekani prisoner. The leg had been severed at the hip of the creature and brought to Ronak still fresh. Its blood now dripped from his beak-like mouth and onto the arm of the throne where he sat, unnoticed. He didn't care anymore about appearances, and he was too busy to eat in his private chambers.

His four remaining counselors stood at the foot of the stairs leading up to his throne, all of them looking down at the ground or fidgeting silently as they waited for him to speak. He'd gathered them together for a briefing, though he hadn't told them yet that it would be the last one on Rajan. He'd decided that recalling all of his warriors would take too long. As far as he was concerned, they were expendable.

It would take a few years to reach the numbers needed to attack Krahn, but he was willing to bide his time. There really was no other choice now. The invasion of Rajan had become a disastrous failure, and he just wanted to escape to his colony ship and get as far away from the planet as he could. He sighed. "I'm tired of this," he said, dropping the bone to the floor. "I'm tired of this world. It's ugly and brown and dry. There aren't enough plants or hills to be seen, the air smells bad, and it makes me feel . . . confined."

Martak was his newest appointed counselor, and much younger than any of the others. He'd been born aboard the colony ship, one of the first broods to hatch there, but he still was only a few years past his last molting. He was a small Krahn with dull plumage and always looked surprised for some reason. "But, Ronak, we've expended too many resources on this invasion," he said. "We need to recoup our losses. The only way we can return to Krahn is—"

Ronak interrupted the counselor. "Do not lecture me, Martak. My father was High Vasin of the Qadira clan. I was raised learning conquest while you were still in the egg. It wasn't chance that left only my brother and me alive to compete for the right to be called Vasin. It was only by luck and betrayal that he was able to seize the title."

Martak bowed, his eyes wide. "Yes, Vasin. I didn't mean to suggest—"

"What's delaying our search for the Stones?" Ronak asked, turning toward Kalik and maintaining the illusion that he still cared about them, when all he wanted was to escape. It had been a mistake to attack Rajan. He knew that now. He would be leaving the planet for good soon. Perhaps there would be other ways to discover the source of the Stones and make them his.

"Mighty Ronak," Kalik answered, his fingertips pressed together in supplication. "As you know, we were unable to capture the Rajani Elder known as the Keeper of the Stones. We were able to question prisoners when we first attacked, but none of them knew where the Stones are kept or how to gain access to them." He paused a moment to gather his thoughts. "The Rajani are secretive, even amongst each other. We've run out of leads at this point, I'm afraid. I'm sorry to say that I cannot see a way of finding the Stones. If what your cousin Sendok says is true, we no longer have the warrior numbers to defend Nestbase One. In my opinion, we must abandon our search for the Stones and leave the planet as soon as we can."

"What?" Ronak asked quietly, spreading his arms and standing before his throne. Kalik couldn't have done better if he'd been coached. Ronak knew what needed to happen now. He'd just found his stooge. He'd been trying to think of a way to leave Rajan, while still saving face with those who left with him on the colony ship. He had to keep his air of dominance. "All of this"—his plumage was up now, as he took a few steps forward to the top of the steps, his voice growing louder in mock anger—"was for nothing?" His claws extended out of the ends of his fingers. "You tell me this *now*?"

Kalik's plumage was down in submission. "Ronak, we tried to tell you many times, even before the invasion, that the current number of warriors would be insufficient for a prolonged offensive, but you wouldn't listen to reason—"

Ronak jumped on his chief counselor, slashing with his claws. "I will *not* be lied to! Where are the Stones! Where are they?"

Just then Mariqa entered the throne room, running up to the Ronak's side. "Ronak! We're under attack."

Ronak turned to look at her. He was covered in blood, still holding the lifeless body of the counselor in his hands. "What? Another ship?"

"No! The Rajani are attacking our perimeter," Mariqa replied. "They're being led by the alien creatures we've been searching for."

Ronak let the body fall to the floor and stood up straight. "Let them come. Call back all of our ships from their mission in the north of the city, and all troops. Tell them to converge on Nestbase One." He looked down at the body of Kalik. "Get that out of here." He licked blood from a finger as two of the three remaining counselors dragged Kalik's body from the room. "And bring me something more to eat, Martak. This exercise has made me hungry again."

"Yes, Mighty Qadira," Martak said, and ran from the room.

"Mariqa," Ronak said in his normal tone of voice when they were alone in the throne room. "Have the preparations been made to leave the planet?"

"Yes," she answered, looking at the trail of blood leading out of the room. She'd been fond of Kalik. "The colony ship should be in orbit over our position soon. My ship incurred some damage to its outer hull from the earlier attack, but that should be fixed momentarily, and then we can make our retreat."

"Not retreat," Ronak said. "A new beginning. This attack from the Rajani plays to our advantage. Our troops will be too busy fighting the attackers to care about us leaving."

Mariqa bowed. "Why did you kill Kalik? I thought our plan was that he would accompany us when we left?"

He looked down at the pool of blood that was slowly coagulating on the steps. "Pity about that, but he'd failed me too many times to take with us. And he was too smart to leave here alive."

◊

Ries woke up to find himself now strapped to the medical bed aboard his ship, the *Digger*. He was surprised that he'd even woken up at all. His antennae ached, and his mouth felt like it was full of Asnurian perfume, but other than that, he seemed fine. He lay there for a while, wondering why he was still alive and what he would do to try to escape this newest predicament. He tried his bonds, but they held tight. All four of his arms had been securely fastened. Finally, after what seemed like hours but was maybe thirty Standard minutes,

Prince Creon walked into the room. Ries said nothing as the prince pulled a chair over next to the bed. He sat down, and for a moment just looked at Ries as if he was contemplating what to do with him. Ries just stared back. The prince would have to be the first one to blink. Ries still had his pride, at least.

Eventually the prince smiled at him. "Still playing the role, eh, Agent Van?" he asked.

"What role is that?" Ries replied.

"The role of unflappable Galactic Intelligence Agent," Creon said.

"That is my job," Ries said dryly.

"It doesn't matter," the prince said, standing up and looking down at his captive. "Once we arrive home, you'll be a prisoner for the rest of your miserable life."

"We're going to Talondaria?" Ries asked. Alarms seemed to blare in the back of both his brains at the news. This would not end well.

"Under the circumstances, I thought it would be prudent," Creon said, beginning to pace back and forth. "Tell me, why are you so interested in finding Odorey T'van's contact on Rajan?"

"As I said, it's my job," Ries said.

"One I'm sure you relish," the prince said, his smile now gone. He stopped and looked at Ries once more. "You're lucky I'm not the same as you. If I were, you might never have woken up. But I want to know who helped you on the space station. If you tell me, things might go better for you on Talondaria."

Ries didn't say anything, and after a few minutes, the prince walked out, leaving him to think about his fate alone.

◊

David ran and kept his eyes on the terrain ahead of

him. He didn't want to run straight into a wall and crush the wounded Sekani leader in his arms. He did feel a sense of resentment, though, toward Zanth. If not for the Sekani leader getting hurt, he could be back at the fighting. He was missing everything.

There was nothing he could do about it, he knew, except run as fast as he could. He took a quick look down at Zath, who was still unconscious. The Sekani's wounded arm was hanging at an awkward angle, probably broken. It felt good for once to be carrying a life in his arms that he was trying to save, instead of one he was trying to end.

His life had been so complicated lately that it was difficult to know just what to think. He'd gone through an emotional roller coaster since waking up aboard the Rajani ship the *Tukuli*. He knew he was past any hope of redemption, but maybe there was still a chance at making up for past mistakes.

He arrived at the medical camp and saw a large canopy set up with cots and cushions beneath it. The rain was coming down in spits as he reached the edge of the shelter. He laid Zanth down gently on the closest cushion and went to find a doctor. He needed to get back to help in the fight where he could, and maybe help himself back to a semblance of normalcy once the battle was finished.

◊

Ronak was in his throne room, pacing before his throne, his face still angry, intent on the problem before him, of when to leave. His three remaining counselors stood waiting for him to talk to them. They'd been receiving messages from frantic couriers who reported the status of the fighting to them, but as yet, they'd been afraid to talk to him. He sighed. "Well," he asked, "what's happening?"

"We're losing," one of them replied.

Ronak was crazed with anger and fear. His eyes were

wide, and his plumage was standing up every which way. He didn't know how to feel, what to show. This wasn't how events should have progressed. His plan to leave the planet and all of his warriors behind was not working out the way he'd hoped. He grabbed the counselor. "Fool!" Ronak broke its neck, shaking the body and screaming at it. Spittle flew everywhere from his open mouth. "I know that!" He threw the body to the side, roaring and turned to Martak, who was bowing to him. "Find Mariqa. Tell her that we can wait no longer on her ship. We must evacuate now."

"Yes, Vasin," Martak replied, turning and running from the room.

Ronak turned to his last remaining counselor. His anger still beat like a frantic drum in his head. "Shut up," he said, turning away from the frightened Krahn.

◊

Ries knew he was in trouble. Probably the worst trouble of his life. He couldn't break free of his bonds, and with every passing moment, they were getting closer to Talondaria. If he was lucky, he'd only be imprisoned for the rest of his life. But he'd heard of the cruelty of the Talondarian king, and he had just tortured the king's youngest son. This wasn't how he thought his life would turn out. He'd had dreams of moving into politics after climbing the ranks of the Alliance Society for Peace. He was going to run for some cushy job in the upper echelon of the Alliance and live the rest of his life in style and comfort.

He sighed, resigned to his fate, at least for the moment. He'd had few visits from the prince in the days that had followed their initial conversation, and those visits were brief, and consisted of the prince giving him a drink of water or a piece of protein bar. Jerboxh hadn't dared to show his face. Ries spent his time sleeping or counting tiles on the ceiling. There wasn't anything else to do. He was beginning to become extremely thirsty as he waited for his daily drink.

Finally, the prince once again entered the room. "We'll be there shortly," he said. "I've already sent word of our impending arrival. Still have nothing to say?"

"I'm thirsty," Ries said. "Could you give me something to drink?"

"I suppose it is time," Creon said. He left for a moment but was soon back, carrying a cup of liquid. "Water is all you seem to have on this ship, I'm afraid."

Ries smiled. Jerboxh had been telling the truth for once. He tipped his head forward as the prince held the cup to his mouth. When it was empty, the prince placed it on the small table near the bed.

"Thank you," Reis said. "You don't have to do this, you know. You could just let me go."

"Why would I do that? So you could go back to torturing others for no reason? So you can make others disappear and not think twice about it? No." He bent closer over the bed. "Like I said before, I'm not like you. I couldn't allow that to happen. You think that just because you work for GI that you can do anything and get away with it. But you can't."

"Sort of like your father?" Ries asked. He watched as the prince stood up straight, his face turning red. Then he sighed and let out a breath that had been pent up in his anger.

"You remind me of him, yes," the prince finally said. "I'm not like him, either." He turned to walk away once more.

"Just tell me one thing," Ries said. He was starting to feel tired all of a sudden, as if the weight of the last few days was crushing him into unconsciousness.

"What's that?" the prince asked, turning to look at him.

"What's the name of T'van's Sekani contact?" Ries asked, his eyes feeling heavy. "I would like to know."

"I guess it doesn't really matter if you know now. You'll never find him, even if he's still alive, which is unlikely. When you wake up next, you'll be in prison on Talondaria," Creon said. "The Sekani's name is Janan'kela."

"Drugged," Ries said softly, realizing what the prince had done, but too late.

"Yes," the prince said. "I didn't want anyone else getting hurt if you escaped when we arrived. Goodbye, Agent Van. Hopefully we'll never speak to each other again."

Ries closed his eyes again, and darkness overtook him.

◊

Zanth woke to the smell of blood and bile and the screams of the mortally wounded. He opened his eyes to find himself lying on a small cushion on the sandy ground. A canopy was overhead, blocking out the incessant rain. He turned his head and looked around the large open medical camp. He saw the Jirina on the cushion next to him was staring at him, and then saw that the Jirina's eyes were clouded over in death. He quickly looked away.

He watched as volunteers frantically rushed about, tending to those in need and comforting those without hope of survival. No one came near him, and he wasn't sure if that was good or bad. His left arm felt cold and dead at his side, but at least there was no pain. He raised his head and looked down at the arm. He saw only the blood-soaked bandage that covered his shoulder. There was no arm below it. He tried his other hand, thinking—no, hoping—that maybe he was only dreaming and that he would soon wake up, whole and well. Then one of the Rajani Elder volunteers noticed he was awake and walked over to him.

"The Human named David brought you here," the Rajani said, smiling. "You would probably be dead if not for him. I'm truly sorry about your arm, but the damage was too extensive. You started bleeding shortly after the Human left here, and we needed to act quickly."

Zanth said nothing. He didn't feel like speaking, especially to a Rajani. Even if that Rajani had just saved his life.

"I'll bring you some water and food when I have a chance," the Rajani said. He turned and hurried off. Zanth paid him no mind. He was contemplating life with only one arm.

Two more Rajani walked by him. They were arguing with each other, from the tone of their voices.

"It's too dangerous, Andraal," one of the Rajani said. "You can't set up a medical station that close to the fighting."

"And I'm telling you, that is exactly where we're needed the most," the one named Andraal said. "We're losing too many patients because it's taking too long for them to get here. I'm taking a group of volunteers and some supplies. Tell Tumaani where I've gone."

Zanth recognized Andraal from somewhere, but he was suddenly feeling sleepy again, and couldn't think of where. It wasn't important, he decided. He wasn't sure if anything was important anymore. He closed his eyes, knowing that his life had changed even more because of the Krahn invasion. He drifted off to sleep, hoping that the fighting would be over, at least, when he woke up.

Chapter 13

James had gathered the leaders of the Resistance for a war council, to explain what to do now that their plans had to be altered. Four of the Sekani lieutenants had come back with Kieren and Gianni. Yvette had returned with Mazal and two of his Jirina troops. There were no Rajani present. They couldn't find any who hadn't gone with Kedar, Welemaan, and Bhakat. The Humans were all in contact with Kieren, holding hands in a semicircle; James wanted to make sure that he and the others were understood by everyone present. David wasn't back yet, though he'd only been gone five minutes.

"We need to avoid a bottleneck situation when we go around the building that's impeding our way," James said. "If we can, I'd like the planned deployment to stay in effect once everyone gets through the area. That means the Sekani will work their way to the eastern side of the base, while the Jirina will go to the north and west. The base should be right on the other side of this building, so be careful going around it. Any questions?"

"And once we get to the wall of the compound?" Mazal asked.

James was looking out at the battlefield before them all

as he answered. "I want concentrated attacks on as many different areas of the wall as possible. Send word to all commanders to give me the signal when they're set. We'll attack in unison. I want you to inform your demolition teams to blow holes in the wall large enough to get our troops through, is that understood?"

The Sekani and Jirina all nodded in general affirmation, though none of them looked very happy.

"Good," James said. "Kieren and Gianni, once we get inside the wall, I want you to help the Sekani as much as you can to limit their casualties. Yvette, I want you to push through the south with the main Rajani force when it arrives. Once David returns, he'll be with you. I'll stay with the Jirina. We'll meet inside. All of you, remember your firing lanes. We don't want friendlies taken out by the crossfire." He sighed, knowing that David had run out of time. "That's it. We can't wait any longer. Get your troops in position."

The leaders of all three species departed with the orders from James, making sure their troops were prepared for battle.

"Are we ready?" James asked, looking around at the faces of the other Humans. They had let go of Kieren's hands now, though they all stayed powered up just in case any Krahn snipers were still around.

"Hey, you know me," Gianni said. "I'm always ready for a party."

"Here he comes!" Yvette said, looking back the way they'd come.

They all saw a blue blur heading toward them. David came to a halt in front of James. He was out of breath, but smiling. "All . . . all right. Let's do it."

While James had been talking, the fighting had almost stopped as both sides regrouped for the final battle. There were wounded Sekani being helped off the battlefield and taken to shelter amidst the rubble. Most wore snarls of rage and pain. Unlike the Jirina, they were born warriors. Some of them had taken to wiping blood on their faces like ancient Sekani war paint.

"I know you may not like it," James said, "but the Rajani Elders have asked that we take Ronak prisoner, if possible. They want him to stand trial."

"Oh, come on," Gianni said. "You've got to be kidding me."

"I know, I know," James said, holding his hands up to forestall any more protests from the others. "But you have to understand. This Ronak is their boogeyman, their Hitler, even. Hell, make any comparison you want to use. They don't need to just kill him, they need to try him and find him guilty. They need to confirm their own way of life by convicting him. Call it therapy or revenge, but it's something they'll need before they can hope to get over all of this." He paused a moment to consider before adding, "But if it comes down to a choice between you and him, you have my permission to fry his ass."

Gianni and David laughed at this, and Yvette smiled, but Kieren kept a worried, almost reproachful look on her face.

"Any questions?" James asked, losing his smile again as he looked at her. When no one said anything more, he nodded. "Good. You know what to do. You know how to do it. Each one of you has a reason to fight, if only to get the hell out of here when it's all over. Be careful, and I'll see you inside."

They said their rounds of good luck to each other, and Kieren and Yvette hugged, and then they started to head away from James, and he watched them go. He couldn't quite overcome the unease he felt as they left for their appointed tasks.

James had never sent troops into a conflict. His enlistment was between wars. In the Marines, they all knew what they were training for. But he knew now that it was much different when the fighting began. James shook his head, clearing it for the fight to come. He waited for their signals and put his fear aside. *They're a good team,* he thought. "They'll be fine," he said out loud, not knowing if he believed it was true, or if he was willing it to be so.

◊

Mazal was amazed that he wasn't more scared. On the march from the north of Melaanse, he knew that he wasn't the only one with misgivings as they headed into battle, but he was their leader now, and he wasn't going to lead from the rear. The Jirina were peaceful farmers, mostly, but he knew they had a courage born from desperation. And they were strong. Backbreaking labor performed for the Rajani had resulted in the ability to shoulder the physical burden of war, at least.

He made his way back from the meeting with James the Human convinced that they had a good plan, if they could pull it off. His faith in James was part of the reason, he knew, that the Jirina hadn't hid in the shadows and let the Sekani and Rajani fight this final battle on their own.

Finally, he reached his troops and spread word of the tasks that lay ahead of them all. They slowly moved toward the Krahn stronghold, their few weapons not doing much to keep the Krahn from firing at them. Jirina dead and wounded were falling all around Mazal. He did his best to block out the screams and the sounds of bullets and lasers meeting flesh, but it was difficult. They made it to the edge of the cover provided by building debris and saw that the Krahn had cleared space around the wall. They would have to cross a large open area. Mazal's heart sank at the sight. More Jirina would die soon. He saw that all of the Krahn warriors were now retreating into the compound, giving him a break in the fighting to position his own troops. Inside the compound, the bodies of Krahn warriors were being scavenged by other Krahn. They took weapons, clothing, and anything else that might be useful. They were bred and trained for this purpose, and they were thorough as they ravaged the bodies of their own dead.

"Bring up the demolition units," he told the Jirina lieutenant at his side. As his lieutenant ran off to give orders, Mazal walked down the line of his troops until he found another of his lieutenants. "When we get the order, I need concentrated fire along the top of the wall. We can't allow the Krahn to pick off our demolition teams."

Just then Mazal saw the demo teams working their way toward the front lines. Each had large canvas bags that carried whatever explosives they could find. Mazal took a rifle and fired it twice into the air. It was the signal they'd been told to use, to show the others that they were in position to attack the wall. It was crude, yes, and also told the Krahn their exact whereabouts, but there was no reason to pretend that the Krahn didn't already know it. "Now," he said quietly, "we wait for word to attack."

◊

The Rajani forces had slowly traveled from the Krahn airfield to the outskirts of the area near the Krahn base. Kedar, Welemaan, and the troops had followed Bhakat's lead. Surprisingly, there were very few Krahn warriors along the way. Ronak had pulled them all back to defend the base. Then Bhakat saw the Jirina troops clustered at the edge of the debris field and guessed that this was the reason for so few Krahn troops in the area the Jirina had already been through. He walked up to see the Jirina preparing to deploy their demolition crew to attack the wall. He sought out Mazal and finally found him, giving orders as he walked down the line of Jirina.

"Mazal," Bhakat called.

Mazal turned and saw that Bhakat was walking toward him, and that behind him were the rest of the Rajani Valderren, now taking up positions amidst the rubble. "Bhakat, it's so good to see you and the rest. But I thought you were supposed to be attacking the airfield."

"Belani did most of our work for us, fortunately," Bhakat said, looking down at the crouched Jirina. "We were able to bring most of our troops with us. What's your status here?"

"The Sekani are deployed on the other side of the base," Mazal said. "We're all waiting for the signal to attack. We'll take the wall and then blow holes in it. After that, we'll begin the assault on the buildings inside the compound. James is back to the north of here. I believe the plan was for you to meet up with Yvette to the south of the base."

"What's the signal for attack?" Bhakat asked, seeing that Kedar and Welemaan were making their way toward his position.

"Gianni the Human will fire up into the air three times," Mazal answered.

"Mazal!" Kedar said, finally catching up to them. "Good to see you're still alive out here."

"Thank you, and you as well," Mazal said.

"The Jirina are here," Bhakat said, turning to Kedar and Welemaan, "and the Sekani are on the east side of the wall. We're to deploy the Rajani toward the south and meet up with Yvette, to make sure that no Krahn escape."

"A good plan," Kedar said. "Welemaan, let's get our troops in position."

"All right," Welemaan said.

"Good luck to you," Bhakat said to Mazal, and went with Welemaan to the south.

"And you," Mazal called after him.

"I'm sorry that your troops have had such a hard time of it today," Kedar said. "When this is over, I hope that you and I can speak more about trying to make things better for all the inhabitants of Rajan."

"Thank you," Mazal said. He stuck his hand out to the Rajani.

Kedar grasped his hand. "I think we've both been hanging out with James the Human too long," he said, smiling.

Mazal was shocked when Kedar's head suddenly exploded in a shower of blood, bone, and pieces of brain. He heard the roar of the Krahn ship a microsecond later, but by then, it was too late to do anything except duck down. He realized he was still holding Kedar's limp hand in his own, and he quickly released it. There was a flurry of activity as Kedar's body slumped to the ground.

"Oh no, oh no, oh no . . ." Mazal was saying over and over when Bhakat found him.

"What happened!" Bhakat asked the Jirina. "Mazal, what happened?"

"Shi-ship," Mazal said, looking down at himself. He was covered in a fine misting of blood and other larger objects. He didn't want to know what they were. He felt something hanging from his right ear and quickly wiped it away.

"No!" Welemaan screamed as he came upon their position, but there was nothing he could do—there was nothing anyone could do.

◊

Bhakat was tired of fighting. He just wanted the war to be over. He was still bent over Kedar's body when he heard the Krahn ship returning. He looked up to see it strafing the Rajani forces that were still moving into position to the south. With a roar of pent-up rage, he began to run toward the wall of the Krahn compound. As he came nearer, the Krahn troops on top of the wall began firing at him. The rounds and laser fire bounced harmlessly off of his energy field. He leaped to the top of the wall, growling in fury as he swept through the Krahn troops, not taking any time to make sure they were dead; they were not his target. He timed his jump as the large Krahn ship came closer to his position. His efforts were successful, and he landed on one of the front guns of the ship. Crawling toward the top, he could see the faces of the Krahn pilot and co-pilot as he climbed over the small viewing window in the front of the ship.

Finally, he made his way to the top of the ship. He slammed his fists down through the hull, breaking it like it was made of paper. He made a hole big enough to fit through, peeling back the thick metal. He dropped into the ship and ran through the main and cross halls of the craft, killing anything he could find, and screaming in rage the entire way. He found his way to the cabin and broke through the door like a wrecking ball. The pilot and co-pilot died quickly, their heads smashed together with enough force to turn their brains to paste. He dropped their bodies to the floor.

Bhakat looked out the viewing port of the ship and pushed the steering yoke down, which caused it to dive directly toward the wall. He made sure that the ship was far enough away that none of the Rajani or Jirina troops would be injured from flying shrapnel. He hardly felt the force of the explosion as the ship took out a good-sized portion of the wall, as well as several Krahn warriors who were still on top of it. Taking a running start, he slammed through the top of the ship and found sunlight and fire. He got his bearings and walked back to the lines of Rajani and Jirina troops.

Almost all of the Jirina looked like they were in a state of shock. They sat and waited for the order to go ahead, but most had a blank stare on their faces. Some were wounded and being tended to by others, though many were just sitting and bleeding. Bhakat could see that Welemaan was still kneeling over the body of Kedar. He slowly walked up to the distraught Rajani. "Welemaan, we must be ready when James gives the signal."

Welemaan looked up at him. "Bhakat, thank you for what you just did. Kedar would have been proud of you." He folded Kedar's arms over his chest and placed a blanket from his backpack over the Rajani's upper body. Then he stood up, wiping his face with his sleeve as he did so. "Let's end this now."

◊

Yvette had killed Krahn in just about every way she could imagine. Now, with the novelty of her abilities having worn off, she killed as quickly and efficiently as she could. She was exceedingly good at it, even as she dealt with her seemingly ever-present nausea. She moved to her position behind the Rajani line, and watched as the large Krahn ship crashed into the wall of the compound to the northwest. She wasn't at all surprised when Bhakat emerged from the flaming wreckage of the ship and joined the rest of the Rajani who had begun lining up next to the Jirina. She walked up to their position and noticed a Rajani body on the ground, covered by a blanket. As she drew nearer to Bhakat and Welemaan, she knew who it was by who was absent. "Kedar?" she asked.

Bhakat nodded; Welemaan said nothing.

"Oh," she said, "I'm so sorry."

Suddenly, she heard a collective groan from the lines of Jirina and Rajani. She looked up to see the signal from Gianni blazing across the sky. It was time to push forward.

"Come with me," Bhakat said, moving down the lines toward where the Rajani had been positioned to the south of the compound. Yvette followed him.

"Attack!" Welemaan called out, and the lines pushed forward into the open space between the rubble of old Rajani buildings and the wall. They were immediately fired upon from the top of the wall.

"C'mon, Bhakat," Yvette said, running toward the wall. "Give me a boost."

As they reached the foot of the wall, Bhakat picked her up and threw her to the top. He then jumped and landed next to her. Krahn troops fired at them both, for all of the good it did them. Yvette moved slowly south along the wall, killing as she went. Bhakat went north, doing the same. Yvette could see a flash of blue now and again as David made his presence known farther south.

Finally, Yvette made it to the large hole that Bhakat had made when he crashed the Krahn ship. The gap was too wide for her to cross without some help from Bhakat, though she wasn't too keen on the idea of him throwing her across. The Krahn ship was still in flames, but they were beginning to die down. She had killed all of the Krahn atop her section of the wall, so she turned around to head back north to help Bhakat. Just then, she felt the wall shudder beneath her feet as the first of the demolition charges exploded, opening a large hole in the wall north of her position. It was quickly followed by other explosions as the Jirina and Sekani blew holes in the wall at intervals. She changed her mind and looked for the easiest way to climb down from her position. She'd find Bhakat inside the compound, if she could.

Chapter 14

Ronak was in a rage still, having heard that Mariqa's ship had been destroyed just as it was making its way down to the base to evacuate him. The fool pilot had disobeyed orders and had attacked the Resistance troops outside the base instead of landing as soon as it arrived. He turned to Martak, his last counselor left alive, and pointed at him. "You! Get my armor. I will show these creatures the mistake they have made by challenging me."

"Yes," Mariqa hissed. "We will ride a tide of blood from this place, killing all who stand before us, as in legends of old."

"Yes. You will call in the colony ship," Ronak said. "It's too large to land inside the compound. We must get past the rebels and to the airfield if we have any hope of getting out of this place alive. Inform the ship they are to lay down suppressing fire. We're leaving."

Mariqa bowed and left the room.

Ronak felt calmness come over him for the first time that day as he watched her walk away. The end was near, he knew. There was a slim chance that he and Mariqa would make it to the colony ship. But he would fight until either he was dead, or all of the Rajani were laid down before him in defeat.

◊

Sendok wasn't a coward, but he wasn't stupid, either. They were outnumbered and fighting a losing battle. For a moment his feeling of hatred threatened to overpower him. But it was not hatred for the Rajani troops, it was toward the leader who had brought him to this miserable planet in the first place. It was all Ronak's fault. He was self-aware enough to realize that it was his fault, as well, for following his cousin in the first place, but this only increased his rage. He'd run out of ammunition for his weapon some time before, and was now fighting with a large knife grasped in his right hand. One of the large, stupid-looking Rajani ran toward him, a huge chunk of rubble gripped in his hands. If he wasn't careful, the creature could easily crush his skull. He waited until the creature was right on top of his position and starting to swing its arms down toward him before moving swiftly to the side.

The creature's initial swing passed close to his head, and he moved in quickly toward its body. He was within its reach now, but too close for the creature to swing freely at him. He brought his knife upwards into the creature's abdomen, feeling the solid jolt run up his arm as he buried the blade fully into its guts. He pulled up on the knife as the creature dropped the large rock, cutting a large gash before pulling the weapon back out. As it fell to the ground, he bent down and wiped the gore from his blade on the creature's clothing. He stood up again, looking for his next foe and hoping that it would all be over soon.

◊

The wall of the Krahn base was soon taken over by the Resistance troops. The Krahn were being pushed back to the troop dormitories and the main house, where Ronak was located. Resistance troops began to pour through the holes in the walls of the compound created by the Jirina demolition units. All of the Resistance troops pushed forward in their attacks. The Krahn had fallen back. Their forces were dwindling. The Resistance troops were swarming toward the Krahn warriors, firing as they went, or if they didn't have a gun, using whatever they could to beat, stab, or crush the Krahn they encountered.

David, Yvette, and Bhakat were now with the Rajani Valderren. David was firing a rifle he'd picked up, and Yvette and Bhakat were fighting hand-to-hand with the Krahn as they pushed through, heading toward the main house.

"We need to wait and regroup once we get to the house," Yvette yelled toward Bhakat as the rain began to come down heavier.

"Agreed," Bhakat replied, as he picked up a Krahn warrior and smashed it into the ground with enough force to crush its bones and rupture its internal organs. He stepped over the body before talking again. "If we try to enter the house while strung out like this, we'll lose too many of our own troops."

"Less talky-talky and more fighty-fighty, please," David said, dropping his empty weapon and picking up a fresh one from the ground, which was littered with empty shell casings and the bodies of the dead. There was no more talking for a while.

◊

Mazal was fighting alongside his fellow Jirina, his heart breaking every time he saw one of them fall. He had a cut on his forehead, and blood covered half of his face, some of it his, some Kedar's. They were using James the Human as the point of a wedge to fight through to the building. He could see now that the Rajani had already made it to one side of the house and had taken up positions next to it. "Jirina, move to the other side of the house and wait for the signal to attack!" he yelled out. He would have to coordinate his troop's movements with the Rajani to make sure they didn't fire on each other in the heat of battle.

They finally made it to the side of the building. Mazal motioned to the Jirina to crouch down next to the exterior until he went to speak with Bhakat. James, Yvette, and David were already conferring near where Bhakat stood.

"What's the plan?" he asked when he finally came near enough not to have to shout over the sounds of fighting. He quickly wiped his face with his already-sodden shirt.

"We don't know how many Krahn are still inside the building," Bhakat said.

"It can't be helped," Welemaan said, coming over to their position. "We need to finish this now."

"I have to agree with Welemaan," James said. "There's no other option." James paused a moment. "Sorry," he said, looking at Mazal and realizing that he'd slipped back into English. "I said there's no other option. We need to push ahead," he repeated in Talondarian.

Mazal smiled at James, showing that he wasn't offended. "The Jirina are prepared and ready to fight on your command."

"Then you can go through the door first," Welemaan said.

Mazal saw James give the Rajani an interesting look, then turn his head to look at Mazal. "Can your troops handle that?"

Mazal nodded. "If it means an end to this, then yes."

"Let's hope it does," James said. "I'll go in first. Tell your troops to follow close behind." He turned to look at Welemaan. "The Valderren need to come in on their heels. Understand?" Welemaan nodded.

"I'll go with you," Yvette said to James.

"We both will," David said.

James smiled at them, and then turned to Mazal. "Tell

your troops the plan. We go through the door in one minute. Stay tight with us. We should provide some cover for them."

Mazal nodded and walked quickly back and told his lieutenants the plan, then waited for James to move. James broke through the doorway, and then he, Yvette, and David stood guard over the Jirina while they entered, making sure there was no counterattack, and using their own bodies as shields from enemy fire.

◊

Sendok knew that everything was lost. He and his warriors were positioned just inside the front door of the former Rajani Elder house in a large, open hallway. The Rajani were overpowering the Krahn warriors, and he was going to die on their wretched planet. He knew now that the only way he was going to survive was if he surrendered, and the only way they wouldn't kill him outright was if he had something of value to offer them.

This presented a problem, because he couldn't think of anything he had that was worth anything. There was no piece of knowledge he could barter for his life. He could just fall to his knees and beg, but from what he'd seen of the Resistance forces, that wouldn't necessarily work, either.

Finally, he did the only thing he could think of. He pointed his weapon at his side, hoping that he would only give himself a wound that looked worse than it actually was, and fired. The burning pain at once dropped him to his knees. He looked at the wound and saw that although it was bleeding, it didn't seem to be bleeding enough that he would die from it. Or so he hoped.

He laid down on his stomach and waited for the Rajani to come, all the while hoping he hadn't already killed himself.

◊

Gianni and Kieren were leading the Sekani forces into

battle, now that Zanth had been injured. Gianni had a large red force shield up in front of him, and the Sekani troops were following closely behind him. They had swarmed over the Krahn wall at the signal to attack and cleared the Krahn from all of the outlying buildings. They were now approaching the main house from the rear, still taking fire from Krahn snipers positioned at some of the windows of the house.

Suddenly, Kieren saw a large Krahn appear at the rear door of the house that the Humans and Sekani were fighting to reach. He wore ornate armor and was surrounded by what looked to her like a small group of bodyguards. Kieren somehow knew the moment she saw him that this Krahn had to be Ronak. She saw that he had a radio in his hand and was motioning toward Gianni while talking into it.

The Humans and Sekani were still a hundred yards from the door when a large energy blast hit Gianni from above. Gianni's force shield and the energy field surrounding his body dropped as he fell to the ground. He was conscious, but rattled badly. The force of the blast had weakened his concentration so that he'd momentarily lost his grasp of the Stone's powers. As far as she knew, she was the only one that this had happened to during their training, and now there was a large hole in the pit of her stomach at the thought that it had happened to Gianni at the worst possible time.

Shots started coming all around the Sekani from the Krahn warriors in the main house. Many Sekani were hit as they scrambled for cover. A Sekani pulled Kieren along, pointing toward the sky. She hardly had time to notice that he was one of Zanth's lieutenants. She couldn't remember his name. "Seek cover!" the Sekani yelled at her. "It's their colony ship. You cannot help him now."

"No!" Kieren yelled at him, pulling her arm away from the Sekani. "I've got to try! Gianni!" she screamed as she ran toward him.

◊

Ronak could tell that he still had a crazed look in his eyes, but this time it was different: now he had the kill in sight, and nothing would stop him from butchering this alien who had presumed to take away his victory over the Rajani. He had counted on the blast from the colony ship being able to knock the alien down, but was delighted to see its energy field disappear as well. The aliens were vulnerable, even with the abilities given to them by the Stones. When he and Mariqa reached the pale, hairy alien, Ronak kicked it in the side as it was beginning to rise from its knees. His foot connected with a satisfying thud as the alien rolled for a few feet before coming to a stop against a pile of stones and bodies. Mariqa walked up to it. She was bending over to grab the alien when a single shot from a laser rifle burned a hole through her shoulder.

"No!" he yelled as Mariqa screamed in pain and fury, blood pumping from the semi-cauterized wound in her shoulder. Ronak looked up to see the other alien creature, flying at them with a rifle, almost growling in its intensity. All thoughts of his bloodmate fled in an instant at the sight of the powered-up alien closing the space between them. He quickly ran for cover, hoping to return to the house. It was a survival instinct that Ronak would question in the aftermath of the fight. He was no coward, and he knew that he would not survive a battle against a Stone-powered being. And yet, this would never satisfy his feelings that if he had stayed to fight, the battle may have gone much differently.

As Ronak ran, Mariqa held her ground, her arms wide, waiting for the alien. "Come to me, creature!" she bellowed, her blood-rage at its peak. This caused Ronak to turn and watch her. He'd thought that she would follow him to safety, but he shouldn't have underestimated her ferocity in battle. Seemingly frozen where he stood, all he could do was watch as the creature flew toward his bloodmate.

◊

A large ship, much larger than any of the other ships the Humans had seen before, was in the sky above them all. It was enormous, simultaneously beautiful and terrible. It made the *Tukuli* look like an SUV in comparison. Gianni slowly rose to his knees, shaking his head, not knowing exactly who had kicked him or why. He'd heard Kieren's cries as if through a fog as pain radiated throughout his entire body from the force of the blast. He shook his head to clear it, seeing the large Krahn standing over him and realizing that it was waiting for Kieren as she flew toward it, head-on, her rifle now forgotten. It took him a second to also see that the large Krahn was not the armored one he'd seen earlier. It wasn't Ronak, but he didn't have a chance to look for the Krahn leader.

Suddenly, Kieren was hit by a bolt from the colony ship. She was pounded to the ground by the force of the beam, only a foot or two away from where he knelt. Her field disappeared. She attempted to lift the rifle to fire it again, but her strength was gone. She was having a difficult time staying conscious. He saw what was about to happen, but he couldn't stand up. "Kieren! Run! Get away from her!" he attempted to yell at her, but his voice came out an unsatisfying croak. It wouldn't have mattered if she'd heard him or not. The large Krahn ignored him. It reached Kieren and picked her up by the shoulders. Its claws dug deep into Kieren's flesh, drawing blood, which ran thickly down her arms.

"Go . . . fuck . . . yourself," Kieren said, looking the Krahn in the eye. She spit weakly at her captor.

The Krahn shook her roughly from side to side and

then savagely bit Kieren's neck, growling loudly as its teeth penetrated her flesh. It unceremoniously dropped Kieren's bleeding body to the ground and walked toward Gianni. The Krahn had blood running down the sides of its mouth, and it was smiling, its teeth long and terrible with the promise of pain. It stood over him for a moment, silhouetted against the colony ship above them.

Gianni's mind grew clearer at the sight of Kieren bleeding, and he felt his body power up again. "No!" he screamed in both rage and sorrow. Energy crackled like red lightning around his head. His hands clenched into a fist, and the power surged around them. A single, enormous blast came from his entire body, almost completely disintegrating the Krahn on its way to the colony ship. It went through the ship in a fiery explosion. The ship began to descend almost immediately, flames erupting from the enormous hole in its hull.

There was still a loud keening sound in his ears, and Gianni realized that it was not made by the crashing colony ship. He looked over to see that Ronak had fallen to his knees. And he was screaming. Yet he wasn't looking at his colony ship as it headed for an inevitable crash into the Rajani ground. He was looking directly at Gianni, more precisely, at where the other Krahn had stood only moments before. In a moment of extreme clarity, Gianni realized that the Krahn leader was crying.

There was a loud cheer from the Sekani at the sight of the falling colony ship, but Gianni didn't pay attention to it. He rose weakly to his knees again and dragged himself to Kieren's side. She was still alive, but bleeding badly. He tried to stop the bleeding, holding pressure on the wound as the bright red blood welled around his fingers.

"Gianni?" Kieren whispered.

"What?" Gianni said as her blood flowed freely over his hands. "What? Oh God!" he yelled over his shoulder. "Help me! Someone help! Godammit, I can't stop the bleeding!"

"G . . . shhh," Kieren whispered. "Please. Just . . . hold me. Please."

Gianni saw that the situation was hopeless. Everyone else was still fighting near them. There was a whoosh of hot air around them as the Krahn colony ship exploded again as it crashed a few hundred yards away from the main house. He pulled Kieren toward him gently. They were both crying.

"Gianni, . . . I-I . . . love you," she said, softly.

"Oh, honey," Gianni said. "Oh God, oh God. Please. Stay with me, baby. Don't leave me alone. I can't stop the bleeding."

Kieren weakly held her hand up toward his face. "Not . . . alone. Never . . . alone." Her hand fell back to the ground, lifeless.

Gianni held her close, rocking her gently. His tears streamed from his eyes and mixed with the rain as it ran down his face.

Chapter 15

There were only a few Krahn left to put up any kind of resistance, and all of them were contained within the main house. Most of the Krahn who had still been at Nestbase One were either dead or dying on the battlefield that surrounded the structure. They groaned in pain and desperation, some digging their claws into the mud to pull their way forward, some giving up any vestige of hope, their faces falling forward to be covered by the ooze created by their dark red blood as it mixed with the mud beneath them. They lay among the bodies of other Krahn, Jirina, Sekani, and Rajani, each one lending its blood to the miasma that surrounded them.

Jirina flooded into the building, screaming and firing their weapons, led by the powered-up Humans. The Jirinas' faces bore a hate brought on by desperation. Their mouths snarled, and they showed their teeth, but their eyes were dead, and they pulled their triggers by reflex only. They were a peaceful species who should never have been involved in this type of hand-to-hand situation, but they obediently followed their leader, Mazal. They fired at the Krahn from behind, hitting many of them before they even know what was happening. Dark blood flew from burning skin as the Krahn were cut down before the enraged Jirina forces. Then the Rajani forces entered the fray, running through the front door and taking up positions at every door, window, and corner. They left the Jirina on the ground floor and began to move their way up the staircases, killing as they went.

The Sekani forces broke through the rear door of the building and made their way inside. They found no resistance waiting for them. Any Krahn present had been killed or wounded by the Jirina that were now standing around as if shell-shocked. A short time later, almost all of the Krahn within the structure were either dead or held prisoner. Those Krahn who were still alive were lined up with Sekani and Jirina guards holding weapons pointed at them. Many of the Krahn were wounded, some badly; some were unable to even stand. There were also dead and wounded Jirina littered about the carnage. The wounded were being tended to; the dead lay where they had fallen.

The walls of the building bore the marks of intense laser and conventional weapons fire. Cracks traced up each pillar of the ground floor main room, disappearing into the gloom near the ceiling. Almost all of the windows were shattered, some altogether missing. The place looked like it could collapse at any moment.

◊

Ronak had finally stood up from where he knelt and retreated to the main house ahead of the Sekani fighters making their way swiftly toward him. The Rajani hadn't yet reached the house, so he'd quickly squeezed through the back door of the structure. He'd thought briefly about just staying where he was, kneeling in the mud and howling like a wounded animal. He'd let the Rajani kill him in whatever way they pleased. But he was too proud for that kind of death. So he'd made his way to the house and climbed the stairs to his bedchamber and waited for the end to come. It was no use anymore. Mariqa was dead. No, not just dead. She had been vaporized by the Stone-powered creature. What had his cousin Sendok called them? He couldn't remember; he didn't care. The information didn't matter now that she was dead. All of his dreams of ruling Krahn had been with Mariqa beside him. All he'd done in the past had been for her. Without her, there was no reason to fight anymore.

He heard the Rajani before he saw them. There was a large group coming up the stairs now. There would be no escape from them. He had no weapon, only his teeth and claws. He stood, poised to make his last fight one the Rajani would never forget. He saw them round the corner, their weapons trained ahead, pointing at him as he jumped in their direction. The end would be swift, if not painless.

Then something happened that he wasn't counting on. The Rajani in the lead didn't fire his weapon, only turned it and hit him full across the face in midair. He felt his mouth burst with pain; his teeth on one side of his face were shattered. He fell to the ground before them as they surrounded him. He prepared to rise again to fight them and felt their feet kick him. He was drowning in the press of kicking, screaming Rajani. He felt his armor being pried off as a rain of rock-hard fists descended on him. He couldn't see anymore, could only feel their fury as they hit him. Every part of his body was on fire. Then there was a yell, and it stopped. He looked up to see a large Rajani with a silly-looking knot in his hair standing over him. The Rajani was smiling.

◊

Yvette, Bhakat, and David were in the Krahn throne room they had discovered while helping the Rajani mop up the remaining Krahn warriors. David was kneeling next to the throne, looking at a pile of small bones that Ronak had left after his last feeding. There were still bodies of the Krahn surrounding the throne. One of the Krahn had a surprised look on its face, as if it hadn't known that its death was imminent. Everyone but David looked at James when he entered, noticing that he wasn't powered up any longer.

"Good job," James said. "Is everyone all right?"

Yvette dropped her energy field and embraced him. "It's finally over," she said.

"Janan?" James asked.

Bhakat was looking at David, who was kneeling next to the pile of bones still, a frown on his face.

James walked over to where David knelt. He rested a hand on David's head. "David, I'm so sorry."

David looked up at him. "Is this over?" he asked. "Please? I just want it to be over."

"Yes, we're finished—" James started to say.

Toruq, who had been hiding in the stairwell that led to the basement, suddenly fired at them, screaming in Krahnish, "Die, creatures!"

Bhakat caught sight of the Krahn just before he fired. He powered up and quickly jumped in front of the Humans. The bullets bounced harmlessly off of his field. The Humans all quickly powered up as well when they saw what had happened.

David looked to James. "James, can I . . . ?"

"Go ahead," James told him. "It's yours. Take all of the time you need."

"Thank you," David replied.

David walked toward the door. The Krahn kept firing, but the rounds bounced off of the power field surrounding David's body. The gun finally died as it ran out of ammunition and clicked repeatedly on an empty chamber. Toruq threw the gun down and then ran for the stairs. He sprinted down them two at a time into darkness. David followed, still walking. When he reached the cellar, he saw that the room had been converted to a dungeon. It had cages lining both walls. All of them were empty except for one. The Krahn was opening the door to the occupied cell. David saw the small form that was huddled within. The Krahn picked up the body and shook it, holding it out for David to see that it was Janan.

"Stop, creature," the Krahn said, menacingly. "Or I'll kill this pitiful Sekani. I don't want to do this. I was helping you all, don't you know that? It was me that informed your rebellion of Ronak's coming. He should have known not to treat me with such disrespect—"

David stopped while the Krahn spouted off something in Krahnish that he couldn't understand. All he knew was the Krahn was threatening Janan. He thought he'd lost his friend forever. Now that he saw he might still be alive, there was no way he would let the Krahn harm him further.

"Good," Toruq said. "Now let me go, and—"

One second David was standing there—a blur, a crack—and the next moment he had Janan in his arms and the Krahn was lying on the ground with his head on backwards, his neck clearly broken.

Janan looked up at David weakly, his eyes barely able to focus. "Dav . . . David. Knew . . . you'd come."

"You're okay now," David said softly. "Let's get out of here." David's eyes were closed as he hugged the form of Janan to him. "Now it's over."

◊

James, Yvette, and Bhakat were still on the main level of the house, speaking in quiet tones about the loss of Janan. They had powered down once again. They watched as a large Krahn was brought into the throne room, surrounded by Rajani and Sekani guards. *It has to be Ronak,* James thought upon seeing the creature. He could tell the guards had not been gentle with their prisoner. They had stripped him down to only a small loincloth that covered his genitals. One of Ronak's eyes was swollen shut, and he had cuts and bruises on other parts of his body. A trickle of blood ran down from his mouth and across his chest. He was also limping as he walked. His arms were bound behind his back with a length of rope. The guards led him straight to James.

"James the Human," one of the Rajani said. "Welemaan has requested that we bring Ronak to you. He said to tell you that the Krahn leader is a gift to you, and that he hopes that your punishment is swift." Ronak didn't look up at all, as if his spirit had already been broken by the treatment of the guards.

"Get this piece of filth out of my sight," James said, ignoring the political posturing of the new Valderren leader. He turned to Bhakat. "Take him to your Elders for all I care."

"He'll face judgment soon," Bhakat said. "I can guarantee it." He bowed to James, and then to Yvette, then turned and led Ronak away, followed by the contingent of guards.

James turned to Yvette. He grasped her hand in his and led her outside the front door of the house. The rain had stopped for the moment, and the freshly scrubbed air was welcome—the inside of the house smelled like gunpowder and death. They looked at each other a moment before embracing again, this time for a long while. The war was finally over.

◊

Bhakat had told James that Ronak would face judgment soon, but he knew that it was his own judgment that weighed on his mind as he led the Krahn leader through the streets toward the Rajani rear lines. As he walked, he saw for the first time the destruction from the recent fighting. There were bodies everywhere, and many injured Rajani, Sekani, and Jirina, still lying where they'd fallen. Some of them were being attended to by their fellow fighters or medical personnel sent by the Elders.

Suddenly, Bhakat saw the Human named Gianni slowly walking along, carrying a body in his arms and weeping. Oh no, he thought, when he saw that it was Kieren. *Not another friend lost.* "Stop here a moment," he told the contingent of Rajani and Sekani who were escorting his prisoner along. He walked over to where Gianni was standing. The Human had stopped when he'd heard Bhakat's voice. As he grew closer Bhakat could see that the female's chest was covered in drying blood. Her neck was ravaged and had bled extensively. His fears were confirmed when he stopped before them. She was dead. "Gianni, I'm sorry," he said softly.

The Human seemed to notice him for the first time, as if waking from an episode of sleepwalking. "Bhakat. I-I don't know where to take her. I didn't want to just . . . leave her."

"It's okay," Bhakat said. "Come with us. We'll take care of her, I promise." He placed his hand on the Human's shoulder and directed him toward the group of Rajani and Sekani who were waiting for them. They all began to walk again. Gianni shuffled along, not speaking or looking at anyone, holding the body close to him as he walked. Bhakat doubted he even noticed that Ronak was walking at the head of the procession.

Finally, the strange parade came to a medical outpost that had been set up by the Elders. There were cots filled with casualties from the fighting and scores of walking wounded milling around, most with at least one bloody bandage somewhere on their bodies. Bhakat saw Andraal bent over a Jirina who had lost one of his arms at the elbow. He walked over to the Rajani doctor. "Andraal," he said, waiting for the other Rajani to finish with his patient.

Andraal turned to see him. His face broke into a broad smile, though Bhakat could see the exhaustion beneath it. "Bhakat, I'm happy to see that you're still alive."

"And you as well. Where can I find the other Elders?" Bhakat asked, not returning the smile. He didn't know if he'd ever smile again.

"I'm afraid I'm the only one here at the moment," Andraal responded, his smile disappearing. "But I think there should be more coming along soon, now that word of the number of casualties has reached them."

"Good," Bhakat said. He motioned over toward his group. "I have two prisoners who must be tended to by the Elders." He looked to where Gianni still stood, holding Kieren's body. "Where are you keeping the dead?" he asked quietly.

"Over behind that building," Andraal said, pointing toward a structure on the far side of the open space, where they had laid out cots for the wounded.

"Thank you, Andraal," Bhakat said, bowing slightly. He walked toward the group of Rajani and Sekani guards. "Sit Ronak down here, and wait for the Elders to arrive. If you can, help out if you're needed, but keep at least three guards surrounding him at all times. Is that understood?"

He once again directed Gianni by gently leading him by the arm toward the building that Andraal had pointed out. They turned the corner and found a wide courtyard filled with bodies, mostly laid out neatly in rows. He found an open space and helped the Human male lay his mate's body down gently on the ground.

"She can stay here for now," Gianni said, kneeling next to her.

Bhakat knelt down as well. He felt tears come to his eyes as he watched Gianni sit down and reach out to hold her hand. He knew Gianni wouldn't leave her, so he didn't even attempt to persuade him. He would tell Andraal to give the Human a sedative later to help him sleep. "I am sorry, Gianni," he said as he stood up. He couldn't think of anything else to say. He placed a hand on the Human's shoulder and squeezed it gently before walking away.

As he came around the corner, he noticed that a group of Rajani Elders had arrived. The Elders were being briefed by Andraal. He walked slowly toward them, wiping the tears from his face as he did. He stopped in front of Tumaani.

"Bhakat," Tumaani said, "Andraal said that you had two prisoners for us, but we only see Ronak. Did the other escape?"

"No, Tumaani," Bhakat replied, knowing what he needed to do. He'd known from the moment he'd escaped the *Tukuli*. "The other prisoner is me," he said, kneeling down and holding his hands out before him.

◊

James went looking for Gianni as soon as he heard the news. Kieren was dead. It was difficult to believe, yet also not a total surprise. The odds were too great, and he'd known it going in. They all had. Still, the weight on his heart threatened to make his knees buckle. He knew, though, that it was nothing close to what Gianni must be feeling at the moment. It had been a roller coaster of emotion in the last few hours. They'd thought Janan was dead, and then found he was alive, and now this.

Yvette had told him that Gianni and Kieren had finally gotten together. He'd been happy to hear it, and fearful of what could happen if either of them were to suffer this fate. And now that scenario had played out. There was nothing he could have done to change it, yet he would never forget that she had died on his watch, under his orders.

He found Gianni sitting alone against a partial wall of a

building close to a medical outpost that the Elders had set up, his knees pulled up to his chest and his hands over his face. As he approached, Gianni didn't move his hands, and he wondered at first if the other man was sleeping. He sat down next to him and wondered if he should say anything. It turned out that he didn't have to.

"She's gone, Big J," Gianni said quietly.

"I know," James said, not mentioning how he felt about the nickname. Now wasn't the time, and Gianni could call him anything he felt like at the moment. He'd earned the right.

"I held her at the end, and I couldn't . . . I couldn't do anything to stop it," Gianni said, taking his hands down from his face and looking at James. "All these powers I have, and I couldn't stop her from bleeding to death."

"I doubt even the Stones give us power over death," James said. "I'm sorry."

"So am I," Gianni said. "So it's over now? We can leave?"

"Yes, it's over," James said. "But I don't think we'll be leaving soon. There's still too much that needs to be done here, I'm afraid. We're still needed too much to leave."

"Then I guess we'll have to have a funeral here for her," Gianni said, standing up.

James stood as well. "Yes, I guess we will. I don't know if we'll be able to transport her home after all of this—"

"Don't worry about that," Gianni said. "I've had time to think about it, and I know a place where she'll be happy. It made us both happy."

James placed a hand on his shoulder. "Good. Let me know if you need any help in planning it. You're not alone in this. Kieren meant a lot to all of us."

Gianni turned to look at him and smiled sadly. "I know. She was a special person. I loved her. I'm glad I got to tell her that before she was gone."

"Good," James said, and a brief image of Jennifer flashed before his eyes. But then Yvette appeared in his mind as the image of his wife faded, and his heart felt like it was whole for the first time in a long while. He placed a hand gently on the other man's shoulder. "Best to keep busy. There's work to be done."

"Lead the way, Big J," Gianni said, though his smile had faded as if it had never been there at all.

Chapter 16

The major fighting had been over for two days as the Rajani began to recreate their world. There had been some Krahn survivors amidst the wreckage of the enormous colony ship, but they were quickly hunted down and killed by Sekani and Rajani forces. No prisoners were taken from the ship, not even the young Krahn who were found in the large hatching rooms deep in the ship's interior. All of the eggs were crushed underfoot or set ablaze.

In the early-morning light, James was gathered with a group of both Elders and Valderren, all facing toward the center of a small square in the north of Melaanse. In the center of the square was a coffin on a stand. The various species of Rajan had begun to bury their dead, though most of the funerals were not held with such a sense of ritual and solemnity as this one. James had been invited to this funeral by Welemaan, who was now the leader of the Valderren.

Welemaan stood in the middle of the square, next to the body of Kedar, and wept. After a moment, he composed himself and continued the speech he had begun a few minutes before. "Kedar was dedicated to what he thought was right. His sacrifice will never be forgotten. As we move forward, we will always have an eye on the past and those we lost."

James was saddened by the death of the Rajani he had grown to know well over the course of the war. He had hoped Kedar would be able to lead the Rajani forward after the fighting was finished. He wasn't sure that Welemaan would be as good of a leader, as the Rajani Elder was far too impulsive and self-important. There was nothing he could do about it, though. He knew his future and that of the Rajani would soon divert along different paths. He'd done what he could to set them on the right course, but it was not up to him to govern them.

After all the words had been spoken, tears had been shed, and hugs shared, James nodded solemnly to Tumaani and the others gathered there as they all made their way out of the courtyard. There were many more funerals to come.

◊

They discovered the small Krahn ship where it had crashed, out of gas and heading toward Melaanse. Of the Krahn who had piloted it and their crew, there were no signs. Perhaps they had made it back to the Krahn base, or possibly they had been killed by the desert, or maybe they had fallen victim to one of its more carnivorous inhabitants. Whatever their fate, they were never seen again.

The search party continued on and eventually found Belani's ship. They landed near the wreckage, which was surprisingly in mostly one piece. When Belani had pulled up just before he blacked out, he'd only been thirty feet off the ground. As the ship rose up, the final engine had cut out, and the ship had fallen backwards and down a large sand dune, tumbling end over end for a hundred feet before finally coming to rest on its engines, the ship pointing straight up toward the sky.

The search party was led by James and included Yvette and some Jirina volunteers. They approached the ship and looked it over carefully, examining it for any signs of a fuel leak that could mean the danger of explosion, but they saw nothing. James powered up and bent open the hatch as best he could to allow entrance to the others. They found Belani still strapped in his captain's chair, lying on his back. James bent over, listening dejectedly for breathing sounds.

"Took you . . . long enough," Belani whispered without opening his eyes.

James smiled as he opened a bottle of water and slowly gave some to the Sekani pilot. "Let's get you out of here."

◊

Tumaani was the last to arrive at the first full Rajani summit since the fighting had started. There were now two disparate groups that needed to work out their differences if the Rajani were to move forward. Now that the war was over, would they be able to overcome their philosophical differences and forge a stronger government? Tumaani didn't know the answer to that question. He nodded to Welemaan as he made his way to his chair. They had agreed to meet in the Valderren headquarters building, and as he looked around the large meeting table, he found that there were few, if any, former Elders on the Valderren side. If he knew Welemaan, this wasn't an accident. The young Rajani Valderren would look up to him as a leader.

"I apologize for my lateness," Tumaani said. He'd been at a briefing of Jirina workers who had been given the task of making coffins for the dead and planning a burial site for all those who had died in the fighting. It was one of many tasks that he had initiated since the fighting ended. There was a long way to go.

"We've already taken a roll call of everyone else present," Welemaan said. "If we may begin now, I believe our first order of business is officially recognizing the Valderren as a valid governing body."

Tumaani cringed inside. *Is this how it is going to be from now on?* he thought. At least Kedar had seemed more tactful. If only he had lived. If only Rauphangelaa had lived. He would have been much better at this. There were so many regrets. So much pain. "The Elders recognize the Valderren's claim to be a part of the governing council on Rajan. Are you the appointed leader and speaker for the Valderren?"

"I am," Welemaan answered, smiling. "What's the next order of business?" The former Elder's smugness was beginning to grate on Tumaani's nerves, but he kept his face emotionless. No need to bring his personal feelings into this.

"There's the matter of the Rajani known as Bhakat, who is accused of implanting himself with a Johar Stone, in violation of Rajan's oldest law," a Valderren named Seliban said. Tumaani saw him look to Welemaan, and Welemaan nod to him. *Politics*, Tumaani thought. He had hoped they wouldn't return so soon to the type of political rhetoric that had plagued the Elders before the Krahn attacked, but it looked like it had only been postponed for a while.

"I don't think either the Elders or the Valderren have the authority to try prisoners of the Krahn conflict on our own," he said. "This includes Bhakat, the Sekani traitor named Belani, and even Ronak and his remaining followers. Their fate needs to be determined by the full governing council in open court. Alliance protocols must be followed." There was a grumbling from both sides of the table at his words. He had known there would be, but so far, he was still strong enough in his position that there would be no open dissent, which is what he was counting on. It was important that the trial process be up to Alliance standards. The Krahn-Rajani war would not stay a secret forever, and when Alliance representatives finally arrived to investigate, they needed to see that the trials were conducted correctly.

"Agreed," Welemaan finally said, though Tumaani could see the disappointment on his face. There would be repercussions to deal with later. Welemaan would not like being shown up, although that had not been Tumaani's intention. He was apt to prove difficult in other matters because of it.

"We now come to a topic that I'm sure everyone has been thinking about," Welemaan continued. "The Humans are talking about leaving soon. Can we truly allow them to do so? The Johar Stones are a valuable commodity, and they make the Humans valuable to us. Their skills are too precious to just let them leave."

"Allow them? What are you saying, Welemaan?" Andraal said from a seat to Tumaani's left. "Are you suggesting that we keep them here against their wills? After everything they've done for us?"

"All I'm saying is that we should not just let them leave so soon after hostilities against the Krahn have been completed," Welemaan answered. "For all we know, reinforcements from the Krahn home world could be on their way here right now. Can we risk our recent accomplishments just to let a handful of off-worlders leave?"

"The key word there is 'off-worlder,' Welemaan," Tumaani said. "They are not Rajani, and I use the word universally for the Rajani, Sekani, and Jirina who live on this planet. The Humans were taken from their world against their will. They should not have been brought into this situation in the first place. Yes, they agreed to help us, and they have done so. It would be dishonorable to not allow them to leave when they are ready. Rauphangelaa promised them that they could. As you have all seen, honor is one of the few things we have left."

"I'm not saying they can't leave," Welemaan said. "All I'm saying is we shouldn't let them leave right now. Not until we know for sure that we're safe. And besides, what ship would they use? As everyone here is aware, our fleet of ships has been destroyed."

Tumaani wasn't sure why Welemaan was attempting to keep the Humans on Rajan, but he didn't like it. He couldn't be sure that Welemaan's stated reasoning gave his true intentions in this matter. He, on the other hand, wanted the Stones as far away from Rajan as possible. And that meant sending all those who were implanted away, and quickly.

"The Humans have saved us," he said. "They've rescued our planet from the Krahn Horde at a great loss to themselves. We can ask no more of them. We need to let them go. They are not prisoners, and I will not stand for them to be treated as such."

There was a round of chest beating from both the Elders and Valderren present, except for Welemaan and his cronie, Seliban. Tumaani knew he had won this battle, but by the look on Welemaan's face, he could foresee a war ahead.

◊

It had been a long day, and James just wanted to get in bed and go to sleep. His hopes were dashed, though, when he opened the door to his room to find Yvette crying.

"Honey," he said, walking over to where she sat on the edge of the bed. "What's wrong?"

"Do you love me?" she asked, looking up at him.

He sat down next to her. "Yes," he said, realizing it was true, but that up until then, he'd been afraid that saying it would somehow change their relationship.

"Then why don't you ever say it?" she asked, wiping her eyes with her shirt.

"I'm sorry," he said. "I guess I didn't want to put too

much pressure on us. On you. I do love you, Yvette. I know I should have said it before now."

"Kieren was supposed to be here," she said, and a fresh sob shook her body. "She . . . was supposed to be here when I told you."

James was confused. "She was supposed to be here when you told me that you loved me?"

"No," she said. "She was supposed to be here when I told you I'm pregnant."

The word struck him like a blow to the heart. "I thought you said—" he began to say.

"I was wrong," she said, looking down. A sob escaped her as she began to cry anew.

James didn't know what to think. Emotions were roiling around inside of him that he hadn't felt in years. He realized that chief among them were happiness and hope. The blow to his heart had quickly turned to a warmth of anticipation and even greater love for the woman sitting next to him. He also realized that he'd been silent for too long. He reached over and cupped her chin in his hand. "How long have you known?"

"Almost three months," she said. "Bhakat confirmed it. The baby is fine, as far as he can tell."

"It's wonderful news," he said, then stopped when a thought hit him. "Are you keeping the baby?" he asked with a feeling of trepidation.

"Of course," she said, an exasperated look on her face. She wiped her eyes again.

He smiled widely. "Good. You can't imagine how happy you've made me."

"Really?" she asked, and he could see that she'd been holding onto her secret from him in fear of rejection. Which explained why she'd wanted Kieren there when she told him the news.

He put his arms around her and squeezed her tightly to his chest. "I love you," he said in reply, feeling tears come to his own eyes. "You know, this is going to be one spoiled kid."

◊

Janan opened his eyes to a low-lit room. He wasn't sure if he was still dreaming or not. His rescue had certainly seemed unreal. He'd slept for an entire day afterward, and was still confined to his bed while he recovered from his ordeal. He turned to see David asleep in a chair next to his bed. His Human friend had seemingly never left his side since his rescue. He was sore and still felt weak, but overall, he felt like he was doing better now that he'd had a few IVs. He also suddenly felt extremely hungry. He didn't know what time it was. There were no windows in the room. He slowly sat up against the wall next to the head of his bed. The room was sparsely furnished, and he couldn't see anything even resembling food. He didn't think he could get out of bed to search on his own.

Just as he was about to try to wake David, the door to the room opened, and a Rajani whom he didn't know came in. The Rajani smiled when he saw that Janan was awake. "Feeling any better?" he asked.

"Yes," Janan said in his new whispery voice. He'd been told that his real voice might never return because of the damage to his vocal cords. "Can I get some food?" he asked.

"I'm sure we can find something for you," the Rajani said, while checking his pulse. "My name is Andraal, by the way. It was a close thing for you, you know? Another day or two, and I don't know if we'd be speaking right now."

Janan looked over at his friend David. No, he wasn't just his friend, was he? More like his savior. "Then I'm glad he came when he did. Has anyone else been here to visit?"

"Most of the surviving Humans have been by to see you, but you slept through it all," Andraal replied. "Which is fine. You needed the rest."

"Oh," Janan replied glumly, disappointed that Rauphangelaa and Bhakat had not made an appearance. He assumed they were too busy taking care of Rajani business to come and see him. "What time is it?"

"Late," Andraal replied, finishing up his examination and punching some keys on a tablet from his pocket. It seemed as though the power was back on, at least. "You should lie back down and try to get some more sleep. I want to push some more liquids through you before you get out of here. I'll send someone back in with some food later."

"Thank you," Janan said. He was feeling tired again. He laid back down and, after one more look at David, closed his eyes again. Just before sleep overtook him, the doctor's words coalesced in his brain. Surviving Humans. Sadness overtook him, as he drifted off.

◊

Tumaani had put off talking to Zanth for far too long. And then Zanth had almost been killed in the fighting with the Krahn. But he was alive, at least, though no longer whole. Tumaani waited at the gates of the Sekani compound for permission to enter. He'd asked the guards to convey a message to Zanth of his wish to speak with him. He was saddened by the fact that he wasn't sure if his wish would be granted. Finally, one of the Sekani guards returned and spoke with the others a moment. Tumaani waited as patiently as he could. Getting angry or frustrated wouldn't help the situation. After a few minutes, the gate began to open.

"He said he'd see you as long as your visit is brief," the guard said when Tumaani walked into the compound.

"That's fine, thank you," Tumaani said.

"Follow me," the guard said.

He followed the guard to a large courtyard in the middle of the compound. He noticed the great many Sekani who were watching him, and the hostile expressions on most of their faces. He wasn't surprised by this; he was sure they knew about his former relationship with his head servant. The guard turned to make sure that Tumaani was still following, then headed toward a large building to their left. The guard stopped at the front door of the building.

"Top floor, last door in the hallway," the guard said, opening the door for him. Tumaani nodded and then entered the building. He saw that the interior of the structure had once been offices, but had been turned into dwelling units. He saw a stairwell ahead and began to walk up it. After walking two flights of stairs and seeing no one else, he arrived at the third and topmost floor.

There were several Sekani males and females on this floor, most looking over handheld charts or sitting at small tables, talking. They all looked up at him from their various activities. Tumaani nodded and attempted his best smile. He walked quickly past the Sekani and realized that the entire floor was actually a medical suite. And presumably the sole patient was located at the end of the hallway.

He arrived at the closed door and knocked quietly. The door opened almost immediately, and he was met there by a rather large Sekani. He came up to Tumaani's navel.

"I'm here—" Tumaani began to say.

"I know why you're here," the Sekani said. "You have ten Standard minutes." He opened the door wider, and Tumaani saw that it was a small room with a single bed and a small window over it in the middle of the wall. There were no other furnishings. Zanth was awake, sitting up in bed, a large white bandage covering the stump of his left arm. There was a tube leading from his right arm to a small medibot that was set up next to the bed.

"That'll be enough for now, Botran," Zanth said. The Sekani at the door bowed to him and managed to frown once more at Tumaani before leaving. He closed the door behind him.

Tumaani turned away from the doorway and toward the bed, wondering if he should have even bothered coming. No, he thought. *If not now, then when?* "I wanted to come here to apologize to you face-to-face," he said, walking toward the bed. There was no preamble. There was no time for it. "How I treated you, how my species treated yours, was wrong, and I'm sorry."

"Am I supposed to simply forgive you now?" Zanth asked. "Absolve you of all wrongdoing and act like it never happened? Are the Sekani supposed to forget years of Rajani oppression?"

"No," Tumaani said quietly. "I'm not naïve enough to think that would happen. I only wanted you to know that I'm sorry. For everything." He was looking at the white stump of Zanth's arm.

"All of your words won't bring it back," Zanth said, bitterly. "But it's a reminder of all the sacrifices my species have made for this planet. We will never forget how it was before the Krahn arrived. We'll never go back to being second-class citizens."

"Nor do I expect you to," Tumaani said. "Everything has changed, for good or ill. I just hope that the Rajani and Sekani can work together to rebuild our world."

Zanth was silent for a moment, looking down at the floor. The moment lingered on, and finally, Tumaani turned and walked back toward the door a few steps. "I'll leave now. Thank you for allowing me to come," he said.

"Wait," Zanth said as Tumaani reached the doorway. Tumaani turned back toward him. "This conversation didn't go the way I thought it would."

"You expected me to start giving orders," Tumaani said, smiling. "Or at least demand that the Sekani conform to Rajani mandates concerning the future of our planet, perhaps."

"Yes," Zanth said. "I admit that I'm a bit taken aback by your . . . humbleness."

"This war has humbled us all, I think," Tumaani said, walking back toward the bed. "I lost my best friend. He died before he could see the war end. He died before I could say goodbye. I learned a valuable lesson because of that. Never take anything or anyone for granted. Our time is too short. Our lives can end between one heartbeat and the next."

"If what you say is true," Zanth said, "then perhaps the Rajani and Sekani can work together to rebuild this world. I'm willing to give it a try. I want peace between our species, Tumaani. I've had enough of war. And I . . . I forgive you, for my part."

Tumaani fell to his knees beside the bed and reached out to grasp Zanth's remaining hand. He could feel tears coming to his eyes. "Thank you," he said, beginning to cry. "Thank you for this, Zanth."

Chapter 17

James felt like he was busier now that the war had ended than he ever was while it was still being fought. He'd formed various units from the Rajani, Sekani, and Jirina to begin cleaning up the carnage of war; some to bury the dead, and others to remove the rubble and other trash from the city. A unit was formed to find and capture any Krahn warriors who were still free. Another crew was tasked with turning the power back on, and yet another with harvesting as much food as possible to ensure there was enough food to survive. This last group was headed up by a Rajani named Dreben.

One entire unit was in charge of scavenging the remains of the Krahn colony ship and breaking down the ship for parts to begin repairs on the Rajani starcruisers that remained. There was also talk of trying to retrieve the *Tukuli* from the bottom of the ocean, but Tumaani said that it would remain entombed there out of respect for the dead Humans still aboard, a gesture that James appreciated immensely. James had also headed up a unit, the search party that had discovered Belani's ship. When everything was in order and all of the units were sent out to perform their various duties, James announced that he was stepping down as military leader, effective immediately, and that he would welcome the new governing council of Rajan, which would be made up of all of the races on Rajan.

Tumaani, Welemaan, Zanth, and Mazal would make up the initial council, until such time that the elections could be made for a permanent council, one voted in by all of the inhabitants of the planet. Their first order of business was to honor the fallen, reading off the names of all those who had died fighting the Krahn or were killed in the initial Krahn attack. A number of individuals had volunteered to read in shifts, but even with an abundance of readers, the Reading of Lists lasted for three days.

James sat in when he could, sometimes hearing a familiar name of someone he had known. Fajel, Mazal's nephew, whom he had met only once; Kedar, Leader of the Valderren, who had died in the final battle; Kieren the Human; Rauphangelaa, Keeper of the Stones. It had been a month, but the names still felt like a knife twisting in his heart.

When the reading of the list was finished, they adjourned, with the agenda set for the next meeting. They would decide the fates of various prisoners, which included Ronak, Belani, and Bhakat. Bhakat had been taken into custody and had willingly allowed himself to be incarcerated shortly after the fighting was over. He would have to face justice for breaking the most sacred of Rajan's laws.

◊

There was a large field a few miles southwest of Melaanse. Long, green grass waved slowly in the wind as the sun shone down and insects and other animals celebrated a brief reprieve from the cold, rainy season. *Such a place as this should not be the sight of such a gruesome discovery,* James thought.

The field was filled with the remains of the Rajani females

and younglings who had been missing since the Krahn first attacked, stacked on top of each other where they fell. They'd been forced to walk to the field, and then they'd been slaughtered. There were thousands of them. Their mouths were open in silent screams at the terror of the last moments of their lives. Things that looked like birds flew overhead and landed amid the dead, still feeding on the rotting corpses. Large alien insects cavorted about the bodies, entering the mouths and feeding off the decayed flesh. The air was dense with the smell of decomposition.

A mop-up team chasing a small number of Krahn south had come across the discovery barely a day before. They'd reported the find directly to James and Tumaani. James thought it interesting that they hadn't reported to Welemaan, since most of the team were Valderren. Obviously there were some who agreed with his assessment of Welemaan. They all missed Kedar.

James and the other remaining Humans now stood looking out at the mass of bodies, still trying to process the horror of what had happened. James held Yvette as she buried her head in his shoulder. David stood to their left. Gianni was off to their right, seemingly lost in his own thoughts.

"My God," James said. He felt like he was going to be sick.

"Why?" Yvette asked. "Why do this?"

"Spite. Terror. Who knows?" James had seen the photos from World War II of concentration camps and the similar results.

Gianni looked down at the ground before him. "Genocide," he said quietly. James and Gianni looked at each other a moment. They both wanted to be open to each other, yet somehow couldn't manage to accomplish letting down their walls. They'd made progress recently, but it was still difficult to change their behavior toward one another quickly.

"Maybe," James finally said, knowing that Gianni said the exact word that wouldn't come to him before. He knew that this was the end of the Rajani species. He didn't know how to feel about that. All he knew was that it was the most horrible part of the entire mission. Even Kieren's death could not compare to the sheer magnitude of what the Krahn had done at that place.

The field became known as Mabata bic Solaa, which was Rajanese for "The Death of a Dream."

◊

Welemaan was sitting in his quarters when the door chime sounded. He was startled, still not used to the recent restoration of power. He pushed the button near the door and, when the door opened, saw it was Tumaani waiting on his doorstep. His relatively good mood vanished immediately, though he was careful not to let his face betray the sudden change in feelings. "Tumaani," he said, hoping he sounded welcoming. "This is certainly a surprise. Come in. Would you like some fernta? Water, maybe?"

"No, thank you," Tumaani answered. "I'm sorry to disturb you, but I've just learned some news, and I thought it better if I told you. May I sit?"

"Of course," Welemaan said. He suddenly had the feeling that no, he didn't really want to hear what Tumaani had to say, but he couldn't very well tell the Elder to leave. Relations were dicey enough between the Elders and Valderren. It wouldn't do to be rude to the Elder's leader. Instead, he sat down on the large chair next to Tumaani and waited in dread for what he was going to say.

"The females and younglings have been found," Tumaani said without preamble.

"What? Where?" Welemaan asked, standing up excitedly.

"Please, sit down," Tumaani said. "Allow me to finish. Please."

Welemaan sat down, the feeling of trepidation now replaced by a tightening of his gut that was bordering on painful.

"They're dead," Tumaani said. "All of them are dead. Slaughtered by the Krahn." Welemaan watched as a tear rolled down the older Rajani's cheek.

Up until that point Welemaan would not have believed what he'd just heard, but the tear sealed his belief. "*All* dead?" he asked weakly. His voice felt like it belonged to someone else.

"I'm sorry, Welemaan," he heard Tumaani say. "They were found in a field south of the city. By their . . . condition, they had been there a while."

"Thank you," Welemaan said, standing suddenly. "Thank you for telling me." He walked to the door of his house. "I'm sorry, but I think I'd like to be alone now." He remembered then, that he wasn't the only one who had lost someone, or even lost the most. Tumaani had multiple wives. Or at least, he'd had them. "Tumaani, I'm sorry for your loss as well." It seemed like his brain had slowed to a crawl and sped to a sprint at the same time.

"Thank you," Tumaani said. "I understand your need for solitude. If you need to talk to someone—"

"Thank you for the offer," he heard himself say, still not believing that the voice he heard was his own. Tumaani bowed slightly, and he returned the gesture. He closed his door and immediately fell to the floor as the strength in his legs gave out. After the waves of grief had flooded through him, he sat up against the wall. He began to go to a very dark place in his heart. He'd held out hope until the end, and that hope had turned to agony in just a few seconds. It was taking all of his control to not go directly to the jail and kill every last Krahn who still lived on Rajan.

No, he thought, *there will be a time for vengeance, but not now.* His failure at the first Rajani summit had showed him that he needed time to gather his own power still. If only Kedar was still alive, he felt like they would have had enough influence together to perhaps carry out their plan to take the fighting to the Krahn. The cold rage in his heart would be there to keep him driven to that end. Eventually, he vowed to himself, there would come a time when all of the Krahn would die. Until then, he would work to bring it about as quickly as possible. He began to immediately make plans for the future.

◊

After the successful attack on the main Krahn base and subsequent capture of Ronak, the hard work truly began. There were still pockets of Krahn to round up or kill. The rebuilding of Melaanse needed to begin, and there were funerals, many funerals to take place. Only one of these funerals was attended by all four Humans, all of the Rajani Elders and leaders of the Valderren, as well as Zanth, Mazal, and many of their followers. Almost all of the Sekani attended, in fact.

The funeral took place above a cliff overlooking a small bay to the north of Melaanse, where large animals called merdin cavorted in the waves and the high calls of the nesting dran were offset by the weeping of the attendees. It seemed as though everyone present was crying. Except for Gianni. He'd been crying ever since she died, but now he sat silently, unable to cry any longer; he was emotionally spent. He sat and thought about the only time he'd come to their special place. How much at peace he'd been, and how he'd known even then that it wouldn't last. But he hadn't known then just how little time he had left with her. He took a deep breath and stood. He vowed to himself that he wouldn't dwell on how short the amount of time he'd spent with her was. She'd been so alive, so vibrant; that's what he would remember, and what he would speak about. He walked to the front of the assembled crowd and turned to face them.

"Kieren was . . . my friend," he began, his voice ringing out through the voice translator. "She was my teammate. And she was my reason for trying to be a better man. I think . . . I think she made everyone around her better just with her presence. She had a way of bringing out the best in people, even people from a different planet." There was some laughter among the members of the crowd, as they all remembered the Human woman who had touched all of their lives in different ways. "I feel lucky to have had her in my life," he continued. "Even though it was only for a short time. I just wish it could have been longer."

He turned toward the ocean and whispered "goodbye," before slowly going back to his seat, ignoring the closed, ornately carved casket next to the open grave. She wasn't there anymore.

She was flying free.

Others took their turns speaking, remembering their time with her—James, Zanth, Yvette. Finally, there was nothing left to say, and the crowd slowly dispersed, leaving Gianni alone with the burial crew, his thoughts, and the high calls of the flying animals that circled overhead and dived toward the ocean far below.

◊

The Rajani had cleaned out the old prison in the north of Melaanse to accommodate the Krahn prisoners who were captured in the final battle, although that number was less than one hundred, including Ronak. Bhakat had been staying in the prison for a while. He didn't know exactly how long he'd been there. All he knew was that it was the most frustrating and tedious time of his life. The only visitors he had were the guards who brought his food and water. At least he was separated from the Krahn by a floor.

Andraal had come very early in his incarceration to see him, but they had quickly run out of things to say, and Andraal had seemed almost relieved to say goodbye. He had not returned, and Bhakat had time to think about which was worse: being uncomfortable in the presence of someone else, or being bored alone. He was contemplating whether or not he should take a nap when the outer door leading to his cell block opened. It piqued his interest because it wasn't time for a scheduled feeding or bathroom break. The cells didn't have their own toilets, so prisoners were herded to a community bathroom at intervals. A smile appeared on his face when he saw who had entered the hallway.

"I always thought I'd be the one who ended up behind bars," Janan said, smiling, though it wasn't his normal mischievous smile. Bhakat noticed that his friend still looked thin, and his voice had a whispery quality to it that hadn't been there before.

"My friend," Bhakat said, walking over to the bars between them. "I heard you've spent enough time in captivity." He knelt and thrust both arms through the bars of his cell. Janan rushed forward and did the same. They held the embrace for a long moment and then broke apart again.

"They told me what you did," Janan said. "I didn't believe them at first."

"I had no choice," Bhakat said, softly.

"They told me that too," Janan said. "And I heard about Rauphangelaa. I'm sorry, Bhakat."

"Thank you," Bhakat said, standing up. His knees were beginning to grow sore kneeling on the hard cell floor. "We'd . . . we'd grown apart at the end. You can imagine what he thought of my decision." He'd known it would happen, and yet, when it did, he'd still felt both sadness and a sense of betrayal. But never regret. He'd done what was needed at the time for both of them to live.

"Well, just so you know," Janan said, breaking him out of his quiet contemplation, "I think it's great. The Stone, that is, not Rauphangelaa being dead. Can you, you know, do the same things as the Humans?"

Bhakat powered up, and then, just as quickly, the energy field disappeared. "Augmented strength and the ability to jump great distances seem to be the extent of my powers," he said.

Janan's expression became sober. "Then why don't you break out of here? Get away before they—" He didn't finish, but they both knew what he didn't say. Everyone knew the punishment for implanting a Johar Stone. "I'd come with you," he finally said.

"I knew the penalty before I implanted myself with the Stone," Bhakat said, softly. He sat down on the floor next to the bars. He was still taller than Janan.

"I'll stay with you here, if you want me to," Janan said quietly.

"No," Bhakat decided. "I'm fine. But I wouldn't mind a visit every so often. Until the end."

"Deal," Janan said. He reached through the bars and squeezed Bhakat's shoulder. "I'll see you again soon."

"Goodbye, my friend," Bhakat said. He'd decided that it wasn't being bored by himself that he wanted, but it was better than seeing pity in the eyes of someone he loved.

◊

Janan had asked around about the Sekani named Golena since being rescued from the Krahn and spending time recuperating. He was now on his way to see Golena's daughter, Kalen. She needed to be told the truth about her father. He knocked on the door he'd been directed to by a few of the Sekani he had talked to, and then waited for an answer. He was still not feeling normal, and his chest still itched as his wounds slowly healed. After a few minutes, the door opened a finger's width or so, and Janan could see a young female Sekani standing on the other side. Judging by her height alone, she couldn't have been more than ten seasons old. Janan felt a painful blow in his chest, thinking about what had happened to her father. He had a moment where he thought he might just walk away, but steeled his resolve. She should know what a hero her father was. "I'm searching for Kalen," he said. "Are you Kalen?"

At that moment, an older female came into view behind the younger one. "Kalen, back away from the door, my sweet," the older Sekani said. She shooed the younger female away from the door, and then turned back to face Janan. "What do you want to see her about?" she asked, sounding suspicious.

"Her father," Janan answered, simply.

The door opened wider. "What about Golena?" she asked, the worried look on her face now replaced with a cautious hope. "Who are you?"

"I'm Janan'kela," he answered.

"What do you know about my father?" the young Sekani asked, pushing through the space between the older Sekani and the doorframe.

"Please, come inside," the older female said, backing away and gently pulling the younger along with her. "I apologize, we're still not used to visitors," she said.

Janan entered the quarters to see a small, simply

furnished living space. There was a single bed in the corner that he assumed both slept in, and a small chair in another corner. He chose to stand. "I . . . I was the last to see Golena alive," he began. He watched as the hope on their faces was replaced by resignation. "I'm sorry if I caused you any fresh pain by my presence, but I just wanted you to know what happened to him."

"When they told us that all of the teams had been killed, I had hoped that my son had somehow escaped," the older Sekani said. "It was a foolish notion, I know."

"When I was a prisoner of the Krahn," Janan continued, "they had me in a small, dark cell, trying to break my spirit so that I'd tell them everything I knew about the Humans. When I wouldn't talk, they brought Golena to me and put him in my cell, in hopes that I would tell him what they wanted to know. Instead, he encouraged me to stay strong and not give up. They took him away, and I never saw him again. I don't think I would have survived without him. I was so close to giving up hope."

The young female began to cry silently, her shoulders shaking. Janan walked over to her and placed his hands on her shoulders. "Your father was a hero," he said. "He was my hero." The girl embraced him, and he held her while she cried, no longer silent. He began to cry as well and looked up to see that the older female was not. She just nodded to him in thanks, as if he wasn't telling her anything she didn't already know. Perhaps he hadn't.

When the girl had begun to settle down again, she pulled back from him and looked up at his face. "Thank you," she said, wiping her eyes with her hands.

"I just wanted you to know, before I left Rajan," he said. He'd made up his mind earlier that he would leave the planet. There was nothing left there for him, and he couldn't bear to see what had happened to it because of one indescribably bad decision on his part. He made his goodbyes and left them standing and holding hands in their small living quarters. He would stay on Rajan, he knew, until the first ship left. He didn't care where he went. He owed his friend Bhakat to at least stay for the trial, but then he would leave Rajan forever.

◊

Belani awoke to find himself back in a prison cell, though a different one than he'd been in before James the Human had come to him with his proposition of a second chance. The last month had seemed to pass in a fog of pain and nightmares. He'd been hooked up to medibots and intravenous tubes for a long time, as he recovered from his crash in the desert. He laid there for a moment, looking up at the ceiling of his new cell.

"How are you feeling, Belani?" a voice asked. Belani turned his head slowly to find that he wasn't alone in the cell this time. A large Rajani was sitting on the floor of the cell with his back against the wall.

"Better," he said quietly. He could only muster a whisper.

When they'd found him, he'd been suffering from extreme dehydration and heat prostration. He also had a concussion, a broken arm, three broken ribs, and a broken pelvis, that last condition needing two surgeries to repair. He was lucky to be alive. *Or,* he told himself, *another way to look at it is that I'm unlucky enough to be alive so that I can spend the rest of my life locked up in a Rajani prison.* He tried to sit up and felt a spasm of pain course through his body from his head to his hips. A low moan escaped his lips.

"Better to rest," the Rajani said. "It'll take some time to heal from your wounds. Especially the broken pelvis."

"Time," Belani said. "I think I have enough of that. At least until it runs out."

"Yes," the Rajani said. "It seems that both of us have had past choices which are only now catching up to us."

"So it would seem," Belani said. "Tell me, what is it you've done that you would expect death from your own species?"

The Rajani sat a moment in silence. Then he powered up without moving, and then just as quickly dropped the power field that surrounded him. It happened so fast that Belani could have missed it if he hadn't been looking straight at the Rajani.

"Amazing," Belani said, his eyes wide. "You must be Bhakat. By the way, how do you know who I am?"

"Yvette filled me in when she brought you here," Bhakat said. "She told me to look after you as a favor to James. Make sure you made it to trial."

That James is a smart one, Belani thought, gratefully. He remembered his treatment at the hands of Welemaan the Elder after first being captured. He also remembered what had happened to the Krahn who had also been captured along with him. "It's funny," he said, quietly. "Before I went out on that last mission, I planned it so that I wouldn't make it back alive. But once I actually got out there again, I realized something."

"What was that?" Bhakat asked, looking over at him.

"I don't want to die," Belani said, and laughed, though there was no humor in the sound.

"I always thought that sacrificing my life for my Master and my species would be the highest of honors," Bhakat said. "I don't regret my decision to save Rauphangelaa, nor my ability to help my species by fighting in the war. But I don't want to die like this either."

"You could break out at any time," Belani said, sitting up slowly. This time the pain was not so bad. Mostly he was just stiff from lying in one position for so long. "I've heard the stories about the power of the Stones. No prison could hold you."

"My honor is my prison," Bhakat said, simply. "My loyalties are its walls, and those I cannot break."

After that, they sat in companionable silence together, as each awaited his fate, whatever it might be.

Chapter 18

One morning, a month after the Reading of the Lists had ended, James was awakened by a knock on his door. He walked to the door in just his underwear, still half asleep. He opened the door enough to stick his head out. He was surprised to see Tumaani and Gianni standing on his doorstep. He was also surprised that it wasn't raining outside. It seemed the rainy season was finally coming to an end, and he was happy to see that there were hardly any clouds in the sky.

"Good morning to you, James the Human," Tumaani said, smiling. "I was hoping you and Yvette could accompany us somewhere, if it's not an impingement on your valuable time, of course."

Although Yvette still had her own place within the Rajani compound, she hadn't stayed there in some time. He looked over to see that she hadn't been awakened by the knocking or the talking that followed. She'd been sleeping more and more recently. The pregnancy was taking a lot out of her. "Yes, I guess," James said, looking at Gianni. Gianni just shrugged and rolled his eyes. "Uh, excuse me just a moment, please." He closed the door and went to wake Yvette up and get some clothes on himself.

"Who was it?" Yvette mumbled from the bed.

"Either we're being arrested," James said, pulling his pants up, "or we're going to get the key to the city."

"How 'bout they give us the key to some other city," Yvette said, sitting up slowly. "This one seems to be broken." James noticed that she looked a little pale.

"How are you feeling?" he asked.

"Okay, I guess," she said. "Just don't offer me any food or I'm going to puke."

"Sexy," he said, smiling at her.

She just looked at him dolefully as she got out of bed. It seemed she wasn't in the mood for jokes. He noticed as she stretched how much she was beginning to show. If word hadn't spread around yet that she was pregnant, it soon would. After a few minutes of wrestling on their clothing, they finally were dressed, and James opened the door again.

"Geez," Gianni said. "Could you take any longer? Should we come back tomorrow, maybe?"

"Sorry," Yvette said, smiling sheepishly. James noticed that her color was beginning to come back, at least, if not her sense of humor.

"Where's David?" James asked.

"He didn't answer his door," Gianni replied. "Maybe he's out with Janan somewhere."

Tumaani made small talk as he led them to the new shipyards, where the Krahn colony ship had crashed nearly two months before. "I wanted to show you all something you might find of interest," he said as they walked past rows of starship parts that were being worked on by Sekani, Jirina, and Rajani workers. He finally stopped before a large Talondarian model starcruiser that seemed to be about the size of the *Tukuli*.

"This is the *Pwyntafa Naa*," he said proudly, holding both arms toward the ship as he presented it to them. "My new starship, which was just finished a few days ago."

"Great," James said. "If you ever want to leave Rajan, say, to take us home, you can." After a moment, he added, "That was a hint."

"But I don't want to leave Rajan," Tumaani replied, turning to look at them all. "There are too many things I need to accomplish here. I couldn't possibly leave for so long a period."

There was silence for a moment.

"Well, nice ship and all," Gianni finally said, "but I have better things to do. See you all later."

"You don't understand," Tumaani said. "I have no need for this ship, which is why I'm giving it to you."

"To . . . us?" Yvette asked, a surprised look on her face.

"Yes," Tumaani replied, happily. "A Gift from the Elders. In appreciation for your great service to my species, I would like for you to have this ship to return home in."

"This . . . this is too much," James said, looking over the ship. It looked fresh off the assembly line—if the assembly line was staffed with blind people. It wasn't that the ship wasn't well put together; he could tell that it was. It was just that it had been pieced back together from various Krahn ships and the body of a Talondarian starcruiser that had been considerably damaged in the Krahn attack. It was an odd match, to say the least. But to James, it was still a beautiful, wonderful sight.

"I insist," Tumaani said. "We all owe you a great debt that can never be repaid. I can at least ensure your safe return home. I even asked your Sekani companion Janan to do his best to teach the ship's computer how to speak your language."

"Well, that should prove interesting," Gianni said, but he was smiling as he said it.

"Yes, well . . ." Tumaani began, and James thought that there was something else that the Rajani wanted to say, but after a pause, he closed his mouth before continuing. "If you would now excuse me, I must attend a meeting with the other members of the Council concerning our upcoming legal proceedings." He bowed slightly and left.

"So," Gianni said, "anyone here know how to fly this thing?"

"I didn't catch the name," Yvette said, ignoring him. "Pwin something?"

"*Pwyntafa Naa,*" James said, still looking up at the ship. Their ship, now.

"Lighted travel?" Gianni asked, looking confused.

"No," James said. "It means Bright Journey. The ship's name is *Bright Journey.*"

"Let's hope that it will be," Yvette said, reaching out to squeeze his hand.

◊

The members of the new Rajani Ruling Council were sitting behind a large, half-moon table. They were in the largest room of a newly constructed building in the center of Melaanse. Though it wasn't as tall and magnificent as the architectural style it replaced, it was built with an eye toward practicality and function. The council building would serve all the species of Rajan.

Bhakat stood before the Council, his hair cut short, though not as short as the Krahn had cut all of the Elders' hair when they'd first attacked. Standing a ways behind him were Janan and the team of Humans. There was no table with a translator in front of them this time. They had all had new translation devices implanted behind their ears, and all of them could now speak at least passable Talondarian Standard. A crowd made up of Rajani, Sekani, and Jirina sat on benches behind them. There had been a line of them waiting for entrance to this trial, but after the benches had filled, many of them had been turned away from the event. They would have to wait to hear about it later.

"Bhakat," Tumaani said, "you stand accused of the most heinous of crimes. The implantation of the Johar Stones has been forbidden for two thousand years. And yet you did willingly do so. Do you have anything to say in your defense?"

Bhakat raised his head proudly, staring straight ahead. "No."

Janan stepped forward to speak in his friend's defense. "Tell them why you did it, Bhakat! Tumaani, tell—"

Bhakat turned around to face the Sekani. "They already know, Janan. My friend, don't you see? They're right."

"Silence in this court of law, please," Zanth said.

"The Council has made its decision at the urging of Rauphangelaa, may he be one with the Kaa," Tumaani said, after everyone had grown quiet once again. "And because you not only saved his life, but also the lives of many others, the automatic death sentence has been lifted."

There were cheers from the team and Janan, not to mention many in the crowd who had fought beside Bhakat in the Krahn war. They'd been witness to his courage as he fought against the invaders, and had seen first-hand how valuable he was in the fight, especially at Nestbase One.

"Yet, this act cannot go unpunished," Tumaani continued. "We must set an example for all to know that this is not, and will not be tolerated. And so . . . Bhakat, you are hereby banished from Rajan and all of its galactic holdings for the remaining years of your life."

As Tumaani laid out his sentence, Bhakat's face was still unreadable, yet grim.

"You have three days in which to ready yourself for your

journey," Tumaani told him. "And then you must go. In the event that you are found on Rajan after this period of time, the death penalty shall be reinstated. This trial has ended. Go with the Kaa . . . and my blessing and thanks, always."

Bhakat bowed to the Council. "Thank you." A set of guards came forward and led him from the courtroom.

"On the matter of the traitor Belani," Zanth said after the clamor of the crowd had died down somewhat, "the Council hereby lifts the death penalty due to his service to the Resistance. He is hereby sentenced to life in prison for the deaths of the members of the strike teams of which he was a part."

Belani nodded, resigned to his fate.

"May I speak?" James said, stepping forward.

"The Council recognizes James the Human," Mazal said quickly. Zanth gave him a look that promised a discussion on proper protocol at some later date. It still made James a little sad to see the stump where Zanth's arm used to be, but the Sekani seemed to have quickly become used to his new disability.

"I ask only for the same punishment for Belani that you decreed for Bhakat. The standards for punishment between the races of Rajan should be equal."

"You would have him banished from Rajan?" Zanth asked, looking confused.

"Yes," James answered.

"One moment," Zanth said. The Council conferred in heated whispers for a few minutes before turning back to the assemblage.

Zanth sighed. "The councilors reluctantly agree with James the Human on this matter," he said, not looking at all happy. "In an effort to maintain fairness in our legal system, let this be a symbol of our unity for all of the inhabitants of

Rajan."

There was a cheer from the crowd, though James knew that it wasn't because Belani had been saved from a life in prison. The Jirina and Sekani needed to know that the court system would be fair in its dealings with all the species of Rajan. It was the second time that the Sekani named Belani had been a pawn in some type of political power play, but James didn't think he would mind this time.

Besides, James had another offer for the Sekani, and Belani wouldn't be able to fulfill it if he was in prison for the rest of his life.

◊

A day after the trial, Tumaani was back at the shipyards, looking for a ship adequate enough to transport Bhakat off of Rajan. He felt bad that he'd lied to everyone about what Rauphangelaa had said to him before he died, but he wanted all of the Johar Stones as far away from Rajan as possible. And if that meant telling a white lie about his friend's final words, then so be it. Rauphangelaa had died before saying anything about Bhakat, but Tumaani had sworn to them that Rauphangelaa's dying wish was for his former pupil to be set free, banished instead of put to death.

Tumaani knew that if Bhakat was killed, there was a chance that the Johar Stone could fall into the hands of Welemaan, and that would be unacceptable. As the new Keeper of the Stones, it was his job to not only make sure the Stones were safe from off-worlders, but to also make sure that off-worlders were safe from the Stones. If it meant that he was the Keeper of No Stones, then so be it. It was imperative that the Humans and Bhakat left Rajan.

Finally, after walking through the yards, he found what he was searching for: a small ship, but one that was nearly complete. From the look of it, it had been a Krahn ship, or at least one that the Krahn had used. Who knew where they'd stolen it from? He walked over to the Sekani workers that were busy repairing it.

"Excuse me," he said, trying to get their attention. When he'd waited patiently a few moments for someone to take notice and they didn't, he walked over to the nearest Sekani and tapped him on the shoulder. The Sekani jumped, turning with a snarl on his face before he saw who it was. The snarl turned to a shocked expression for a moment.

"Apologies, Elder," the Sekani said. "I guess I'm still a little jumpy. It's still too early after the fighting—"

"I should be apologizing," Tumaani said. "I shouldn't have startled you."

"What can I do for you today?" the Sekani asked, wiping his hands on a cloth.

"I was wondering, who owns this ship?" Tumaani asked.

"The Resistance, as far as I know," the Sekani answered. "This here is the ship that the traitor Belani used to attack the Krahn air base. A salvage team went out and brought it back from the Ambraa Desert. It was in relatively one piece, so we decided to fix it."

"Perfect," Tumaani said. "Thank you."

The Sekani nodded to him and turned back to continue his work on the ship. Tumaani began to head back to his house. Since the ship belonged to the Resistance, and the Resistance technically didn't exist anymore, then that meant that the ship had no rightful owner. Bhakat could use the ship to leave Rajan, and there would be one less headache for him to deal with. After thinking about it a little more, he changed course and headed toward Bhakat's quarters. He'd tell him right away. The sooner Bhakat was told, the sooner he could leave. After that, he'd make sure that the Humans were on their way as well, and hopefully get back to the business of putting things right on Rajan.

◊

James had mixed emotions about leaving Rajan. On the one hand, he was anxious to return to Earth after so long. He still had dreams about eating a hot dog and sitting in the stands at a Tigers game with his father and brother. Or simply sitting on his fire escape and listening to the sounds of the city. On the other, he would miss the challenge of coordinating the war and the thrill of discovering something new every day. But most of all, he would miss all of the friends he'd made while there. Rauph, Bhakat, Zanth, even Welemaan and Tumaani. The one he would miss the most of all, though, was the first being he had met on Rajan, which was why he found himself back at the Jirina housing area. It brought back a lot of memories as he walked slowly along the road toward where he'd lived for a little while after first crash-landing on the planet.

He had turned invisible, not wanting to create a scene or impose his presence on the Jirina. He was surprised at how different the entire area looked since the first time he'd been led there, shortly after rescuing Mazal from the Krahn. Gone was the rubble and trash strewn about and blocking the streets. The area was bustling with activity as the Jirina set about cleaning up the buildings, parks, and fountains.

The rainy season had ended, and the sun now shone down brightly. Younglings ran through the area, laughing and playing tag or throwing small balls to each other. Flowers bloomed in gardens, and clean water flowed through the fountains. One of the first things that happened after the Krahn were defeated was the restoration of electrical power. The Jirina were not used to having electricity; they rose with the sunrise and retired with the sunset, when it became too dark to work. Mazal had told James that the situation would change in the future. Whoever wanted power in their homes could have it, but he had also added that he thought that most would refuse. They were content with their connection to the cycles of day and night.

James finally found the Jirina leader helping to rebuild a Rajani Elder's house. There were a number of Jirina males helping to replace the roof of the structure, as well as one of the walls.

"I'm surprised you're helping build a house for the Rajani when you have more important things you could be doing," James said, materializing next to Mazal.

Mazal jumped back in surprise, before realizing it was James. Suddenly, the two were surrounded by Jirina, all of them smiling and calling out "James the Human!" Younglings gathered around him, all of them wanting to touch their savior.

"Enough," Mazal said, laughing. "Go on and play somewhere else now. Let us talk. Go on."

James waved to the younglings as they ran off, most of them waving back. It made him happy to see them bouncing back so soon after living in hiding for so long. *At least the Jirina still have a future,* he thought, as a picture of silent, screaming Rajani faces played across his memory for a moment.

"I wish you wouldn't do that," Mazal said, turning serious again as he looked at James.

"Do what?" James asked, smiling mischievously. "Come to visit you?"

"No," Mazal answered, leading James inside the house. "Sneak up on me like that. I can't forget as quickly as those younglings out there, I'm afraid. I wake up some nights thinking I've heard the sound of Krahn warriors approaching. Other times, I relive Kedar's final moments, and I wake up in a cold sweat."

James grew serious. "My apologies. I was just hoping to not disturb the Jirina too much with my presence. Guess it didn't work out so well."

Mazal smiled. "Oh, don't mind me. I'm just grumpy today. I've been dreading this. I do not wish to say goodbye to you."

James could see that the Jirina was tearing up. "Now stop that," he said, clapping Mazal on the back. "This isn't goodbye. I told you I would come back and visit someday. Let's call this farewell for now."

"Whatever you may call it," Mazal said, "it makes me sad."

"I'll miss you as well, my friend," James said as Mazal embraced him in a tight hug. "Take care of yourself, and the Jirina too."

"I will," Mazal said. "I promise they will live free from now on."

"Good," James said. "I look forward to seeing the progress you've made when I return. What you've done here already is very impressive."

"Thank you. And by the way," Mazal said, finally stepping back and rubbing his eyes. "This is no longer a Rajani Elder's house. It's . . . mine."

"Really?" James said, smiling.

"At first I refused," Mazal said, looking sheepish. "But some other Jirina told me that I'm their leader now, so I must look more prestigious to the Rajani and Sekani, or else they won't respect me. I really hate all of the politics that come with the job of being on the Rajani Council."

"Well then, you have my apologies for getting you into this," James said. "But I've seen how you've grown into this role, and I have every confidence that you'll do well in the future. Even if it's against your will. Sorry."

Mazal looked around the inside of the house and smiled. "No apologies are ever needed from you, you know that. And some of the perks are worth it, I guess."

They laughed, and then shook hands one last time before James gave a little wave and disappeared once more.

◊

The *Bright Journey* sat in a field outside of Melaanse. Another, smaller ship was fifty yards away. Between the two ships were David, Yvette, James, Janan, and Bhakat. Gianni had gone aboard to help the *Bright Journey's* new pilot prep the ship for the voyage back to Earth.

"You could come back with us," James said to Bhakat and Janan. "Both of you could come to Earth."

"No," Janan said, sadly, nodding toward Bhakat. "I don't think he knows where he's going, to tell you the truth. Besides, we've seen how Humans treat those who are different. We won't come back to Earth with you. I don't think either one of us would feel safe on your planet." Janan smiled, pointing over his shoulder at Bhakat. "And since he needs someone with a brain to watch his back, I'll go along with him to keep him out of trouble. Plus, he flies like he's had one too many glasses of fernta."

Bhakat only growled at him, though fondly. "Janan is correct on one account," he said. "Neither of us would survive on Earth, I think. But there's more to it than that. I just need to get away for a while, from all of this."

Yvette walked up to Bhakat and put her hand on his arm. "Well, I for one will miss my favorite doctor," she said, and hugged him. "Take care of yourself, Bhakat."

"Thank you, my friend," Bhakat said, returning her hug. "Go with . . . go in peace. And take care of that youngling."

"You could come with us, David," Janan said. "There's

room for one more on the ship."

"I'm staying on Rajan," David said. For a moment, everyone stopped and looked at him in surprise. "I can at least help them here," he continued. "I have nothing to go home to, and in fact, it's better if I don't go back to Earth." He turned to the others and lifted up his shirt. "I don't know what will happen if I do."

James could see the tattoo on David's side. It wasn't an eight, as he had told Kieren on the *Tukuli*.

It was the symbol for infinity.

"Oh my God," James whispered. "The dead girl on the *Tukuli*—"

"Didn't commit suicide," David interrupted.

James took a step toward him, but David powered up, and in a blur was suddenly standing ten feet behind him. "You can't catch me," David said. "So don't even try. You see now why I can't go back? It's better for everyone this way."

"David, what are you saying?" Janan asked, confused. He'd been off duty when Rauph had witnessed David throwing the girl from the roof, and had then transported her to the ship.

"I'm sorry, Janan," David said. "Truly I am. I can't explain to you what my father did to me. It would take too long, and none of you would understand, anyway." He turned back toward James. "Goodbye. You were a worthy opponent back on Earth, and an even better leader to all of us here. I'm sorry it has to be like this."

"You really think I'm going to just leave you here after what you've done?" James asked angrily, judging the distance between them.

"You'd better," David said, turning hard and serious. None of them had ever witnessed this side of him, except for Gianni, when they'd fought in the Sekani courtyard. He slowly backed away from James, guessing the other man's intent.

Suddenly, there was a force shield behind him. He bumped into it, and as he turned to look at what was blocking his way, Yvette powered up and sent a lance of energy from her arm, piercing David's side through his field, obliterating the infinity symbol that rested there.

David screamed in agony as she pulled it out. "You'll pay for that, bitch!" he said through clenched teeth. He looked around quickly and saw that Gianni was walking from the ship toward him. All of the Humans were now powered up, as was Bhakat. Still holding his side, he disappeared in a blur, running toward the city.

"James, we—" Yvette began.

"We do nothing," James said, dropping his field. "He's right. We can't catch him, and we don't have the time."

"But," Gianni said, "if he's really the Infinity Killer . . ."

"No," James said. "If he wants to stay here, then fine. We'll inform the Council and let them deal with him as they see fit. I just want to leave. Let's go home."

◊

It felt like David's side was on fire. He was going into shock from the wound he'd sustained from Yvette. Nothing had gone right. He'd thought that the others would be happy to know that he wasn't going back to Earth. One less murderer in Detroit. He'd even tried to give James some peace of mind, letting him know that the Infinity Killer was gone forever.

He hadn't counted on that bitch Yvette being so quick. It had surprised him that she was even able to penetrate his energy field. He hadn't thought it was possible after all the times he'd used it. Clearly there were still mysteries to be solved about the Stones and how they interacted with each other. But there was no time for that at the moment. He was bleeding profusely from the wound in his side. He needed medical treatment quickly if he was going to live. As he came closer to the clinic, he felt like he was going to either vomit or pass out, or both, and he knew he wouldn't make it to the medical building before it happened. He altered his course and headed for the only other place he could think of at the time: the home of his new friend and ally.

They'd talked extensively about their hatred for the Krahn, as well as David's past on Earth and the things he'd done since coming to Rajan. His friend didn't judge him, could even sympathize with his burning need to kill. He got as far as the doorstep before dark spots appeared in his vision and he fell down, unconscious. His energy field disappeared just as the front door opened.

"David?" Welemaan asked.

◊

James and the rest of the Humans were finally aboard the *Bright Journey*, having said their final goodbyes to Janan and Bhakat. They were all still in varying stages of disbelief about what had just happened with David. James felt like he'd been punched in the gut. He'd been so happy to no longer be a police detective, and so busy running the war against the Krahn that he'd let his instincts go lax. The Infinity Killer, the man he'd spent so long searching for back on Earth, had been right in front of him the entire time, and he hadn't even suspected it.

They were all emotionally drained, and James wasn't surprised when they had all begged off coming up to the bridge for the takeoff.

"I just want to be alone for a while," Gianni said. "I'll catch you guys later. I'll be in my quarters if you need me for anything."

"Get some rest," James told him as he walked away. He

turned to look at Yvette. "You need some sleep too."

"I know," she replied, and yawned as if on cue. "You sure you don't need me to come with you to the bridge?"

"No," James replied, kissing her on the forehead. "I'll be along shortly after takeoff, I'm sure. You go on ahead."

She leaned up and kissed him softly on the lips. "Wake me later if you need to talk about . . . well, about anything."

"I will," he said, knowing that he would have to talk about David sooner or later. It was a long trip back. He was sure he'd have time. James could understand how the others felt, because he felt the same things—a need to be alone, along with a feeling of exhaustion, both mental and physical. But he couldn't rest just yet. He had too much to think about.

He walked down the main corridor and was soon sitting in the command seat on the bridge of the *Bright Journey*. "Okay, let's see what this piece of junk can do. Computer?"

"Acknowledged," answered the cold, impersonal voice of the computer over the ship's communication system.

"Have you programmed and verified our flight path?" James asked.

"Affirmative," the computer said.

"Damn," James said, with a slight smile. "I'm going to have to work on giving this computer a better personality. Pilot?"

"Yes, sir?" Belani said, turning to look at him from the pilot's chair.

"Take us home," James said quietly, already lost in his own thoughts as he felt the engines come to life.

"Cry not for the fallen, for in their time, they were heroes."
- Ancient Rajani Proverb

The End - War

**This ends
The Rajani Chronicles Trilogy**
by Brian S. Converse

Look for other writing by Brian!

Updates on

www.BrianSConverse.com